About the Author

NATALIE CHANDLER studied at St Chad's College, Durham, and went on to work in behavioural education, specialising in social, emotional and mental health issues. After turning to thriller writing, her fiction delves into the workings of the human mind, the tricks it can play and the darkest places our deeds and desires can take any one of us. Her novels *What We Did* and *Believe Me Not* hit the national and international ebook best-seller charts. Natalie has lived and worked across the world including in Argentina and Georgia, before moving to her current home in the north of England, where she lives with her husband and their collection of cockapoos.

Real Readers Love
Natalie Chandler

'I preordered it. And aren't I glad! I was gripped from the get-go. A real page-turner, with a twist I never saw coming!! (And I'm usually good at guessing!!)' ★★★★★

'A marvellous debut. The storyline is both realistic and unbelievable, but all in a good way. The characters felt authentic and the mystery kept me wondering what was real and what wasn't' ★★★★★

'A brilliant ending. It really makes you understand the way the mind works' ★★★★★

'Great story. Hooked from the beginning and couldn't put it down. Look forward to more from this author' ★★★★★

'Couldn't put this book down. It was so gripping I read it in two days. Couldn't wait to find out what happened in the end' ★★★★★

'Full of intrigue. Enthralling' ★★★★★

'Things that happened in your past – mistakes made and lies told – can't be covered forever. This book will show how it all catches up to you' ★★★★★

'The characters were fully fleshed out and likeable. I'm already looking forward to the author's next book!' ★★★★★

'This book really hooked you with such good twists and turns, and so real! Absolutely loved it!!' ★★★★★

'A compulsive read. You will not be disappointed with this book' ★★★★★

'Couldn't put it down. Kept me guessing until the end!' ★★★★★

'Suspense to the end; brilliant' ★★★★★

'Can't wait for the next book' ★★★★★

NATALIE CHANDLER

THE
VOICES

Harper
North

HarperNorth
Windmill Green
24 Mount Street
Manchester M2 3NX

A division of
HarperCollins*Publishers*
1 London Bridge Street
London SE1 9GF

www.harpercollins.co.uk

HarperCollins*Publishers*
Macken House, 39/40 Mayor Street Upper
Dublin 1, D01 C9W8, Ireland

First published by HarperNorth in 2025

1 3 5 7 9 10 8 6 4 2

A catalogue record for this book
is available from the British Library

ISBN: 978-0-00-866672-9

Printed and bound in the UK using 100%
renewable electricity at CPI Group (UK) Ltd, Croydon

This novel is entirely a work of fiction. The names, characters
and incidents portrayed in it are the work of the author's imagination.
Any resemblance to actual persons, living or dead, events or
localities is entirely coincidental.

MIX
Paper | Supporting
responsible forestry
FSC™ C007454

This book contains FSC™ certified paper and other controlled
sources to ensure responsible forest management.

For more information visit: www.harpercollins.co.uk/green

For Sabrina, my actual first-favourite Irish person
(but don't tell Sara).
Remember who you are.

Prologue

I suppose I was meant to die.

My life should have ended, torn apart by shards of metal and crumpled fibreglass as viscous puddles darkened from red to black.

I felt Death's cold fingers stroking my arms, persuading me to release my grip on life and be guided to a warmer, kinder place. It was too tempting, that comforting embrace beckoning me, and I felt myself being drawn into the darkness.

The weak kick barely registered amongst the more urgent sensations – the white-hot darts stabbing through my nervous system, the rasp of ragged breath in my throat, and the acidic stench of petrol – but it was enough.

My baby was not ready to follow me. She needed me to stay with her.

My eyelids refused to open but I could see the blue strobe lights even behind them. I heard the crunch of running footsteps, sensed the bulk of big men clad in heavy clothing that smelt of smoke and soot. A hand pinched my ear, knuckles rubbed briskly across my sternum. It hurt and I tried to cry out, to pull away, anything to make it stop.

'Non-responsive,' was the last thing I heard them say.

1

Tamsin – Now

My brain instructs my little finger to move.

Just the slightest twitch. A flicker of motion. Anything.

But my body is as ignorant of the order now as it has been for years, and the effort of trying to produce an action only brings a weighted cloud of exhaustion.

I am awake, but I'm not. I exist in a land of perpetual stillness while the world carries on around me as if nothing has happened. Invisible but present. Ignored yet considered. A half-life, neither dead nor alive.

The doctors call it a permanent vegetative state. I call it limbo, an uncertain borderland between the heaven of a second chance and the hell of an eternity trapped in my own mind. I will soon turn forty but the frozen recesses of my mind are stuck, perhaps forever, at the age of thirty-seven.

Morning announces its presence via the swish of the heavy curtains as they are yanked opened. I know by the overpowering aroma of daisies that it's Hannah on the early shift. She always spritzes her uniform tunic, which I have decided is baby blue, with fake Marc Jacobs in an attempt to disguise the stale smell of damp which always permeates her washing.

It is hard to be sure what day it is – my internal calendar is easily disrupted, especially on days when no visitors come to break the monotony. I try to track the weekly routine: physio, movement therapy, sensory stimulation, visits from Jamie, Lucia and Dan. Occasionally there are others but not often, not like in the early days after the accident, when a steady stream trooped into my ICU room to offer a morale boost or stare in horror.

Wednesday evening and Friday morning are Jamie's visiting times, when we pretend our marriage is still functioning and he doesn't resent the constraints I put on his time. He used to come with Lucia, my best friend, but now he's usually alone and Lucia has switched to Tuesday afternoons.

Monday is Dan, my boss of sorts, who comes out of hope and stays exactly ninety minutes. The routine helps them, like it does me. It's human nature, the need to organise our lives into compartments of time we can control.

I always know when Jamie arrives, even before he speaks. His shower gel and aftershave combine pine forests and icy, crystal-clear streams, as if we are walking together through the Scandinavian wilderness of our honeymoon. I sense his agile movements, easy strides and even, steady breathing. When his hand takes mine, I can picture the olive tones of his skin from the warmth of his touch, mentally trace the smooth, toned definition of his arms as if I am caressing them with the fingers I cannot move.

It is only in those moments that I feel like my past self, happy and secure in the life we had created, never for a moment believing it would ever be different. A past that had been a distant memory even before the crash changed everything.

I have no recollection of the events that led to my current predicament. They are lost to a grey, stormy sea of swelling emotions, unidentifiable voices and whispered rumours. On occasion, crystal-clear images pop into my mind, but they are lost before I can absorb any details.

Sometimes, Jamie brings Elise. Every few weeks or so. It is confusing for her. She doesn't know who I used to be. It hurts when I hear her little voice call me Mummy, the uncertainty in her tone, as if she has been told this motionless figure gave birth to her but she doesn't fully believe it.

Does she understand what happened? Why I can't smile or tell her I love her?

Does she even realise, beneath the tubes and wires, that I am a real person?

Today, it feels like a Thursday. When my room door opens and closes as Hannah sweeps about, I catch the faintest whiff of Mexican spices telling me it's fajita day, even though lunch must be hours away and I know from the conversations that happen around me that only a few residents are on solid diets. The staff enjoy their meals – Milena, my favourite carer, often brings her plate to my room and talks to me as she eats, describing the flavours in her lyrical accent.

I know a lot about a place I have never seen.

I sense Hannah's presence beside my bed. She blocks the light in a way Milena never does. Her breathing is always slightly laboured, as if the physicality of her job is a constant challenge, and I can feel her warm breath on my skin as she raises me to a sitting incline and begins the daily tasks. The peppermint tang of her toothpaste just about prevents the nausea that regularly rises from the pit of my stomach. I have never liked people invading my personal space, but dignity is a distant memory for me now.

Hannah's hands are cold and, although she isn't rough, she performs every movement with a sharp efficiency that makes me feel like a machine being maintained. She doesn't talk to me. She never does, only whispers the occasional reminder to herself as she follows the routine to the letter or issues an instruction to a junior staff member if they dare interrupt her.

The smell of artificial flowers is replaced by the fresh, subtle fragrance of the genuine article and a glass vase thuds onto a wooden surface close by my ear. If Milena was on duty, there would be rustling as she arranges the flowers to her satisfaction, but I doubt Hannah has even snipped the band binding them together.

They call this a rehab facility, even though I know they don't think I can be rehabilitated. Maybe it's difficult to label a place people are sent to await death. That is what they're really expecting. They are waiting for me to catch an infection or for my lungs to shut down or for my heart to simply give up. They don't know me very well, these medical experts who peer and prod and talk about me in the same confident, well-educated tones I used to use.

When I arrived here, all those months ago, I had assumed we were still in London as the ambulance curved across crunching gravel, drawing to a gentle stop as if I were a precious artefact. I hadn't been sentient long enough to have adjusted to the loss of vision and I was still learning how to interpret my dark environment, too many details still escaping me.

It was only when I was carefully unloaded that the breeze ruffled my hair and I smelt freshness – cut grass, newly sawn wood and spring flowers. I heard the rustling of branches laden with bright young leaves and I realised we had left the city behind. Free of traffic's steady drone and the fug of pollution, my senses sparked and a rush of joy snaked through me at my new-found ability to enjoy such simple pleasure.

As my stretcher was wheeled inside, I pictured a manor house, sandstone, with double oak front doors and sash windows, its Georgian features carefully preserved alongside the necessary modern amenities and medical equipment. The scent of original floorboards and the airiness of high ceilings guided the mental image I swiftly sketched. The rubber soles of my guardians' footsteps echoed and padded softly by turns, telling me of woven rugs and large rooms.

Later, I would find out the place is called Rushmore. Ironic, considering the residents within it will probably never rush anywhere again. Not that I've met any of them. I have gathered from the conversations that go on around me that, not only is this facility small, only six beds, but it is wincingly expensive. I think of Jamie's money woes and wonder how he can possibly afford this place when creditors had been relentlessly pursuing him.

I can't ask him, and he gives me no information – not that he ever liked to talk about money before the accident. I just have to hope there will be enough left for our daughter.

Our daughter. Elise. Jamie remembered my preferred name as he was left to organise the birth certificate alone. He calls her Els and, even though I have never seen her, I know what she looks like. I know she has silken blonde hair, several shades darker than my own, and bright cerulean eyes. I can picture her peachy-soft skin and her willowy limbs. I have missed two birthdays and am about to miss another. I have missed first steps, first words, the start of nursery and the end of nappies. Elise has lived her entire life without ever having a kiss from her mother.

Sometimes, I think it would have been better if I had let the darkness claim me that day.

Most people have a set idea of what emerging from a coma is like, whether based on TV dramas, books or their own imagination. They expect the slow fluttering of eyelids, a gasp around the ventilator, a clenching of fists or a sudden strike from a previously useless limb. Like waking from sleep, dull-minded and slow, brain thick with fog as realisation gradually dawns.

My experience was nothing like that. It was sudden, abrupt. One moment, it was the blissful suspension of light and sound, a black void in which I had been drifting, without thought or feeling, for what seemed to be a few moments. The next, I was *there*.

I was aware. And I was petrified.

The darkness was no longer absolute; it had become shadows. Soft, like rippling velvet, with gradients and movements. When I tried to move, it seemed I was trapped beneath its steady trickle, drowning slowly. I had no idea where I was, no idea what had happened to me.

I would later learn the only physical signs of the storm erupting within me were from the monitors – pulse, respiratory rate, brain wave activity all sending their alarms into panicked shrieks.

I heard pounding shoes and urgent whispers, sensed frantic movements all around. Hands touched me, strangers' voices called my name, asked me questions I couldn't answer, gave me instructions I couldn't follow.

Can you hear me, Tamsin?
Open your eyes.
Can you squeeze my fingers?
Tamsin, do you feel this?

I tried to nod that I could hear them. I tried to open my eyes and squeeze their fingers and tell them yes, I could feel the testing rod running along the soles of my feet.

I tried.

I failed.

At first, I thought I was paralysed. My brain was sluggish, reluctant to fire. The void of inability scared me as much as the paralysis.

There was a moment's silence in the volley of urgent discussion going on around me, a relief from the sudden assault that had been launched on my senses.

Senses.

I couldn't be paralysed. I was able to feel. I just couldn't move. My skeletal muscles were frozen, as if the neurones were failing to carry the increasingly frantic messages my brain was sending.

My terror began to escalate, a rapid tick of a clock inside my skull as my pulse thumped a tattoo. The strangers' voices asked more questions, issued more instructions, implored me to respond.

Why couldn't I do as they wanted?

I tried to lash out. Cough around the tube I could feel running down my throat. Anything to show them I was here.

Nothing.

The darkness implored me to return, a heavy blanket of exhaustion settling over me. I wanted to fight, screaming at my brain to keep trying.

I failed.

The next time I was aware of anything, the frenetic activity in the room had ceased. I could hear two voices, both male. I got the sense it was later in the day; there was no sunlight caressing my closed eyelids.

'Look, activity is registering again,' one man said, the sound becoming clearer, as if the stranger had turned towards me. He was well-spoken, sure of himself, his words delivered in such a way that told me he was used to being in charge.

'So she's awake?' Jamie. That was Jamie's voice, but not like I remembered it. Uncertain, tentative. I heard his fear. What he was afraid of, I didn't know, and I didn't have the capacity then to find an answer. 'Her eyes aren't open.'

'Open eyes aren't always the key indicator. We need to organise tests, but the signs are all suggesting Tamsin is no longer comatose.'

'Can she hear us?'

'We'll know more after the scans. I've notified the consultant at the Royal London. We'll arrange transfer back there as soon as we can.'

Did that mean I wasn't in hospital? Where was I?

I heard a finger tap insistently against a screen. 'She's definitely responding. Talk to her, explain what's happening. Her vital signs suggest she might be agitated.'

I heard a chair creak, felt warm skin against mine, a hand touching my forearm.

'It's OK, Tam,' Jamie said. 'You're in a rehab centre in Lewisham. You've been here since you were stable enough to leave the ICU.'

I waited for more. I had always hated receiving scant information. Details were important to me. I needed to have all the facts.

'You were in an accident. A car crash.' Jamie's voice caught, gravel scratching at his throat. 'It was pretty bad. You suffered a traumatic brain injury.'

That would explain why I had been comatose. But how did I crash the car? I had always been a careful, alert driver. I treated driving like a chess match, always several moves ahead, spotting hazards long before they became an issue.

Questions crowded my mind. Where did it happen? Was Jamie in the car with me? What caused it? Was I even driving?

I examined each query in turn but there were no clues in the dusky recesses of my memory. I couldn't even remember what car I used to drive.

'You've been in the coma a long time, Tam. The doctors weren't sure if you'd ever come round.'

How long? I tried to shout the question, urgency throbbing in my throat as this new issue snatched my attention away from the accident's details. Weeks? Months?

'But don't worry,' Jamie continued, not noticing my disconcertion. 'Elise is safe. She's doing fine.'

Again, I searched the shadows for clarity. That name was familiar, yet I couldn't put my finger on it.

Comprehension dawned, a sun reaching its peak above a cloudy sky. I had been pregnant. I remembered the feeling of tiny feet drumming against my ribcage, the pulse of a second heart beating in tandem with mine, the skin taut across my swollen abdomen.

I could feel the difference now, the emptiness where there had previously been life, movement, feeling. Even without being able to see for myself, I knew I was no longer pregnant.

Elise. My baby. My reason to live.

I wondered if she would be the one to realise. Whether she would understand the true situation that no one seemed to have grasped.

That beneath my wasted muscles and useless nerves, inside my bodily prison, my brain was as capable as ever. I could hear, smell, think and process, just like I always did.

I was in full control of my senses.

I just didn't have any way of showing it.

2

Tamsin – Now

'Good morning, Tamsin.' The ever-cheerful voice of the physiotherapist floats across my room. 'Happy Thursday! How are you today?'

I have known this woman for the year I have been at Rushmore, and she always greets me in the same positive way, as if certain that one day I will reply to her. She always takes care to tell me which day it is and what the weather is like, and I wish I could let her know how I appreciate her thoughtfulness.

'It's a beautiful day. The sun's lovely and warm.'

Her strong, supple hands pick up my right forearm, flexing and straightening the elbow. She raises the whole arm in the air, rotating the shoulder, stretching my hand towards the ceiling. Her fingers glide the length of the wasted muscles in firm strokes, sending warmth flowing through my skin.

She chats away to me as she moves to the other arm and repeats her actions, carefully avoiding the thick, raised scar on my left palm as if she can sense it is still sensitive to the touch. She will believe it is from the crash.

Next, she starts on my legs, the long levers I had always kept toned and strong with runs and spin classes and boxercise. Now my knees creak as she bends and straightens them, and the definition to my calves and quads I had worked so hard to maintain is lost. When she leans her weight on her palms to work the big muscle group, I can feel the pressure against my femur and know just how emaciated they have become.

These sessions are never rushed, not like some of the other therapies that are done as a duty, a routine, without hope. This woman believes she is helping me, preparing me for a recovery most of the other professionals don't think will ever come.

I enjoy her visits because I can relax with her. I don't have to analyse and second-guess every move. Too often, my own medical knowledge is a curse rather than a gift. I understand too much, and the blissful ignorance of laymen would be welcome when I am faced with my own very fragile mortality.

Maybe if I had followed my professors' advice, taken the path to neurosurgery and risen to the top of my speciality by treating the brain as a mechanism instead of an entity, I wouldn't have found myself in this mess. If I had listened, if I hadn't chosen to become a psychiatrist, if I had studied CT scans instead psyches, perhaps it would all have been different.

I have a lot of time to question some of the choices I made.

The physio has finished rubbing oil into my limbs, leaving a lingering scent of calming lavender, and is methodically packing up her bag.

'Good morning, Milena,' she says as the door hinges groan. 'Hi, Hannah.'

Milena returns the greeting with her usual brightness, but Hannah is silent, and I imagine her merely nodding in response. I wonder if there is anyone here she does talk to.

The faintly damp smell of her reaches my nose. I consider her home life, picturing a small flat, perhaps in a tower block, windows clouded with condensation as she hangs her uniform tunics over an airer. She can't put the clothes on the Economy 7 heaters for risk of fire, though she will turn them on once darkness falls to try and speed up the drying. Too expensive to run in the daytime. Despite all the luxuries of Rushmore, I know the staff are paid a pittance. I often listen to them complain about struggling to balance their minute budgets.

The physio says her goodbyes to me and leaves for the next room, the next unresponsive body. I can guess it is a shower day by the presence of both of my assigned carers and, sure enough, I hear the whirring of the electric hoist being brought to the bedside.

This is the most humiliating part of my week, when I am stripped naked and shipped to the ensuite wet room to be hosed down like a racehorse. I am exaggerating the cruelties; I am treated gently and humanely, as much as it is possible, but I cringe throughout the whole sorry procedure. I was a private person before all this and the sensation of strangers touching my bare skin is nauseating.

When Milena has time, she shaves my legs for me, as if she understands my dislike of the stubbly regrowth. She is a good carer, instinctive and patient. She has told me she had intended to pursue a new career when she left Poland for the UK, after several years caring for dementia and stroke patients. I'm glad she didn't.

Today Hannah hurries us through it, then orders Milena to change the bed.

'We have five more patients to wash, get a move on!'

I am lowered back onto the clean bed. This is one of my favourite sensations. Who doesn't love fresh sheets?

'I'll make a start next door,' Hannah loudly bundles up the old linen. 'Finish off in here and come through. Be quick.'

Milena doesn't reply, snorting softly as the door closes briskly behind her superior. Moving with deliberate slowness, she dresses me in a soft merino jumper. She is tiny, much smaller than Hannah. I can tell the height difference when she leans over me, and I can hear the lightness of her footsteps. She tells me each time she changes her hair colour, painting vivid pictures with her words so I can see the magenta, the electric blue, the bubblegum pink as she brushes my own platinum locks, murmuring wistfully of her desire to have my natural colour instead of her own boring dark brown.

A phone buzzes and I hear Milena search her tunic pockets to locate it. She gives an impatient sigh before she taps the screen. She speaks rapidly in a language I don't know. I recognise the sounds as belonging to the Slavic group, but it isn't Polish. I always liked to learn the polite necessities for any country I visited, and I had taught myself enough phrases when I'd stayed in Warsaw, a city I had loved in a past life, to know the basics.

Milena's voice becomes sharper, words spilling in a torrent, barely pausing for breath, very different from her usual relaxed tone. I can feel her tension, the abrupt tightening of her muscles. I don't need to comprehend her words to understand their meaning.

I wonder who she is talking to. Her lack of hesitation suggests familiarity but there is cold rage in her words, and she barely gives the caller a chance to respond. She is close to the bed, and I can just catch enough of the quiet voice on the other end of the phone to be sure it is female.

She ends the call while the other woman is still speaking, cutting her off in mid-sentence. She is rough with her pocket as she stows the phone safely away.

'Sorry, Tamsin,' she whispers, her accent stronger from the abrupt switch back to English. 'I am not so calm today. You know how that feels. The ants when they are under your skin.'

I know exactly how that feels.

Milena leans over to adjust my pillow. 'You are trapped, and so am I.'

Trapped in a job she doesn't like? In a country not her own? By a failing relationship? My mind automatically begins to analyse her words, weighing up the possibilities. People often struggle to say what they really mean but, if you are paying attention, the words they unconsciously choose can give the game away.

She sighs softly. 'Life is never easy.' She clears her throat and I sense her straightening up, drawing her shoulders back. When she speaks again, there's a forced positivity in her tone. 'You have a quiet day now. Shall I put the music on? It can keep you company till I come back for lunch.'

As if she has heard my agreement, she taps the iPad that lives on my bedside table, brought by Jamie when he had decided I wouldn't enjoy silence. In the evening, the wall-mounted TV will be switched on and I cannot explain I hate having no control of the remote.

For now, the sounds of Chopin soothe me as I set my mind to deconstructing Milena's secrets.

It is a relief to have a brief respite from my own.

3

Jamie – Now

J amie Shaw dreads Fridays.

He has to take the whole morning off, which he's come to resent as the months creep by. He prefers being at work, where he is in control. His career in commercial property lettings suits him well. He has the easy chat and ready smile that relax his clients, reassure them that he is the same as them – sociable and socially acceptable in equal measures.

He prefers not to remember the darker days when the opposite was true, when he didn't dare answer the phone and cringed every time the doorbell rang. Things are different now. It is easier to pretend those times never existed, just as he pretends he was saved through hard work and dedication.

He always makes an early start on Fridays, far earlier than when he's in the office, keen to get his task done for another week. He can't summon guilt that it has become a chore after so long. Next week it will be three years since the accident. Wednesday will be both the anniversary and his daughter's birthday.

It takes nearly two hours to drive to the North Wessex Downs, his thoughts his only, and distinctly unwelcome, companions. He manages to hold the distractions at bay on the busy motorways but, as soon as he hits the country lanes, his concentration wavers and the voices surround him.

By the time he pulls into the long gravel driveway that leads to the gault-brick manor house, his head aches from replaying the same old arguments with everyone he has wronged.

There is no relief as he approaches Rushmore's front doors and pulls the bell cord – the convenience of an intercom would spoil the pretence of luxury. The stately *dong* announces his biweekly sentence, and he is as conditioned to it as Pavlov's canines. He can feel himself starting to sweat, and his shoulder muscles bunch in readiness for the fight-or-flight battle that inevitably rages within him.

Hannah answers the door today, with a generic greeting. She is tall and stocky, broad-shouldered and thick-necked, with calves that strain against her uniform tights. Her hair, so black it is surely dyed, is always slicked back in a bun tight enough to tug her eyes up at the corners, making her look like she is slyly amused. Jamie is wary of Hannah.

She only looks at him for a moment before she presents the visitor book for him to sign. He does so mechanically, not bothering to glance at the other signatures he knows will be listed under Tamsin's name for the week.

He always prefers it when it is Milena who meets him, with her ready smile, her vibrant hair dyed a different colour every few months, her graceful, effortless movements that remind him of *Black Swan*, Tamsin's favourite film. Milena's accent makes the English language sound beguiling, and she is quick to laugh at herself if she uses the wrong word or her pronunciation slips.

He has barely removed his coat when the facility's director appears at the top of the wide, sweeping staircase, her high heels soundless on the thick carpet as she descends like royalty meeting their adoring public. Her suit jacket is buttoned, her lipstick too bright for her pale complexion, but she moves with the authority of her position.

'Good morning, Mr Shaw.'

He has asked her to call him Jamie on too many occasions now, so he doesn't bother to say it again. 'Good morning.'

'Do you have a few moments before you see Tamsin?'

He feels like a troublesome schoolboy as he follows her very straight spine up the stairs. The first floor has been converted into offices; the ground floor exclusively for patients who will never be able to ascend. The director's office was presumably the master bedroom in a former life, a large room with a sweeping bay window and the original cast-iron fireplace.

Jamie takes the offered seat in front of her mahogany desk.

'How are you, Mr Shaw? How's little Elise?'

'We're both fine,' he replies stiffly. He is asked the same questions every three months or so, when the boxes need to be ticked.

'And you're happy with the care Tamsin is receiving?'

'Yes, Milena and Hannah look after her well.'

'You have a long drive here every week. Not easy to juggle family life and visiting hours.'

'The distance isn't an issue.' In fact, it has been an advantage. 'We manage. Lucia helps.'

'It's nice that friends still visit.' The director shuffles a sheaf of papers, drawing a line under the small talk. 'The matter I wanted to discuss with you is about the next steps for Tamsin.'

Jamie isn't aware there are any next steps. 'Her diagnosis was a permanent vegetative state. That seems pretty definitive to me.'

That sounded passive-aggressive, but he has no expectation of the Rushmore staff to perform a miracle. He doesn't believe Tamsin will ever open her eyes, no matter how good her care is.

'Tamsin was in the coma for a considerable amount of time.' The director chooses to explain anyway. 'They rarely last more than four weeks – hers was nearly eight months. Her brain function tests showed less than fifty per cent of normal brain activity at the time.'

Jamie can feel his legs growing restless and he begins to fidget in his chair, struggling to keep his attention focussed as the monologue continues.

'Tamsin has been here for twelve months. She is an extremely dependent case, which means she cannot survive without medical intervention. Once a patient has spent over a year in a vegetative state without improvement, guidelines state that options should be offered to family members, to decide whether it remains in the patient's best interest to continue providing care.'

Jamie frowns. 'I don't understand.'

'After so long without any sign of recovery, you can choose to withdraw Tamsin's treatment.'

'What?' He still doesn't get what she's trying to tell him. He feels himself sit more upright as he tries to decode the formal language. 'Let her die? Is that what you're saying?'

'In cases where there is little chance of recovery, it's a choice that some relatives consider when prolonged intervention may not be practical.'

Jamie has no idea how to respond appropriately. This is a conversation he had never imagined would happen, and he is entirely unprepared for it.

'I know this must be a shock, but Tamsin's quality of life needs to be taken into account. She spent six months in the Royal London's ICU before she was stable enough to move to the Lewisham rehabilitation centre. Then an eighteen-month stay there, before she came to Rushmore. To keep her alive indefinitely, when her outlook is so poor, may not be advisable.'

Jamie nods dumbly, robbed of speech as his mind races in circles, a hamster on a wheel. A shiver runs through him as comprehension finally sinks in.

'I appreciate that,' he forces himself to say.

'I understand how difficult this must be. But it's our responsibility to offer options and try to help patients' families.'

'We don't need help,' Jamie interrupts. 'We're fine … as fine as we can be in the circumstances.'

He won't reveal he still sees a counsellor once a month, to try and atone for his guilt. Nor will he admit that Elise goes to play therapy because sometimes she wakes in the middle of the night, screaming, 'No, Mummy!' at the top of her little lungs.

He braces his hands against the chair arms, preparing to stand. 'I need to think. I should get down to see my wife.'

'Please update me on your long-term wishes once you've had time to consider.' The director begins unnecessarily tidying her desk, and Jamie takes that as his cue to leave the office.

As he stands at the top of the stairs, a wave of vertigo strikes so unexpectedly that he nearly loses his balance. Possibilities fly through his mind as he imagines sitting by Tamsin's bed, watching her heart tracing gradually flatten, her chest ceasing to rise and fall. He sees himself, calm, composed, trying not to show his relief when the solemn confirmation is delivered.

Three years of limbo. Could it be over soon?

Can he really be free – of the guilt, and of his marriage?

4

Tamsin – Now

J amie has arrived late today.

Even though the exact hour is always a mystery, unless it is a feed time or someone happens to read their watch aloud, I have learned to use sunny days as my timepiece. Usually, the light can be detected on my ear from the right-hand window when Jamie arrives and, by the time he leaves, it has moved to the left-hand window and my left cheek.

Jamie settles in the armchair beside my bed and his smell envelops me, as familiar as the smooth, symmetrical planes of his face. He drops a kiss onto my cheek as usual. He never used to have this long stubble he favours now, which smarts when it scrapes against my skin. He always preferred to be clean-shaven, but I imagine the beard suits him, a sandy scattering below his defined cheekbones.

I wonder if his hair is still short back and sides, if it remains precisely razored into the nape of his neck where I loved to caress the bristly strands, if the cowlick still falls over his forehead.

'You look exhausted.' I only realise Milena is in the room when her rolling accent sounds.

'Too much stuff in my head,' Jamie says, his voice quieter than usual, a weight to his words. Milena's clean scent fills my nose –

no perfume, just fresh linen and soap, telling me that she has moved closer. I hear her palm run across clothing and imagine her giving Jamie's shoulder a reassuring squeeze.

Her gentle fingers brush a few strands of hair from my eyes as she leans over me, monitoring the equipment that surrounds the bed as if she expects it to fail me. Her voice is slightly muffled, telling me her head is turned towards Jamie.

'Something is bothering you.'

'I had a meeting with the director.'

'About what?'

Jamie takes too long to answer. 'Tamsin's care,' he eventually sighs. 'I need to think about it.'

Think about what? Whether to continue paying a king's ransom for my comfort? I can only hope he's not considering choices other than Rushmore. I don't think I could bear another upheaval.

Milena doesn't press him for answers he is clearly not prepared to give. 'The director has to update the care plan every year Tamsin is here. She will know it is the anniversary soon. Of the crash.'

'And Elise's third birthday,' Jamie says heavily.

My daughter's birthday. The seventh of October, just nine days before my own date of birth. How I wish I remembered the moment she was born, even if it was behind a surgical screen. Had they laid her on my breast as the ventilator expanded my lungs? Or was she swept away immediately, denied even a glimpse of me?

I have worked backwards to ascertain Elise was born prematurely. I have regained enough memories of scans and appointments to join the dots and I am certain she was around eight weeks early. I hope she breathed unaided, screamed for me after her abrupt entry into the world, but I can't be sure.

There is a pause that tells me Jamie's mind is elsewhere, still fixed on whatever the director had said. He has never been able to focus on a conversation when preoccupied. His brain compartmentalises by default. Mine is the opposite, always seeking connections.

'It was in the news today,' Milena says. I hear her lift the iPad from my bedside table.

'In *Kent Online*?' Jamie is dismissive. 'They'll take any excuse to rehash the story. The crash was the most exciting thing to happen in that village in decades.'

'Don't you want to know what it says?'

I hear Jamie huff a sigh, but he is always patient with Milena, considerate, and he tells her to go ahead with a note of fondness in his voice that tells me he is humouring her.

'*Almost three years on from the catastrophic road traffic accident on the Hoo Peninsula, which left a man dead and a woman with life-changing injuries, victim Tamsin Shaw still lies comatose in a hospital bed.*'

The lazy description that Milena haltingly reads enrages me. They can't even be bothered to fact-check the difference between a coma and a vegetative state.

'*Celebrated Michelin-starred chef Benicio Aguero, a London-based Argentine with a second home in Cliffe, was pronounced dead at the scene. Mrs Shaw, an eminent psychiatrist, was ejected from the vehicle on a lonely lane, sustaining massive head injuries.*'

Did they do *any* research before publishing the article? The slapdash content needles at me, sharp prods to my brain as I register each medical inaccuracy as much as their failure to even use my correct title. More infuriating is the fact it provides me with almost no memory aids. It tells me nothing I didn't already know, except that I was thrown clear of the mangled vehicle.

This is the first time anyone has read a report of the crash aloud within my earshot, and it should be an opportunity, a chance to learn what I cannot recall, not this clickbait.

Jamie doesn't speak immediately. Tension radiates from his silence in powerful waves I can almost physically feel.

I wait. I have never known why Lucia's husband, not Jamie,

was my passenger that day, and the promise of new knowledge calms my frustration.

'Bad memories,' Milena says quietly. 'I'm sorry.'

'It had been nice, that weekend,' Jamie murmurs, as if talking to himself. 'All of us together in the countryside, me and Tam, Lucia and Ben. I was hungover, wasn't in any rush to head back to London, but Ben and Tam had stuff to do, so they left first.'

The explanation jars me. I don't remember Jamie or Ben ever joining us in Kent. It was mine and Lucia's place, where we escaped our responsibilities for lazy weekends of wine and charcuterie and reruns of *Sex and the City*. There was no reason we'd have all been there together.

'Sometimes it is fate, these things,' Milena says, with the certainty of faith. She went to church back home in Warsaw. She has told me about the peace she found there.

Jamie laughs weakly but offers no further comment, as if he wants the conversation to end as quickly as possible.

Silence sits for a few more moments as Milena continues with her tasks. Jamie always struggles to find things to say, and looks to Milena for help to talk to me like I'm still a human being. He has never been comfortable with quiet – extroverts rarely are – unlike me, who could tolerate it indefinitely, a trait that has undoubtedly saved my sanity in recent times.

'When are you next bringing Elise?' Milena asks.

'Not sure. She gets upset sometimes …'

'It's important, though, that she knows her mother.'

Another sigh. 'Maybe I'm making it worse by bringing her to visit. Since she's started nursery, she's realised she's the only one whose mother lives in a hospital bed.'

I feel my heart rate quicken, bird wings fluttering beneath my sternum. Elise has already learned we are different, that other families don't exist like this. How bemusing it must be for her, how painful, to see her nursery friends being collected by their mothers, lifted onto their hips and smothered in kisses, laughing together as they head for their cars.

Yet, selfishly, the thought that Jamie might stop bringing her to visit makes my throat constrict with dread. There is so little in my life that brings me pleasure, and my daughter is a ray of hope that I have come to depend on.

'It's all she has ever known,' Milena says. 'She's strong, that little one. She will cope.'

I can only hope she is right, this perceptive woman who always seems to know if I'm in pain or distress, who reads my daughter in the same way she does me. She will have noticed the rise in my pulse rate. Sure enough, her cool hand comes to rest on my wrist, a reassuring touch.

As Milena bustles about, Jamie sits quietly as if staring into space, lost in his own thoughts, though I am sure his eyes are on me, watching for any sign that his wife knows he is there. Without the calming sound of his voice reading aloud to me, usually one of the classics he remembered I love, time seems to stand still, and I lose track of how long he has been there, drifting away into my own little world.

I startle back into vigilance when a new arrival suddenly announces their presence with an awkward clearing of their throat. This is rare, unless another visiting doctor has come to make a case study of me. A man, standing in the doorway, if the direction of sound is anything to go by. I can hear change jingling in a trouser pocket, agitated by restless fingers.

Jamie stands too quickly, his thighs pressing against the edge of my mattress as he steps closer to the bed. 'I thought you came on Mondays,' he snaps.

That tells me it is Dan, my literal partner in crime, although we used to fight the causes rather than commit the acts. Dan is the probation service executive who deals with the people society would rather pretend don't exist. And I was his link between depravity and justice, a psychiatrist determined to reset minds that knew only danger.

I have already identified him by the smell of leather from the jacket he always wears. That is why Jamie has stood. Dan's six-foot-four height dwarfs his five-foot-eleven and Jamie doesn't like being made to feel small.

'I didn't know it was your visiting day,' Dan says tightly.

That is a lie. There will be a visitors' book to sign, if only for fire regulations, and Dan is too astute not to have checked the names written there. He will have known exactly when Jamie visits.

'I can't make it next week, so I thought I'd stop by today.'

'I'm sure Tam wouldn't mind if you missed a visit,' Jamie mutters, his voice muffled by gritted teeth. He does not like Dan. I understand why, but it is uncomfortable, lying here listening to the loaded silence, knowing they are staring each other out like warring schoolboys.

'You mean you don't think she'd notice.'

'Hello, Mr Attwood,' Milena interjects. She doesn't usually call visitors by their surnames, but there is something about Dan's demeanour that grants him authority, a gravity in the way he carries himself.

I hear Milena pull another chair up to the other side of the bed, even going so far as to pat the seat. 'More than one visitor is no problem.'

Dan doesn't move from the doorway. He is used to taking charge and I am sure, beneath his show of awkwardness, he is expecting Jamie will make way for him.

He doesn't know Jamie well.

'It's fine, I'll grab a coffee and come back later.'

'Good luck finding a café in the middle of nowhere,' she says. 'Sit down, I'll go make you both one.'

Jamie sits again, marking his territory by reaching for my unresponsive hand. His palm is damp and his grip slightly too tight. I hear Dan's measured footsteps cross the room and I picture the Chelsea boots he favours. The leather jacket creaks as he sits and presses his back firmly into the chair.

There is silence and I am almost certainly the one who finds it the most discomfiting, these two men facing off over my motionless figure.

'How's Elise getting on?' Dan eventually asks.

'Fine.' Jamie isn't about to help make the conversation flow.

Dan doesn't know what to say in response to that. I feel him lean forward, resting his forearms against his thighs, observing me. Jamie's fingers twitch around my hand.

'How you doing, Tam?' Dan asks softly, a sing-song quality to his tone.

His visits are rarely silent; he talks easily to me, telling me of his week, updating me on the clients he and I have shared. It has done his career no harm, forming a working partnership with one of the UK's foremost psychiatrists, one of the very few women to specialise in sex offenders. I have a lot of letters after my name and there were a lot of certificates lining the walls of my Southwark office, where I used to explore the minds of men who have committed the worst acts imaginable. Not that those qualifications are any use to me now.

'Do you believe she can hear you?' Jamie asks, a note of challenge ringing out.

Dan's jacket rustles as he shrugs. 'Some of the research suggests it's possible. Don't you talk to her?'

'Of course I do!' Jamie retorts.

'But you don't think she's listening.'

Jamie releases my hand, shoving back his chair. 'No, Dan, I don't. I don't think Tam has any idea we come here every week and jabber nonsense at her. I don't think Tam is in there at all. And I'm glad. I wouldn't want my wife to be trapped in a never-ending hell with no way out.'

Dan shifts but I know by the direction of his voice that he is still looking at me. 'This is hard for everyone.'

'Hardest for her *family*,' Jamie emphasises. 'That's why we've got tough decisions to make.'

'What tough decisions?' Dan's attention, and mine, is caught by the odd comment – one I suspect Jamie had not intended to make.

I am grateful to him for asking the question I cannot.

'None of your business,' Jamie blusters, caught out. He will hide behind avoidance tactics now. 'You know what, I'll leave you to it. I might as well spend some quality time with Elise.'

'Say hello to her.'

'She's no idea who you are.'

Dan is silent as my stomach squirms. Jamie pauses to place a kiss on my forehead, taking his time, and I feel the imprint of his lips even after he has moved away. The door opens and closes smartly, and with him leaves my chance to find out what tough decision needs to be made.

I file it away in my mind, ready to retrieve it when the opportunity for further investigation presents itself. I'm good like that now, able to pick up trains of thought at will, no longer floundering to recollect previous days' events like I had been in the early months. I have worked hard on my capabilities and, although they are very different from ones I used to have, I am proud of them nonetheless.

Dan sighs gently and picks up my hand, resting it on his upturned palm. His fingers intertwine with mine, longer and slimmer than Jamie's, cooler to the touch. His thumb begins a rhythmic caress that sets my teeth on edge, the sensation too much for my paper-thin skin.

He begins to speak, like he expects me to respond at any moment, and I wish I could. Especially when the first words out of his mouth are, 'Tam, we need to talk about Richard Mandeville.'

5

Tamsin – Before

I insisted on meeting Dan Attwood early, before my first client of the day, but he was always delayed, in demand from the moment he switched his work mobile on. Rather than wait alone in my little office and allow anxiety to pluck away at my nerves, I walked the short distance to Borough Market and the kerbside coffee shop where Lucia started her working mornings.

The place was popular and always rammed. The air was alive with voices and footsteps, rush-hour traffic, the clink of china and cutlery. Hot, delicious smells of fresh coffee and frying bacon and toasting bread made my stomach growl.

'Espresso's not a good idea,' Lucia warned as I sat beside her, clutching my tiny cup. 'You're already twitchy.'

'It's not from caffeine. I've got a new client starting today.'

'You don't usually worry about new starters.'

'This one's a bit different.'

Wariness cast a shadow across Lucia's warm eyes. 'Tell me more.'

I shrugged as if I didn't have a firm answer. 'His file didn't make for pleasant reading. He's just finished half of a sixteen-year sentence.'

'I don't know how you do it, sitting in that room alone with that sort of man.'

'There are panic buttons everywhere. The security guard's desk is just down the corridor, and I have an emergency radio.'

I had told her this before, but Lucia needed the reassurance of repetition.

'I chose the job,' I reminded her. 'It's what I want to do. I'm good at it.'

She couldn't suppress a shudder. 'I worry about you, anyway. You put yourself at risk.'

'Don't we all?' I sipped the thick, bitter coffee and immediately felt bad, watching Lucia's knuckles whitening around her cup. 'It's worth me taking the risk, if it prevents other women being exposed to it.'

She twitched her head and shrugged, plastering a smile across her lips. 'You and Jamie are still coming tonight, aren't you?'

'Absolutely. We're looking forward to it.' The latter wasn't true, but she had earned her reprieve. Lucia had put a lot of effort into organising the celebration of her husband's second Michelin star at his Canary Wharf restaurant.

Porteños was Ben's dream. It was the culmination of years overcoming his rugged upbringing in the far north of Argentina, born into the gaucho tradition in Salta province, before he ran away to Buenos Aires as a teenager. He loved to tell the story of his meteoric rise to celebrity chef at every opportunity.

There had been a lot of sacrifice, mostly on Lucia's part, but it seemed to have paid off. That was a quiet relief, for me as much as my best friend, since Jamie was now also heavily invested in Ben's success.

I looked away from Lucia. I was not comfortable with Ben and his infamous Latin temperament being responsible for the financial security of my marriage. My fingers automatically found my left palm, and the thick raised ridge running across it, as it always did when I was ill at ease. Since the day I got that scar, I had been constantly on the alert for danger, even in circumstances that should have been safe.

'Let's just hope he keeps the damn star and doesn't upset every other chef in London showing off about it.' Lucia batted my fingers lightly to stop me worrying at the scar. 'Who knows, it might make the TV producers up their offer for season two.'

It was Lucia's PR expertise that had catapulted the Aguero empire into the public eye and kept it there, capitalising on Ben's sultry pouts and sensuous caresses as he seasoned his mouthwatering steaks. His flamboyant habit of tossing cuts of meat high into the air to impale them on churrasco skewers had won him millions of Instagram followers and an Amazon Prime docuseries. I had never been able to bring myself to watch *La Cocina Loca* and hadn't realised there was going to be another season. Even the title made me cringe.

'Tell me who's coming tonight. Has Ben lined up all of London's celebrities?'

'Tons.' Lucia rolled her eyes at my sardonic tone. 'You'll hate it.'

'It'll be interesting to talk to a different demographic.'

'You make it sound like a social experiment.'

'That's exactly what it is.' I laughed. 'And I bet Mateo's excited to hobnob with the influencers.'

'He just wants to meet the grime artist I've banned him from listening to.'

My twelve-year-old godson, Mateo, was no stranger to pre-teen rebellion. He would make sure to enjoy himself while his mother was distracted.

'I'll keep an eye on him for you.'

'Thanks. How are you feeling, anyway?'

My unscarred palm moved to my stomach. Lucia was the only person I had told so far. Like me, her first reaction had been disbelief. Both us of had sat on the floor of my ensuite, three positive tests before us, undeniable proof of an impossible result.

'Fine, I think.'

Lucia swished a spoon through her cappuccino foam, creating patterns in the fluffy white froth. 'Have you told Jamie yet?'

'Tonight, once he's had a few drinks.' I had to prevent myself from picking at the skin around my nails. I could feel the strength of the espresso, ants trotting through my veins, and I knew I must give up the habit, but I couldn't, not just yet, not until I knew for certain about my future.

'I don't know what you're so worried about.'

'Jamie accepted it was never going to happen years ago. He's too used to his freedom now.'

'Ben was the same when I got pregnant.'

I kept my own counsel on that. 'It might not be what he wants. We haven't talked about kids for years.'

Not since the events that had put paid to us having a family, that had robbed me of so much. We didn't talk about that day either. It wouldn't have made a difference if we did.

Because Jamie could never know the truth of what really happened, when we lost our chance to have children. Or so we thought.

Lucia checked her watch again. 'I've got to go, Tam. I'll see you tonight. We'll get Jamie drunk before you tell him.'

I forced a smile, happy for her to think she understood the reason for my reticence.

She power-walked away, heading for the bridge, and I denied myself another espresso. A notification pinged on my phone – Dan letting me know he was at the Elephant and Castle roundabout. Five minutes for me to slip into the safety of professional mode as I strode back to the office. I had missed my morning run and I could feel the restlessness in my calves instead of the familiar, sweet ache after a brisk ten miles. I wondered how I would be able to maintain my strict exercise regime in the coming months.

For once, Dan was waiting when I arrived at my practice's nondescript, brick-clad building, his BMW idling throatily against the kerb despite it being a no-parking zone. I slid into the passenger seat before he could get out and greet me.

'Good morning,' he said, sending me a questioning glance. I saw him assess me, deciding if I would be safe at work today. He didn't need to worry. I was dressed in a regular work outfit: olive green linen trousers and a cream polo neck. I would never wear anything clinging or revealing to the office. Not worth the risk of offering myself as an object of desire. Nor did I ever wear makeup, or any jewellery apart from ear studs and my wedding ring, or let my hair hang loose. I made every effort to appear plain, unremarkable, in my appearance.

'We don't need to do this inside,' I said. 'It won't take long.'

'Then why couldn't you phone me?'

I ran my fingers along the straps of my handbag, making sure they were both identical in length. 'Because I wanted to see you.'

I saw him smile out the corner of my eye but couldn't raise my gaze to meet his. He turned in the driving seat, angling his body towards me. His shoulders looked wider without his leather jacket, his rower's physique evident in his long, lean body.

He wasn't classically handsome, not like Jamie, who was so effortlessly attractive that women stared at him wherever he went. Dan had a slight underbite, a nose that was just a little too hooked and denim-blue eyes that sat a tiny bit too close together. His power was in his forceful presence, his natural gift for commanding attention and acquiescence with equal ease.

'Richard Mandeville,' I said, quickly, before he could speak. 'It's his first appointment today.'

'I know that.'

'What do *I* need to know about him?'

Dan's eyes hardened as his jaw clenched. 'He's been deemed fit to be part of society again.' He spoke as if reading the party line.

'There's a "but" coming.'

'You've read his file, you know his crimes. You know what he did to those women.' Dan shook his head, barking a laugh devoid of humour. 'Eight fucking years served. They call that justice. There must have been more victims – an attacker like that doesn't just stop at two. Too traumatised to come forward, I bet.'

I refused to get sidetracked by his futile hypothesising. 'You've met him. Tell me your impressions.'

'Charming. Clever. Controlling.' A muscle jumped in his face. 'Dangerous.'

'Did you deliberately put them in alphabetical order?' I tried to lighten his mood despite knowing he didn't respond well to teasing.

'I didn't want him seeing you,' he said abruptly. 'I tried to arrange a different psychiatrist. I even told the bloody executive director you weren't the right psych for him. You should never have been amongst his selection in the first place.'

My professional pride roared. 'That's my reputation you're undermining!'

'I'm trying to keep you safe, Tam! Richard Mandeville is one of the most twisted offenders I've ever come across. Yet, because he's got a title and nice manners, he gets to make demands.'

'He chose to work with me,' I stated firmly. 'All participants in this programme have the right to choose their psychiatrist. Mandeville got no privileges.'

Dan snorted softly, refusing to reply. He ran his fingers roughly through his hair, which was just long enough to touch his collar, his way of rebelling against the civil service's conventional neat haircuts.

I knew my qualifications, my experience, were not the real reason I had been paired with Richard Mandeville. Dan may have been certain he had been granted special treatment but that couldn't have been further from the truth. If anything, it had been the opposite.

'Parole surely wouldn't have been granted if he was so dangerous.' I spoke quickly, hoping my thoughts hadn't been broadcast across my face. I didn't need Dan's suspicious nature interfering in my work.

'The board fell for him hook, line and sinker. He convinced them he's a changed man, sickened by his own past, desperate to make amends. With intense psychiatric help, of course.'

'He must have been an exemplary prisoner to have halved his initial sentence.'

'Didn't put a foot wrong.'

'Then I'll give him the same chance I give every client. And if he puts a toe out of line, I'll let you march him straight back to Wandsworth.'

Dan grabbed my hand, making me jump with the suddenness of his movement. 'Text me after every appointment, as soon as he leaves.'

'You're being ridiculous. He's just another offender.' I tactfully slid my hand free. 'And stop making dramatic statements. You're clouding my judgement. I'll never be able to work with the man if you impair my neutrality.'

Finally, a grin played on Dan's lips.

'"Impair your neutrality",' he mocked softly. 'Christ, you always were cleverer than me.'

Momentarily relieved, I grinned back, but I knew it was a short-lived respite.

'Dan, there was another reason I wanted to speak in the car.'

His eyebrows rose but he waited, biting his lip to prevent himself from rushing me.

'I'm pregnant,' I told the dashboard, staring straight ahead until I could summon the courage to glance sideways.

The silence was deafening. Dan's entire body jumped, as if he had been punched, before he went very still. I could practically hear his keen mind working, trying to solve the puzzle.

'How long?' he whispered.

'Eight weeks. I did a test at the weekend.' I forced a laugh. 'Took me too long to notice I didn't get my period –'

I didn't have the chance to continue waffling nervously. The next moment, Dan's long arms were wrapped around me, and he was beaming and laughing and hugging me as if I had given him the best news in the world.

My capable, methodical brain, which always knew what to do, chose that moment to desert me and I had no idea how to respond.

'Dan, stop,' I whispered. 'It's Jamie's baby.'

He released me like I was suddenly tainted. The car became so claustrophobic I tried to move away too, the passenger door trapping me. I pressed the pad of my thumb along the length of my scar, focussing on the texture of the damaged tissue.

His hands gripped the steering wheel, his knuckles whitening. The ropey muscles of his throat flexed as he swallowed hard, and I heard him draw a sharp breath.

'How do you know it's not mine?'

'Because it was one time.'

'*One time* is all it takes,' he rapped out. 'Why are you telling me, if you're so sure?'

'So you're not left wondering, once I start showing.'

'Thanks for your consideration.'

His brittle sarcasm stung, especially when he'd been so concerned for my welfare just moments before. There was no trace of solicitousness as he reached for the start button, punching the engine into life.

'For the record,' he said, 'I didn't think it would just be "one time".'

I stared, unnerved by the intensity of his agitation. 'It was –' I just managed to catch myself before the wrong words spilt from my lips, '– wasn't meant to happen. We were drunk, we weren't thinking straight.'

'I wanted it to happen,' he snapped. 'I've waited years for you, for God's sake.'

The conversation was rapidly going out of control. 'Dan, we've not been together for over a decade! You're my friend, my colleague. There's nothing more between us.'

'Then why did we sleep together?'

'I'm sorry,' I said, fingers reaching for the door handle. 'My life is with Jamie and that isn't going to change. If I gave you any other impression, then I apologise, but I certainly didn't mean to. We'll talk another time.'

'If you can fit me into your busy schedule.' I had never heard Dan sound this childish. Even in our twenties, when everyone lived by their impulses, he had seemed so mature, so adult.

As I escaped onto the pavement, he barely waited for me to close the door before pulling away from the kerb. I watched him swing out into the traffic, blaring his horn at a bus that had the temerity not to give way. I found I was shaking, adrenaline and caffeine combining in a flammable cocktail.

Pressing my hand to my abdomen, I silently apologised to my baby for the mess I had got the two of us into.

Richard Mandeville arrived exactly on time.

He walked into the room with long, purposeful strides, his hand already extended to me. His grip told of power, but he was careful not to tighten his fingers. The contact was over in a moment, and I was left wondering at the sudden fizz of electricity his skin had caused against mine.

Richard's full lips pursed as he examined his surroundings, as if he had been expecting the opulence of my former premises on Harley Street, rather than a practical shared office block in the maze of narrow streets behind London Bridge station.

I took my opportunity to assess him as he did the same to my work space. I noted the rapid movements of his grey eyes, the carefully styled dark-blond quiff that spoke of a fresh haircut, the rhythmic clenching of his fists in time with the rise and fall of his high, firm chest. His feet were shoulder-width apart, a planted base, and he held his spine very straight, making him seem tall even though he only just reached average height.

'Please take a seat,' I said, an instruction as much as an invitation.

He waited for me to sit before folding himself gracefully into the tub chair, an etiquette that seemed to come as naturally to him as breathing. He wore a navy blazer over a thick cotton dress shirt, striped with pale blue, and pressed chinos with well-worn espadrilles. He would have looked equally at home on a Saint-Tropez yacht or at a table in Boodle's.

'Thank you for seeing me.' His voice was softer than expected, precise vowels, a pleasant timbre. 'What would you like me to call you?'

I pretended I wasn't set off-kilter by the question I usually asked all first-time clients. 'I prefer Dr Shaw. Are you comfortable with Mr Mandeville?'

'I heard my surname rather a lot in prison. It would be nice to be addressed by my Christian name.'

'As you wish.'

He removed his blazer and draped it neatly over the arm of his chair before rolling up his shirtsleeves in measured and even folds. Finally, he sat back, his shoulders relaxing, but his eyes still moved, taking in every inch of space around him. I had seen it before in newly released prisoners. They were often on guard, but this man had a poise rarely found in ex-convicts.

He had those classic features that foretold of his status: the aquiline nose, high cheekbones, carved jawline. A dimple sat perfectly in the centre of his square chin. The Right Honourable Richard Mandeville, the fifth Earl of Southvale, was devastatingly good-looking and he knew it.

'How are you finding life on the outside?' I asked, deliberately casual, as if it hadn't been a momentous change for him.

He flinched, just slightly, and it would have been undetectable if I hadn't been looking for it. He didn't have an easy time in prison. The scars were deep and still painful.

'A little unsettling at the moment. I'm not used to busy streets and crowded restaurants anymore.'

He had served his time in the VP unit, protected from other inmates who might take umbrage at his crimes. A solitary existence.

'But being able to go to bed when I choose, select my own meals, lock my own front door – that's a pretty magical feeling.'

A disarming grin deepened the laughter lines around his eyes. It gave him the air of a vivacious host, welcoming his guest with the guarantee of a good time. His skin bore no trace of prison pallor. I'd have been forgiven for thinking he'd just returned from a trip to the Amalfi Coast, if his licence terms didn't forbid him from leaving the country.

'I invested in a sunbed,' he confided, smile widening as he laughed at himself. He had not missed my visual evaluation of him. 'I resembled a corpse when I walked out of those gates. My own mother barely recognised me.'

For once, I didn't know how to reply. 'You look very well,' I settled on.

'The diet of carbs upon carbs didn't quite finish me off,' he agreed. He propped his elbows on the chair arms, his forearm muscles cording into sinewy planes. 'So, perhaps you could tell me how this works? It's all new to me.'

Once again, I was wrong-footed. Usually, I controlled the session, leading the client through the plan, making sure they understood I was in charge, not them. Richard Mandeville had shown no signs of dominating, no manipulation of the conversation, yet he had somehow taken the reins.

As if reading my thoughts, he raised his palms. 'My apologies, Dr Shaw. I was too used to taking charge before recent circumstances. I didn't mean to talk over you.'

He had a formal way of speaking despite his relaxed body language, as if he was addressing an audience. I wondered how he behaved in private, whether he let the mask of propriety slip.

'Thank you for the apology.'

He smiled again, a genuine smile that turned his flinty eyes a dove grey and softened his features.

I realised then that I was enjoying Richard Mandeville's presence in my office.

6

Tamsin – Now

Dan stays by my bed longer than usual, and I wait for him to finally get to the reason why he can't visit on Monday. He seems determined to delay telling me.

Instead, he talks about the old days, of how we met, of when he realised he had fallen in love with me, as I grow increasingly impatient for him to make his point.

I squirm mentally as he describes his memories of long nights talking in the cramped living room of the Shepherd's Bush flat we had shared with two others. A cheap bottle of red and whatever takeaway Dan had ordered for us both, despite knowing my aversion to junk food.

I was in my third and final foundation year at St Mary's, about to choose my specialty rotations. Dan, several years older, was on the prison service's graduate scheme after failing to make the cut for the GB rowing squad. Hence the kebabs and pizzas, his way of sticking two fingers up to the selectors.

We had been members of the same gym, usually the earliest arrivals, and I had offered him pointers on his deadlift form, fresh in my mind from my orthopaedic rotation. After he'd patched up his punctured ego, we had drifted into a daily routine of spotting each other on free weights and competing on the ergometers.

Sometimes he would let me win and I would soundly condemn him for what he insisted was chivalry.

When Team GB later rejected him, and he couldn't bear to flat-share with his fellow rowers and their success any longer, I invited him to take the spare room vacated by another St Mary's junior, who had turned to whisky to get him through the trauma of A&E shifts. He had given his soul to a career I had sworn only to apply my brain to.

'Do you remember the night I swam across the river?' Dan asks, and I hear the grin in his voice. I had been less impressed, clutching my phone ready to summon the lifeboat, despite knowing how strong a swimmer he was. All for a £10 bet from one of our other flatmates as we walked towards Wandsworth Bridge in the wee hours.

'You wouldn't speak to me for days, would you?' he continues. Rhetorical questions are a necessary part of conversing with the vegetative, preventing the speaker's voice from becoming a painfully monotonous drone, but they only highlight my inability to answer. 'That was when I realised. You were angry I might have drowned, not because I was being a show-off. You cared about me.'

In reality, I had been livid at the prospect of having to waste the lifeboat's time, angry that I may have had to perform CPR on his inconsiderate corpse and furious that he had made me wait in the freezing cold as he powered his way across the fortunately calm, black waters.

It seems Dan had seen it quite differently.

'That's why I asked you out,' he says, his fingers squeezing mine. 'I knew we had a connection then.'

For once, I am glad I am unable to speak, because I would have struggled to resist putting him straight.

I had dated Dan because he was steady and reliable, despite the occasional stunt to paint himself spontaneous. It wasn't love; it was security. He was big enough to make me feel safe when we walked through dark, cramped London back streets. He didn't waste money on pointless items he didn't need. He didn't start arguments with strangers in pubs.

'I'd have done anything for you,' Dan continues.

That was true. He was an unselfish partner, attentive, but in a way I often found suffocating. He never understood when I tried to explain how I valued my alone time. He was not an introvert; he just wasn't keen on many people. But he expected his inner circle to stick close to him, and that included me.

'I went back to Lito's the other day,' he tells me. 'I like to go every so often, remember the good times.'

I adored trying new restaurants, different cuisines, but Dan was a creature of habit. He loved Lito's, a tiny Thai café just off Battersea High Street, and would have happily eaten there every date night, complaining whenever I managed to drag him elsewhere.

'I should have asked you to marry me when I had the chance,' he is saying, bringing my attention back to his words again. 'I shouldn't have waited.'

It wouldn't have mattered. I would have said no.

'We had a good time, didn't we, Tam? We were a good couple.' If I were awake, his voice would have held more than a hint of neediness, but the persistently vegetative aren't brilliant at assuaging their visitors' insecurities.

I understand why he doesn't mention the less appealing parts of our history. People prefer memories to be sanitised, just like they canonise the dead. It is easier to see through rose-tinted spectacles than the cold lenses of reality.

Dan won't talk to me about his possessiveness, how he came to hate me going anywhere socially without him. He won't own up to checking my phone when I showered or discuss his defensive behaviour when I caught him. He won't acknowledge that he disliked all my male friends or that he was once certain I was having an affair with an anaesthetist.

I didn't love him. That was the biggest problem. Because it made his love overwhelming to me. I ended it, as soon as I realised he felt so much more strongly about me than I ever would about him. As my psychiatry career began to flourish, I landed my dream position at Broadmoor. A few months later, I was introduced to Jamie at a party.

'Do you remember when we got back in touch?' There is more confidence in his tone now the silence has sat for a few moments. 'I wasn't even sure you'd take my call. I'd followed your career but I hadn't realised just how stratospheric you'd gone.'

It had been a bit of a shock, my secretary announcing I had a call waiting from Daniel Attwood, regional director of the probation service for London. I had been in private practice for several years, needing the flexibility for my own research, and kept a deliberately small client list for discretion's sake.

'I got the feeling you weren't up for it at first.'

Of course I wasn't. He'd explained his impossible task – reducing the reoffending rates of paroled Category 1 sex offenders – and the almost limitless budget he had been given to try and make it happen. Would I design a bespoke programme, engineered to reset the urges of this reviled population? Could I rewire their brains, to see if that would stop them committing their terrible crimes?

I had nearly laughed in his face.

Why would I have risked my reputation entering into a partnership with my ex-boyfriend, for a scheme that seemed certain to fail? Those types of men could not be rehabilitated. It was their base nature, their lizard brain. No amount of plaudits to my name could change that.

And yet, I admit, despite myself, I was curious. I loved a challenge and, even though I dismissed it as ridiculous at the time, Dan's suggestion had piqued my interest.

'I'd decided you wouldn't be calling me back.' He laughs softly. 'I'd already started researching other psychiatrists when you turned up at my office. Must admit, it didn't fill me with confidence when you said this went against your every instinct.'

Without sounding too egotistical, I was respected in my field, my opinion in high demand, and I wasn't comfortable gambling everything I had worked for on an experiment.

Yet I hadn't been able get it out of my mind. The possibilities, the intricacies of such complex treatment, tormented me, but it was the potential for glory, the chance to be a trailblazer and the plaudits that would doubtlessly follow, that enticed me.

So I'd signed on the dotted line and agreed to let some of the most twisted individuals in the UK offending system into my professional world.

'You want to work with your *ex*?' Jamie had demanded when I told him, as if I would be sharing my daily life with Dan once again.

'That's the main issue that's bothering you? Not the rapists?' I'd rolled my eyes. 'I'm happily married, Jamie. We're not going to be sneaking off for trysts.'

He'd grinned. 'Thank you for saying "happily".'

'I'll barely see him. He's only sending me the clients, not sharing my office. I'll need to find new premises, by the way.'

'You love your office.'

'Bringing a steady stream of sex offenders to Harley Street is not going to go down well. Better somewhere more anonymous.'

'Place above a massage parlour, maybe? Or a chicken shop might be better. Save you skulking the mean streets trying to find a Pret.'

The trial group had been a huge success. Dan had been applauded by his bosses. My reputation soared again, and I was invited to give lectures to probation services and psychiatric associations around the globe.

'You were so good at your job,' Dan sighs. 'The things you did for men like Richard Mandeville, no one else could have managed that.'

My muscles can't react, but my brain can, and it steps up a gear again at the mention of Richard's name. Finally, we get to the point.

'That's why I can't visit Monday. His case has finally come to court. He claims he'll prove his innocence.'

Of course he does. Richard Mandeville, determined to show the world he was wrongly convicted on all charges, would move mountains to make sure his denials were heard loud and clear. He has waited a long time for this retrial.

'How has it taken this long to decide the jury was unsound? If it wasn't a fair trial, why the hell wasn't it obvious back then?'

Richard's resolve to clear his name, start afresh as the injured party, no doubt with a massive compensation cheque, had been unwavering from the start. He wanted his old life back, as it had been before it was tarnished beyond repair.

'We could do with your testimony, Tam, I tell you. The jury would listen to you.'

But what did Dan think I would tell them?

'I've submitted your reports, and I found your notebooks when your office was cleared out.' Dan pauses. 'They're quite … different from your usual notes.'

I remember them. I wrote throughout each session with Richard, instead of a brief summary afterwards, like I usually did. I recorded his gestures and mannerisms, his deflections and his admissions, the shades his eyes turned. 'My boss said we had to declare them, as well as the reports. The defence requested them.'

I cringe at the thought of my private notes being quoted in court, so different from my concise, factual, clinically worded reports. I picture myself taking the witness stand, buttoned into the armour of my Dior pinstripes, delivering my expert opinion to ultimately guide the deliberation of my client's fate.

In many ways, I crave to have that control. But a part of me can't deny the relief of being excused from such a responsibility.

'He's already throwing "miscarriage of justice" around like it's a brand name,' Dan sneers. 'You should see him, Tam, sitting in the dock in his Savile Row suits, smiling at the jury. He thinks he owns the place.'

Dan is not being objective. He disliked Richard from the beginning, before the man had ever set foot in my office. I hope he will at least try to maintain a professional detachment, for his own sake. Richard is more than capable of seeing Dan out of a job, though I suspect his current focus will be solely on his own fight for freedom.

Milena comes back with another coffee for Dan. He usually gulps down three or four mugs over the course of each visit, not even waiting for the drink to cool. I wonder if she senses the taut atmosphere, whether she casts Dan a questioning glance, because he seems to feel compelled to offer her an explanation for his off-schedule visit.

'I was just telling Tamsin about a client we shared. She didn't get the chance to finish his treatment programme before the crash.'

'Her rehabilitation programme?' I hear interest in Milena's voice. She doesn't know much about Dan. He deliberately plays his cards close to his chest during visits, giving little away about our shared past or professional relationship.

Dan must have nodded confirmation. 'She was certain she could make a difference, keep women safe from those offenders. This client was convicted of some horrific things but now he's trying to prove he didn't commit his crimes.'

'But you think he did?'

'I'm certain he did. Tamsin would have been the key professional at his retrial. Without her, I think we're going to struggle.'

'She would have helped you prove he is guilty?'

'I hope she would.' Dan sounds uncertain now, and it chills me. 'She seemed to like him. I've no idea why.'

'Maybe she saw something in him that you don't.'

'Believe me, Milena, I saw enough in Richard Mandeville to give me nightmares for years. I never wanted Tam working with him in the first place, but she was so sure she would be OK with him.'

Milena's fingers tighten in a reflex reaction, a vice around my wrist. 'That's his name?' Her voice sounds strangled.

'Nice-sounding name for a monster.'

Milena's grip becomes painful. She will leave bruises on my fragile skin. What has unsettled her so much? Past trauma needled by the mention of violence against women, or something else, something closer to home?

'And when the crash happened, she was still treating him.' Her palm is damp with sweat. Her own pulse beats against mine, faster, like frantic wings.

Dan is too fixated on Richard Mandeville's guilt to recognise the edge to Milena's words. I will him to display some curiosity at her reaction, but he seems oblivious. Milena seems to be making a connection between my work and the crash. I don't have the memories to support or deny her theory, but it puts me on edge.

'Did you see the pictures of her car?' Milena asks. 'They've been in the newspaper.'

'I saw them at the time. It was a complete wreck. Miracle that Tam survived.' Another silence and, finally, Dan's cloud of preoccupation lifts. His voice softens, as it always does when he is considering his next move. 'What are you saying, Milena?'

But it is too much for her. Perhaps her instinct for self-preservation has warned her to watch what she is saying, and her confidence has faltered.

'Nothing,' she stumbles. 'It doesn't matter. Just thinking out loud, that's all.'

Ask her, I scream silently at Dan. *Ask her what she really means!*

Something has spooked her. And I have to find out what.

7

Jamie – Now

Jamie drives back to London on autopilot, barely noticing the roads before him, his mind a maelstrom of contradictions. He jumps violently when his phone rings out through the car's system, bringing him abruptly back to attention.

He doesn't recognise the number but answers anyway. The calls from unknown numbers are usually the ones he dare not ignore.

'Jamie, it's Dan Attwood.'

Jamie's shoulders drop in relief, even though he is annoyed by the sound of Dan's voice. 'Didn't know you had my number.'

'Sorry to bother you.' Dan manages to sound awkward and dismissive at the same time. Clearly, he is as uncomfortable with this call as Jamie is. 'I need to ask a favour.'

Jamie stays silent.

'Have you seen the big retrial on BBC news this morning? It's one of Tamsin's clients.'

'I don't keep up with the news much.'

'Did Tam ever mention a Richard Mandeville?'

Jamie grits his teeth at Dan's persistence, and at the use of his wife's shortened name. 'Tamsin didn't talk about work.'

'That's why I'm calling. I need to check through the boxes from Tam's office, in case we've missed anything that could help the prosecution.'

'You took all her paperwork when the office was cleared.'

'I have to be sure, Jamie. We need everything we can get our hands on. Are the boxes in storage?'

'No,' Jamie sighs. 'They're at home.'

'Can I come and look? I wouldn't ask if it wasn't urgent. I'm heading back to London from Rushmore. I can swing by your office.'

Jamie considers refusing, but that would only prolong the inevitable. 'I'll meet you at the apartment. I'm not far away.'

Jamie hangs up without saying goodbye and tries to focus on the road. He wasn't about to tell Dan Attwood that Apollo Point, their Isle of Dogs apartment building on the curve of the river, is no longer his home. It lies empty, nearly three years since it was last occupied.

He parks in his assigned spot in the underground car park as if he is still here every day and takes the lift up to the fifteenth floor. The apartment's stillness unnerves him as he steps inside. It smells of loneliness and stale air and old reed diffusers run dry. Once, he had adored this place, with its floor-to-ceiling windows and limitless views of the Thames, so close he could throw a pebble into the waters from the wrap-around balcony.

In the early days of their marriage, he had loved to sprawl on the corner sofa in the open-plan living space, watching Tamsin cook, appreciating her competence in the kitchen compared to his own ineptitude. They would watch the sun go down together as they sipped a good Malbec, a burning heat between them that was entirely at odds with the ice queen persona Tam presented to the outside world. That was before the cracks began to show, before their relationship was scarred by secrets and lies.

Now, the only regular presence in this once happy home is the cleaner, who keeps the place sparkling, as if expecting them to return any day and resume their privileged lives. It can't be sold, not since Jamie had the bright idea of transferring the deeds solely into Tamsin's name to avoid his creditors getting their hands on it. So, as long as Tamsin lives, their home sits empty, a reminder of a marriage now frozen in time.

He tiptoes up the spiral staircase as if afraid to disturb the slumbering ghosts. Wrought-iron spindles and oak boards, chosen for beauty over practicality. If circumstances had been different, could they have lived here as a family?

Jamie runs his hand along the smooth banister, imagining himself carrying a squirming infant up the stairs or an adventurous toddler attempting to descend independently. He tries to imagine his daughter in this place she has never called home, learning to walk, decorating the lowest expanses of the windows with her little handprint smudges, saying her first word. Revelling in the attention of both her parents. All those things feel impossible now.

And how is all this making Elise feel? Raised by a clueless father and a woman of no relation who she calls Lu-Lu. No wonder she needs play therapy.

Jamie directs his mind to the job in hand as he strides into the master bedroom, barely glancing at the views across to Greenwich and the O2. He opens Tamsin's expansive wardrobes, staring at the neatly hung clothes, his fingers gliding over silk, linen, cotton. He has no real idea which items go with what, or which colours complement each other. Tamsin just always looked good – her style seemed effortless.

He closes his eyes as a wave of his wife's J'adore perfume drifts from the rails. He's made such a mess of all this, when it should have been so simple. He drags several deep breaths through his nose to expel the unwanted reminder of his old life.

He has never removed her belongings – a kind of superstition has stopped him. But won't he be forced to shake that off when he makes the ultimate decision?

He can't think about that now. He straightens his shoulders and sets about dragging the taped cardboard boxes, neatly stacked beneath the hanging clothes, out onto the carpet.

The buzzer sounds, announcing Dan's arrival. They nod warily at each other as Jamie permits him entry.

'Thanks for this.'

Jamie leads him through to the bedroom, gesturing to the pile. 'Best of luck finding anything. There's no order, it was all just thrown in.'

'I'll manage.'

Jamie is twitchy now, eager to leave. He doesn't want to make small talk with Dan or hear about Tamsin's former clients, in case he lets slip something he shouldn't.

'I've got to get back to work. Close the door behind you when you leave.'

He doesn't retrieve his car. Instead, he walks away, without looking back, onto the next road lined with tall redbrick terraced houses. Number 4 was always 'Ben's place' before, but now Jamie calls it Lucia's house, not yet daring to claim it as his own home. He lets himself in with the key that still sits unfamiliar in his palm. The rich aroma of garlic and herbs greets him like a hug and Jamie realises he has forgotten to eat again.

His daughter is perched on a high stool in the kitchen-diner, scribbling enthusiastically on a piece of paper.

'Daddy!' She launches into his arms, her little hands gripping his neck. 'Look, I drawed a flappy fly!'

Jamie holds her close, breathing in the scent of strawberry shampoo and custard creams, until she wriggles to freedom. He dutifully admires the drawing that looks surprisingly like a 'flappy fly' – Elise refuses to use the correct name for butterfly – and asks her about her day at nursery.

She shrugs, uninterested. 'It's done now.'

Lucia turns towards him from the hob, her neat fingers holding a wooden spoon stained red with tomato. 'Doesn't dwell on the past, this one.'

'If only we could take a leaf out of her book. Thanks for picking her up.'

'She's no trouble. We went to the aquarium after nursery.'

'I saw a horsey fish!' Elise proudly announces.

'She means a sea horse,' Lucia whispers confidentially. 'How was visiting today?'

Distracted by his daughter, Jamie takes a moment too long refocusing on their conversation. He checks to see if Elise is listening, even though he knows she can't comprehend the enormity of what he is facing.

'They said Tam's been vegetative for over a year now,' he tells Lucia quietly.

'Yeah, that'd be right. She was moved to Rushmore just before the second anniversary.'

'That changes things, apparently.' He is being deliberately vague, unsure whether he is ready to have this discussion, unsure how to voice his thoughts even to the woman he trusts most of all.

'Like what?' A hint of impatience enters Lucia's voice.

'We can decide whether to let her go. If her quality of life hasn't shown any signs of improving, her support can be withdrawn.'

Lucia's busy actions come to an abrupt stop, her spine stiffening. 'That means she would die. She would starve and dehydrate until her heart stops.'

Jamie reflexively looks to his daughter, but she is absorbed in her artwork. 'Jesus, you don't have to be so graphic. You make it sound like we'd be killing her.'

Tears swell in Lucia's eyes as her voice wobbles. 'She could live for decades with the interventions.'

'Lying there day after day with no clue of what's going on around her. That's not a life, Lucia. Tam's not coming back and, let's be honest, would you really want her to after what happened?'

A sob claws its way out of Lucia's mouth and her palm against her lips isn't quite quick enough to smother it. Elise's head jerks round at the noise.

'Lu-Lu?'

'I'm OK, sweetie,' Lucia chokes out, turning so Elise can't see the tears streaming down her cheeks. 'I'm just going to the loo.'

She almost runs to the downstairs cloakroom, rubbing fiercely at her eyes with clenched fists. Jamie steels himself, praying she's not about to shut down on him when he needs her support the most. Just like Tamsin had once done.

He can't let this relationship go the same way as his marriage.

She returns before he can go after her, but she doesn't make eye contact. He reaches out to her and, after a moment, she allows him to enfold her in his arms. He blows out a long breath of relief.

'I don't know what to do,' he murmurs into her hair, aware of Elise watching them closely.

'Neither do I,' she whispers back. 'This is madness. Rushmore shouldn't be asking this of us. Did they tell you after the visit?'

'Soon as I arrived. It was like the director needed to tick the box as fast as possible.'

'It must have been hell, sitting with Tam after hearing that.'

'I kept looking at her, hoping she'd give me a sign.' Jamie lifts his head, his hand finding Lucia's. He laces their fingers together, trying to ground himself.

'How can we make that choice? What gives us that right?' Lucia demands.

'Tam can't make it for herself, can she? Who else is there?'

'The doctors. They must know more than us.'

'They can't make the decision. Only next of kin.'

Lucia stiffens. 'I'm not next of kin.'

Jamie tightens his grip as she tries to pull away. 'You're as good as.'

'It's *your* decision.'

'And I can't make it without you.'

She steps back sharply enough to break the circle of his arms. 'How is that fair on me? Giving me that sort of responsibility?'

'You think *I* want it?' Jamie can't prevent an incredulous laugh. 'This was the last thing I expected when I set off this morning. I don't want to play fucking God!'

'Daddy!' Elise admonishes him and he catches himself before he says anything she will comprehend.

He shakes his head warningly at Lucia. 'Let's not talk about it now.'

'It's not going to go away.'

'No,' he murmurs. Now the can of worms has been opened, the lid won't easily fit back on. 'But we have time. No one's giving us a deadline.'

He winces as he realises just how inappropriate that last word was, but it is enough to draw a hoarse laugh from Lucia. She moves to scoop up Elise, depositing her into her highchair and placing a bowl of pasta in front of her. Elise examines the meal suspiciously, poking her spoon into it, but finally decides it is acceptable and commences shovelling.

It wasn't good food that had cemented the bond between Jamie and Lucia. Rather, exactly the opposite. They'd spent an uncomfortable hour at the hospital, staring at each other over Tamsin's motionless figure, the silence broken only by the hiss of the ventilator and beeps of the monitors as hunger gnawed at their bellies. Only a month old, Elise slept the sleep of the innocent in her buggy, blissfully unaware of the significance of her surroundings.

They had emerged from the Royal London that evening needing something to fill the emptiness, though they both knew food was not enough to satisfy such a void. Jamie had made the choice, a touristy Greek restaurant near Spitalfields Market, and swiftly regretted it. Lucia had taken one look at the rubbery calamari and limp dolmades before whisking them off to the back streets of Cheapside, to a tiny Vietnamese eatery no visitor could ever have stumbled across.

When Elise had finally woken, her tiny mouth puckering into a pained lament, it had been Lucia who picked her up. Competently teasing the teat of a formula bottle between the baby's protesting lips, she had rescued Jamie at the moment he needed it most.

It was there, in the candlelight flickering off handmade paper lanterns, senses enveloped by heat and spice and the contented noises of Elise feeding peacefully, that Jamie had finally accepted he was hopelessly in love. Not with his wife, but with her best friend. A year of secret meetings and snatched moments, and it had taken an event of total devastation to make Jamie realise what had been staring him in the face. He loved Lucia.

It was both a relief and a stark reminder of what his life had become, that he was admitting his love for one woman as another fought for her life.

Heavy footsteps make Jamie start as Mateo thumps into the room, insolent-eyed and sulky-mouthed. The teenager doesn't even acknowledge Jamie's presence as he greets Elise and his mother, but his eyes flick suspiciously between the two adults.

'Why do I get the feeling I'm interrupting something?'

'Nothing to interrupt.' Jamie attempts a breezy tone, wincing at the sound of his own voice. He usually tries to blend into the background when Mateo's in one of his moods.

'Then why are you sweating?' Mateo challenges. 'Why does Mum look like she's been crying?' His stare is intense, ice-cold, boring into Jamie, and it is so much more unnerving than just a fifteen-year-old's fury against the world. He holds himself at his tallest, barely shorter than Jamie these days, demonstrating the breadth of his shoulders and the solidity of his chest. He's so nearly a man now – a man too like his father.

'Elise is trying to eat her dinner,' Lucia says pointedly, between gritted teeth.

Elise's spoon stalls in mid-air, a piece of pasta balanced precariously. Mateo hesitates, glancing across to the little girl, his expression softening.

'That looks nice, Els,' he says, giving her a thin-lipped smile. Then with one last glare at Jamie, he stalks out again, slamming his bedroom door moments later.

Lucia sags against the edge of the worktop. 'Sorry, I know I shouldn't let him talk to you like that, but Jesus. It's like he's turning into Ben, and I can't face another row.'

Jamie has to clear his throat before he can reply. 'It doesn't matter,' he lies.

He can't talk about Ben. He never goes to Mateo's room, not only because the kid would hate it, but because a picture of his father sits by his bed. When Jamie had first started staying over, the hallways had been lined with family photos, Lucia trying a little too hard to document a once happy life, and it had physically hurt every time he had glimpsed his ex-business partner's grin.

Since then, the pictures have gradually been replaced by South American artwork and shots of Buenos Aires, Lucia's tribute to her son's heritage. But Mateo occasionally rips one off the wall in a fit of rage.

He has had counselling, like everyone else in the household, but it doesn't seem to have helped him to process his grief. His father was mostly a distant figure in his life, working all hours, quick-tempered due to fatigue and other reasons they'd all fought to hide, but Mateo chooses to forget those flaws. He permits himself to remember only the golden times, even ones that never existed. His loss is still raw, evident in his clenched jaw and obsidian eyes, his sharp movements and biting remarks.

He blames Jamie.

Jamie blames himself, too.

8

Tamsin – Now

Night is the only time I can truly think. In daylight hours, my focus is on trying to gather information from limited sources and I do not have the energy to process or analyse as I always, constantly, did before all this. Back then, I was a force to be reckoned with in my ballet pumps and tortoiseshell glasses; now, daily life, such as it exists within the four walls of my room at Rushmore, exhausts me.

It is only once the sounds and motions have settled, the curtains have swished closed and the night staff have retreated to their stations, that I am calm. The tension that buzzes through my body amid visitors, therapies, treatments and care routines finally abates. Behind my eyelids, the shadows and colours become lighter and, as the voices that surround me every day are finally silenced, my thoughts slow their frantic pace.

It is a relief to begin putting some order to them, reflecting on what I have gleaned that day. Often, it is nothing more than Hannah's complaints that her partner didn't do the dishes *again*, or Jamie's obsession with his new Tesla. How he's afforded that *and* my care here when we were on the verge of ruin prior to the crash, God only knows. I hope he's not simply piled more debts on top of the mountain.

Today, however, I have something interesting to chew over. Milena's fearful reaction at the mention of Richard Mandeville's name niggles me. Why did she leap to associate him with the crash? What connection has she made that I have missed? I am tired, and my thoughts are sluggish, but I fight to stay awake.

Usually, I am relieved to sleep. Outwardly, there is no variance between my waking and slumbering states, but I have the same cycles as a fully conscious person. I look forward to sleep. It is my only respite.

When I first emerged from the coma, I couldn't dream. My brain didn't have that capacity, too busy trying to come to terms with my useless body. It is only recently that I have started to regain the ability.

At first, it was a blur of images and muffled voices with no sense or order. Now they are becoming sharper, in a vibrant rainbow of colours so different from the darkness of my waking hours, and with crystal-clear sounds, as if this is the only space where my senses can truly excel and they are determined to put on a high-definition show.

I dream of freedom. Of long runs along the Thames, of creating complex, unhurried recipes in my beloved kitchen, of luxurious spa days. Travelling to far-flung corners of the world, eating delicious food cooked on open, sizzling coals, sipping ice-cold white wine in tiny taverns. Reading a book at my own pace instead of it being narrated to me, so slowly I am somehow both bored and infuriated. Snuggling on the sofa with my daughter to watch a film, sharing my own childhood Disney favourites with her.

But that makes it worse when I wake up to the cold, harsh reality of my situation.

At first, it made my frustration spiral to the point where I felt on the verge of explosion, and the staff worried about the spikes in my blood pressure and heart rate. It's not easy to avoid dwelling on your deepest desires but I understood that, ultimately, it was causing more problems than it was worth.

So I distract myself with memories. I remember many things. School and university, med school, my stints at Guy's and St Thomas' hospitals. I remember my first position as a psychiatrist, the thrill of danger working in a high-security unit. I remember meeting Jamie, our wedding, buying our apartment. I remember telling him I was pregnant and the shocks that followed my announcement.

But the vital memories are missing. The day of the crash is gone, lost in shadows. I don't remember the events or circumstances. When I was at the Royal London and consultants spoke of my traumatic brain injury, discussing my scans over me, I knew those memories may never be recovered, but that didn't stop me trying. I resolved to search those hazy recesses, seeking out any little chink of light.

Before all this, mine was a rational, ordered mind. I relied on facts and evidence; I was not prone to whimsy or flights of fantasy. Grounded, level-headed, cynical even. But it changes you, an experience like this. When you have nothing else, hope is the only comfort you can cling to. And she is a dangerous mistress.

I developed a wild, fanciful motivation that my old sensible, scientific self would have refused to tolerate. An irrational belief that my lost past will be the key to unlocking my future.

If I can remember, I am convinced I will break the cycle, and that will allow my return to consciousness. My brain has done its job well, safeguarding me at my most vulnerable by shutting down, instinctively creating a shield between life and death. Now I need to persuade it that the time has come to release me from my shadowy cocoon. There is something left for me to do – I'm sure of that – but until I know what happened that fateful day, I can't begin to decipher my challenge. No matter how hard I stretch, it remains beyond my grasp.

Even after all these months, I am as much in the dark as ever.

Just like tonight, as my frustration grows at my inability to decipher what may have spooked Milena. I have devoted several hours to weighing up possibilities, yet I remain at square one.

And I have become convinced that consciousness will remain beyond my grasp, until I can finally find a way to answer my questions.

Without Dan's visit, Monday was a quiet morning. Milena was on the evening shift and the day staff had left me in peace after the necessary tasks. I had been calmly drifting, far from Rushmore, in a tranquil sea of turquoise and aquamarine the colour of my daughter's eyes. It was no effort to picture Elise there beside me, floating on her back, a natural water baby like me.

'There you are, at last.'

The male voice takes me by surprise, startling me back to attention.

I think it is late morning from the position of the weak sunshine, maybe not far from lunchtime, and I must have been asleep for a couple of hours.

I struggle to identify the voice. I'm sure I recognise it.

'Are you in charge?'

'I'm the senior nurse, yes.' That is Hannah in the doorway, but she sounds different from normal, more alert. 'You haven't visited before, sir.'

'I've been living abroad. I only found out about Tamsin's accident when I got back to the UK. I thought her eyes would be open.'

'Tamsin isn't in a coma anymore, but she doesn't respond to any stimulus yet. We call this a permanent or persistent vegetative state.'

'She'll be like this forever?'

'There's no way of knowing. It means her life isn't in danger, not like when she was comatose. She looks like she's asleep but she's technically awake.' Hannah is usually so curt that I can easily surmise she is flattered by the new visitor's attention. 'Tamsin is in an unusual state for PVS. Typically, patients can open and close their eyes, follow basic commands, respond to pain.'

'Why doesn't she?'

'Traumatic brain injuries are unique events, so each person is affected differently. You can sit here. Most visitors find it difficult at first but, if you talk to her, tell her your news, it gets easier.'

'She can hear me?'

'We don't know. Some studies suggest yes, others say not. Can I get you tea, coffee?'

Hannah must really like this new arrival; I've never heard her offer to make coffee before.

'Thank you, coffee would be lovely. Black, no sugar.'

The door closes and the man comes closer, leaning over me for a better look. I smell sandalwood and cigar smoke.

Oh God, it's Richard.

Richard Mandeville has come to visit me.

'Hello, Tamsin,' he says softly. Not Dr Shaw anymore. He doesn't touch me or take my hand, but I can feel his eyes roaming over me, taking in all the equipment. 'I'm sorry it's taken me so long to come.'

He hasn't been living abroad. I know that for certain. He won't have been allowed to leave the country while the preparations for his retrial were underway.

'I could say I've been too busy or make some other excuse, but the truth is I've avoided visiting. It would have been easy enough to track you down, but it never felt like the right moment. I didn't expect it to turn into three years, but time flies, doesn't it?'

Not for me. Time crawls for me.

'I wanted to come on Wednesday. It seemed more fitting to visit on the anniversary of your accident, but my schedule didn't allow for it.'

I am glad. I wouldn't want his presence to taint my daughter's birthday.

'You don't get many visitors, do you? I had a look when I signed the book. I always did imagine you with a small circle of friends when we worked together. You didn't seem the type to trust many people.'

He begins to pace, observing his surroundings. He had always been perceptive, rarely missing a thing.

'This is a lovely place. I wish you could see the architecture, you'd adore it. Must have been a grand house in its time.' I hear the smile in his tone. 'It reminds me of home. I think you must have the best room. It looks out over the formal gardens.'

He pauses as if studying me.

'It's easier talking to you than I thought it would be. I expected it to be awkward when I was so used to our debates.' A gentle laughs huffs from him. 'At least now I get free choice of our topic of conversation.'

The chair creaks as he finally sits, and I picture him neatly crossing his legs, settling back into his familiar pose.

'I was shocked when I was told what happened to you. I'd only seen you earlier that day, hadn't I?'

This is new. I have no idea how I spent that day before going to Kent. I must have been at work, but I don't remember which clients I saw.

'Those roads are so tricky out there.'

It seems sensible that Richard would have read the newspaper reports, seen their photos of the crash site, but he almost sounds as if he is familiar with those twisting, barren lanes carving their way through the marshes.

'It was Dan Attwood who broke the news. That man really doesn't like me.' Another gentle laugh. 'We're currently facing each other across a courtroom. He can barely bring himself to look at me. He always was a little too *invested* in our sessions, wasn't he, for someone in such a responsible position? He's itching to explain your notes to the jury, like he can interpret them when no one else can. Comes across as a little desperate.'

Richard exhales a long, slow breath.

'That's the reason I decided it was time to visit. I know what you're thinking – why the hell bother, after all these years? What good can it possibly do to rekindle what we had?'

If only I could grimace, smirk, do anything to dissuade him

from the notion that he can read my thoughts, that there is any kind of deep bond or affection between us.

'I've never forgotten you, you know.' His tone becomes reflective. 'I can go months without thinking of you, then suddenly I'll see a pair of tortoiseshell glasses, or I'll smell J'adore and you're there again. Did you ever realise you had such power, Tamsin? Did you know what a hold you had over me?'

My heart begins to thud painfully. His words would be concerning at the best of times, and I am acutely aware I am powerless, lying here.

'So, why am I here, you're asking me.' Since my arrival at Rushmore, no one has ever spoken to me with such ease, as if I am replying, as if I am part of the conversation. Once again, his confidence is his compass. 'My retrial has finally started. They're beginning to refer to your notes and reports almost daily. They haven't got very far into our sessions yet but it's unsettling. Like hearing your voice from someone else's mouth.'

I sense him leaning closer to me. The intensity of his gaze is almost tangible.

'It always felt like you really understood me,' Richard murmurs. 'You saw a lot deeper than most other people ever have.'

Too deep. Our working relationship had been different from the start, unlike any I had experienced with previous clients, and Richard knew it. We crossed the line early and never really returned to the right side.

'I trusted you to see the real me. But I was a fool to believe you'd truly understood me. Wasn't I, Dr Shaw?'

I can feel the blood thumping in my ears at such a definitive statement. Danger crackles, electric and tangible, a lightning strike too close for comfort. He thinks my notes will deny him his freedom. I have become the enemy, a threat to his campaign.

I am not capable of having a panic attack, not in my current condition, but my brain hasn't grasped that, and it is starting to divert blood to my limbs in a futile preparation for fight or flight. The band around my chest is growing tighter, forcing me to take short sips of precious air. Behind my eyelids, the darkness is agitated by flashes of jarring colours, red and white exploding from the black.

I hear a sharp intake of breath from Richard as the alarms begin to sound. His palm hits the call button, efficient as ever.

Hannah appears quickly, no doubt concerned I might die on her watch and cause all sorts of additional work for her.

'Her monitors just started going crazy,' Richard reports.

Hannah's fake daisies overwhelm the sandalwood as she moves around me, performing the routine checks without bothering to tell me what she is doing with her cold hands.

'Could be an infection starting,' she mutters to herself, though I am sure I hear doubt in her voice. She has no idea what has caused me to react like this.

'Is she alright?' Richard interrupts.

'Her vital signs are different from normal.' Hannah's explanation is smooth, professional, reassuring everyone that she knows exactly what she's doing. 'We'll monitor her closely for twenty-four hours and, if we're concerned, we'll bring in our on-call doctor. Don't worry, it happens sometimes. It isn't an emergency.'

I want to flail my arms about in protest. I hate being spoken about like I am nothing more than a breathing corpse, the casual way Hannah discusses my very existence. Can she not realise I have emotions just like her? Her business-like tone leaves me on the verge of tears I cannot produce.

'Do you need me to leave?' Richard asks, the embodiment of quiet cooperation.

'You're welcome to stay unless anything changes.'

I listen to her leave the room and suddenly feel very alone.

'What was all that about?' Richard asks, as if expecting me to reply.

Even though I can't answer him, I am certain we both know the reason for my reaction.

It was because of him. Because the Devil himself has walked back into my life.

9

Tamsin – Before

'How did it go?' Lucia practically roared into my ear as she passed, a glass of champagne in either hand, both for herself.

I checked quickly about me, even though the music was too loud for anyone to overhear us. The thumping beat seemed to make the walls of Porteños quiver, and all around us fairy lights twinkled, glasses clinked companionably together and raucous laughter rang out amid a sea of attractive, well-groomed faces. Ben's guests were far more interested in themselves than other people, anyway.

'What?' I asked.

'The psycho ex-con!'

I let out a breath disguised as a laugh. 'Oh, that! It was only a short introductory session. He was fine, perfectly polite and well-behaved. He was wearing a cravat, can you believe it?' That last part wasn't true – Richard Mandeville did not need a fashion statement to emphasise his status – but I knew it would distract her from asking further questions.

Lucia pursed her lips. 'And a matching pocket square, I hope. Do you want another mocktail? I assume Jamie hasn't noticed you're not drinking.'

I raised my flute of sparkling orange juice, which I'd been passing off as a mimosa, in my husband's direction. 'He's busy making new friends.'

As I cast around for something to look at other than Jamie, my eyes alighted on my godson, casually sipping a bottle of Quilmes as he chatted to several older teenagers dripping with designer clothes and gold jewellery. Mateo glanced at his mother and attempted to hide the beer.

Lucia summoned him with a glare, and he slunk back to her side, reluctantly handing over the bottle. Lucia drained it in a couple of gulps, blatantly ignoring his scowl.

'Who are they?' I asked my godson.

Mateo rolled his eyes and spouted off a list of names I had never heard of. 'YouTubers!' he exclaimed impatiently when it became clear I was clueless.

I nodded cooperatively, pretending to be impressed as I looked around. I recognised almost no one except a few famous chefs and a couple of well-known actors. I didn't have Instagram, never watched YouTube and hated football – it was not a social setting I was comfortable in.

Jamie, on the other hand, was holding court across the other side of the room, gesturing expansively as his audience laughed, entirely in his thrall even though he had no celebrity status, no lights to his name. He found networking, a task that made me want to bore a hole in my own skull, effortless.

'Ben!' Lucia waved up to her husband on the mezzanine, where he was showing off his knife skills to his admirers.

Ben pretended not to see her beckoning him, wielding the Japanese steel with a wicked flourish as he sliced up a fillet of pampas-reared beef.

'Fuck's sake,' Lucia hissed under her breath as she maintained her wide smile. She turned so only I could see her face. 'He never even mentioned me or Matty in his speech. Jamie, sure, but not his family. Bollocks to everything we put up with from him.'

I winced for my friend. Ben hadn't always been like this. Through the leaner years, while battling to make it as a commis chef in touristy restaurants, he had been a family man, finding time for his wife and son even when working fourteen-hour days. That had all changed when he achieved his dream, when his own success had blinded him.

I had witnessed how badly Lucia had struggled since Porteños became the priority, five years previously. We were old friends by that point, having met at a community pottery class just after Jamie and I moved to the Isle of Dogs. We were seated beside each other, and quickly bonded over fits of laughter at our mutual incompetence as we attempted to manhandle wet clay that seemed determined to escape our wheels.

We had given up after the second class ended in equally abject failure, bunking off the next in favour of the pub. Soon, we were meeting regularly, introducing our husbands, enjoying double dates. When Ben had suddenly become obsessed with baptising Mateo, despite his son having survived his first five years without the protection of the Catholic church, Jamie and I were first choice as godparents. It had all been so easy back then, before everything began to fall apart.

Jamie finally left his new fans by the bar and decided to join us. He threw an arm round Mateo's neck, playfully ruffling his hair. Mateo jerked free, casting his godfather a withering scowl.

'I'm going up to Dad,' he muttered to Lucia.

I watched Jamie stare after Mateo as he jogged up the solid glass staircase, seeing the tightness in his jaw that told me he was gritting his teeth. It was rare for Mateo to be moody around Jamie, the one person who could usually be guaranteed to tease him out of his hormones. Even rarer for Jamie to react badly to a pre-teen sulk.

Before I could ask if they'd had a row, Jamie had flagged down one of the waiting staff and was gulping a glass of champagne with the thirst of a shipwrecked man. Perhaps the gladhanding had worn him out for once.

I shook my head when he held a flute out to me, pretending I didn't see his questioning look. Ben unintentionally saved me, yelling over the frosted glass barrier for Jamie to join him in yet another toast. Jamie threw us a grin, but I was sure I saw him hesitate before he went to take his place beside his business partner.

I definitely saw him wince as Ben gave a roar of triumph and hurled several churrasco skewers high into the air, piercing the ceiling that had been designed, at great expense, to look like a night sky. He had forgotten his son was beside him and Mateo dodged out of the way as plaster dust rained down onto the heads of Ben's delighted guests. They whooped and ate up the spectacle as Lucia and I simultaneously rolled our eyes.

'He's acting like this because the TV producers are here,' Lucia confided. 'I wish he wouldn't make such a show of himself.'

'Have they signed for season two yet?'

'They're still working out the details, apparently. Which probably means Ben is demanding more money than they're prepared to pay.'

'*Salud*!' Ben bellowed as his spectators egged him on.

I raised my glass obediently, determined to ignore the squirming unease in the pit of my stomach. Jamie tapped Ben's shoulder, speaking rapidly into his ear. Ben's expression darkened and he pulled abruptly away.

Jamie's eyes met mine and, almost imperceptibly, he tilted his head.

Let's get out of here.

I met him at the cloakroom, where the attendant scrabbled to retrieve our belongings.

'He knows how much that ceiling cost,' Jamie growled under his breath. 'If it reminds him so much of the sky over the pampas, why does he want to poke holes in it?'

'You know what he's like, he can't resist blowing his own horn.'

'The bill for all this will be insane.' Jamie gestured sharply around him. 'Did he really need fucking ice sculptures?'

'He told Lucia it reminds him of Patagonia.' I made my voice as dry as the large glasses of Argentine Riesling currently being circulated. 'Come on, let's go home and have a nightcap on the balcony.'

Outside, the crisp night air was a blessed relief from the hot and heavy restaurant atmosphere.

Jamie hailed a black cab and held the door open for me. 'Don't think I haven't noticed you're not drinking,' he said as I stepped in.

I bumped my head on the padded roof as I whipped round to look at him. As hard as I tried to keep a neutral expression, I could feel the skin around my eyes had gone taut. Observation was not generally one of Jamie's finer skills.

'Tell me at home.' He took my arm and guided me into the far seat.

I tipped my chin up, suddenly needing the reassurance of his touch, but he only dropped a brief peck on my lips before leaning his head back. I watched his shoulders relax as he took several deep inhalations through his nose. His eyes closed.

Safely back home, in the apartment we had shared all our married life, I poured him a double Laphroaig and glanced wistfully at the bottle of my favourite Kyrö pink gin.

I wrapped a pashmina round my shoulders and joined Jamie on the balcony. He sat close to the edge, his forehead resting against the glass barrier as he gazed down at the gentle roll of the water's velvety, black surface.

'Thanks.' He took the tumbler from me, looking pointedly at my own sparkling water as he hooked another chair for me with his foot.

I tugged the pashmina tighter against the wind swirling up from the river, pulling my feet up onto the chair so I could hug my knees.

'I missed my period this month.' I decided matter-of-fact was the best tactic. Jamie got lost in excessive explanations. 'I did a test. I'm eight weeks pregnant.'

Jamie had already tensed, waiting for a blow. 'Fuck,' he whispered, the word slipping from his lips as if he was unaware of it.

'Is it such a disaster?' I kept my voice light even though my stomach was clenched.

'You're infertile, Tam, you can't be pregnant. You had it confirmed, after –'

'I know what happened,' I interrupted, before he could say any more – my own equivalent of clapping my hands over my ears and humming.

'So surely that can't have changed ...' He trailed off, grasping at straws.

'I'm a psychiatrist, Jamie, not a gynaecologist. I can't tell you the science behind it, only that the test was positive.'

Jamie took repeated sips of his whisky, his eyes moving rapidly, never focussing on one spot, especially not on me.

'Talk to me,' I found myself begging. 'I know it's a shock.'

'I don't know what to say.'

'Then tell me what you're thinking. I can see this isn't necessarily positive news for you.'

'Stop being a shrink!'

I was aware that was a character flaw of mine, and it wasn't the easiest to control, but aggravating Jamie wasn't going to help the situation.

'Sorry. I just want to discuss this calmly.'

He looked at me for the first time. 'Discuss what we're going to do?'

I didn't know how to interpret the hope that had appeared in his tone. 'What we're going to do?' I repeated dumbly.

'This isn't a good time to have a baby, Tam.'

'I know we're a little older than we'd planned to be, but that doesn't matter –'

He dropped his head into his hands, cutting me off. 'There's no money.'

I stared at him, not comprehending what he was saying. 'Of course there's money. My salary alone is enough to raise a child.'

We had a joint bank account. Our lifestyle wasn't cheap. The mortgage was enormous, the bills were high. Jamie was good with money; he had built his company to be one of the foremost commercial property businesses in the south-east. He contributed more than I did but in big chunks at the end of each tax year. He hadn't put the lump sum in yet, but we'd never struggled to make ends meet, so I hadn't been concerned. Until now.

He stayed silent, shaking his head like he was trying to clear water from his ears.

'Jamie, how can there be no money?' My voice came out more insistent than intended and it seemed to startle him into a reply.

'Porteños,' he snarled. 'Ben is haemorrhaging cash. The restaurant is in massive debt. It hasn't been able to pay rent for months.'

'But your company owns the building.'

'And I still have to pay a mortgage on it, Tamsin!'

I realised my own naivety. I had nothing to do with Jamie's company or its finances, and I had never questioned what he told me. Evidently, I should have done.

'How big is your share in Porteños?' I hardly dared ask.

He had put money into Porteños without bothering to discuss the implications, only thinking to inform me after the deal had been agreed. Apparently, it had made sense because his company owned the building, and Ben had offered a generous share in return for reduced rent. It had not made sense to my risk-adverse mind but that hadn't seemed to concern either man.

'I bought out fifty per cent,' he mumbled. 'It seemed a safe bet. Ben was coining it in.'

'Then how can it have gone from massive success to haemorrhaging cash, all while getting a second Michelin star and a new season of *La Cocina Loca*?'

'Ben's fucked it all up.'

'How?!' The word came out as a demand.

Jamie sighed into his glass. 'He started using coke to cope with all the hours in the kitchen. Now he can't function without it.'

That explained the erratic behaviour, the mood swings, the abrupt energy crashes Lucia had confided in me about.

'His habit's that big?'

'His debts are. His dealer was refusing to give him any more on tick, so he panicked and borrowed money off a loan shark, then started channelling the restaurant profits to pay him back. Now Porteños is nearly broke, Ben owes the sort of people who take late payments in fingernails, and he still can't control his fucking habit.' As if the floodgates had opened, everything came spilling out. 'Amazon are wondering whether they dare take a risk on him. He's so unpredictable and they're worried he won't take direction or he'll bury his meat cleaver in a cameraman's head or something. But we're relying on their contract to pay off a chunk of the mortgage debt.'

'My God.' The enormity of the situation began to dawn. 'Does Lucia know?'

'Leave Lucia out of it.'

'She deserves to know they're about to go bankrupt, let alone that her husband is a cocaine addict!'

'I knew I shouldn't have told you!' Jamie leapt from his seat, pacing the balcony like a caged animal. 'Fuck, Tam, you don't get it. If Ben goes under, so do I. I'll be bankrupt too, everything I've ever worked for – gone.'

'Then tell me what we do.'

'*We* do nothing. *I'll* take care of it.' His knuckles whitened around the glass, and I heard his struggle to inject reassurance into his tone. 'It'll be OK.'

If only I could believe him. I picked up my drink and went back inside, shivering.

In the back of my mind, even as I tried to make sense of what I had learned, I noticed he hadn't even mentioned the pregnancy again.

Like with most of Jamie's problems, he had simply blocked it out.

* * *

Richard arrived, as usual, precisely on time. I knew from his file that he had served as an army captain. He would have excelled at Sandhurst; he had that disciplined approach, an air of decisive commitment to whatever he had chosen to undertake. I also noted how he had justified his visits to me as a choice rather than a directive.

'How are you, Dr Shaw?' Again, he waited for me to be seated before taking his own chair. It seemed to be a genuine question rather than polite convention; he was waiting for my answer.

'Fine, thank you,' I said vaguely.

'You don't sound too sure. Are you alright? You're very pale.'

He couldn't know I'd been fighting morning sickness, but I was taken aback that he would notice my pallor and lethargic movements. It was an effort not to cradle my churning, aching stomach and I was slumped low in my chair, my usual commitment to good posture abandoned.

'I'm not feeling well.' I was surprised by my own admission. It was a firm policy of mine not to reveal anything personal to clients.

'Can I get you anything? Sparkling water? Tea?'

'No. Thank you, but I'll be OK.' I straightened up with some effort. 'I must have eaten something that's disagreed with me. Please don't concern yourself.'

Richard raised his palms in acquiescence, responding to my overly formal language as I had intended. 'If you change your mind.'

'We're here to talk about you, Mr Mandeville.'

His eyebrows jumped. 'I thought we'd agreed on first names?'

'I don't recall agreeing to my first name being used.'

'Damn,' he grinned. 'You're not susceptible even when you're ill. But you did promise to call me Richard.'

'I did.' My use of his surname, to restore formality, had not gone unnoticed. 'My apologies, Richard. May we begin the session now?'

'Please.' He leaned back comfortably, as if we were about to have brunch.

I had to shake myself to get back on track. My brain had forgotten the steps that were so familiar to me.

'Today I'd like us to discuss your convictions,' I finally said, forcing myself to concentrate after his expression became quizzical. 'This is the first step of the treatment programme, to confront the crimes you committed before we begin to dissect the motivations behind them.'

Richard's entire body tensed noticeably but his face remained neutral.

'I haven't committed any crimes.' His voice was entirely even, as if he was giving a casual statement of fact.

My pen stilled. 'Your convictions –'

'I pled not guilty,' he pointed out, mildly.

'Yet the jury convicted you.'

'I'm not a stupid man, Tamsin. I couldn't prove my innocence, that was clear very early into the trial. I was forced to take a risk, to gamble my freedom on twelve strangers with their own agendas and prejudices. I had to trust them to make the right decision.'

I barely noticed his use of my forename. 'Isn't that exactly the reassurance the justice system should provide? That the innocent will be found so.'

A smile curved the corners of his mouth. 'You're not that naïve.'

'Perhaps I am.'

His head tilted. 'Somehow, I doubt that.'

'So you've served eight years for crimes you didn't commit?'

'Better than sixteen.' Another smile. 'You don't believe me.'

'I'm not here to judge you, Richard.'

'Are you here to understand me?'

'In some ways, yes.'

'I'm not going to tell you no one has ever understood me before, if that's what you're waiting for.'

I met his gaze. 'I wasn't expecting you to.'

I saw the spark in his eyes, the enjoyment of our discussion. This was what he thrived on, a rapid back-and-forth, a challenge.

'I'm a privileged bastard and I know it.' He leaned back in his seat again. 'My father didn't beat me, except at squash. My mother didn't extinguish her cigarettes on my skin. The masters at school kept their hands to themselves. There are no scabs for you to pick away at, Dr Shaw, though I'm sure you'd like to find some.'

'You have a very set expectation of psychiatrists.'

'Perhaps. You're the first I've ever met.'

'How did you feel when you found out seeing a shrink was one of your licence terms?'

'Forgive me if I sound rude, but I felt it was a completely unnecessary clause.' A shrug. 'It didn't matter. I was willing to agree to whatever terms were set. I told the board what they wanted to hear.'

'That's probably not something you should shout about.'

'There's only one thing I'm going to shout about, and that's my application to the Court of Appeal.'

I refused to give him the reaction he was seeking. 'What grounds are you appealing on?'

'Unfair hearing. The jury was a joke. I didn't stand a chance.'

I made a note, keeping my eyes on the page in front of me. 'Appeals are tricky things. You're risking a lot to clear your name, especially when you've already lost eight years behind bars. What if you end up back there?'

'I have no intention of that happening.' His confidence was incredible considering his situation. 'It's a gamble, I acknowledge that, but I like my odds. Hence why I expect your report will be vital.'

He sat forward over his knees again, a fluid transition. Usually, I would have sat back, ensured distance between us, but I fought the usual compulsion for personal space.

'I've read several of your research papers,' he said.

'You must be the first client to ever do that.'

'I had plenty of time on my hands. Why do you think I asked to be treated by you?'

His eyes roved momentarily over my face and I hoped my expression didn't betray my internal reaction.

'Don't look so alarmed,' Richard chided gently. 'No ulterior motive, I promise.'

I kept my eyes fixed on my notepad. It was too early in his treatment to challenge him – that would only antagonise – but this suddenly felt too intimate.

I nudged the papers on the table between us with my pen.

'This is what I'd like us to consider today.'

'You're the boss.' He obligingly scooped one up, his eyes flying over the text. 'This is about the victims of a crime?'

'We're going to talk about your victims.'

'*Alleged* victims,' he gently corrected.

'Richard, you were convicted of these crimes. In the eyes of the law and of society, that means you committed them.'

'Society is such a flock of sheep. People are happy to believe what they're told, without question.'

I gave that statement due consideration. 'I like to think that I don't conform to that generalisation.'

That earned me a smile. 'Glad to hear it, Dr Shaw.'

10

Jamie – Before

Jamie's head dropped in humiliation as he rolled away to the far side of the mattress, his cheeks burning. He grabbed at the sheets, pulling them around his naked body, an ineffective shield.

'Sorry,' he mumbled.

'You don't have to be sorry.'

Her words didn't make him feel any better. He closed his eyes, trying again to stir a reaction, focussing on the smooth, soft skin pressing against his as she scooted over to him. He reached for her breast, caressing the welcoming flesh, willing himself to respond.

Nothing.

He flopped back against the pillows, defeated.

'Don't worry about it,' Lucia whispered, her lips tickling his ear.

'It's not you.'

'I know. It's not you either. There's just too much going on right now. I'll get us a drink.'

'Mateo will be home soon.'

'We're safe for at least another hour. Stay there.'

She strode off downstairs. Jamie didn't even bother to watch her naked figure; usually, he couldn't take his eyes off her tanned curves, so different from Tamsin's ivory lines.

She returned clutching a bottle of Argentine Cabernet from Ben's private stash, and poured them each a glass with cheerful carelessness despite the light-coloured carpets surrounding the enormous bed. She cuddled up against him, not bothering to cover herself. She was so at ease with her body, no hang-ups, no complexes. Comfortable within her own skin.

'Did you know Tamsin is pregnant?'

Lucia averted her eyes. 'Yes, I knew. She wouldn't have told anyone else first.'

'You could've let me in on it.'

'How could I? I've already betrayed Tam enough. It wasn't my secret to share. And yes, I do feel like an utter hypocrite lying in bed with her husband while I say that.'

Sometimes, they tried to justify their sins. They sought explanations in their strained marriages, pretending Jamie's relationship was as damaged as Lucia's, even though they both knew it wasn't true.

They hadn't meant for it to happen. It had only been about desire in the beginning, the thrill of forbidden danger amid lives that had become dull and heavy. That was all it was meant to be, a release of frustrations, but it had somehow become a connection that continued to deepen. Lucia had made Jamie feel like he wasn't a failure, in spite of his poor investments; he had provided safety for her, so different from Ben's rages. They had come, entirely without intention, to depend on each other for emotional support.

Even now, several months in, they promised each time would be the last, acknowledged they were doing wrong and swore not to repeat their mistakes.

Neither of them believed their own words. It was a rush they couldn't relinquish.

'You know she'll go through with the pregnancy,' Lucia said gently. 'She won't change her mind.'

'I know,' he sighed. 'Maybe she would, if I told her about us.'

'We can't do that.' Lucia's tone sharpened. 'You know that. We both have too much to lose.'

'If we have that much to lose, we shouldn't keep doing this.'

'This is the only thing that gives me any pleasure in life.' Lucia's hand ran across his chest. '*You're* the only thing. I can't give you up.'

'Then leave Ben, and I'll tell Tam. It'll be absolutely shit but we'll get through it.'

'He'll take Mateo.'

'You can fight him for custody.'

'Matty has dual nationality, Jamie! Ben would have him out of the country before I could blink. He'd make sure I never saw my son again, that's how he'd get his revenge.'

'It might not be that extreme.'

She fixed him with a look. 'As if you believe that.'

Jamie winced at the mere thought of his business partner's instability. Ben was more than capable of exacting revenge on Jamie too.

'Don't lose your head now.' Lucia softened her voice. 'We said from the beginning, this isn't about us starting afresh together. We both get what we need, and that should be enough.'

Jamie took a gulp of his wine.

How could he have a baby with a wife he no longer loved?

'I didn't realise you and Tam were still having sex,' Lucia said carefully, and he wondered if she could read his mind.

'Once in a blue moon. She'd get suspicious if we didn't occasionally.' That wasn't true. His physical relationship with Tamsin was unscarred, even though he much preferred Lucia's warmth to his wife's sinewy frame. It was their emotional connection that had been damaged beyond repair.

'You two never used to be able to keep your hands off each other.'

'I loved her so much in the beginning,' he mumbled. 'It was like an addiction. I couldn't get enough of her.'

'I remember,' she said, with just the hint of an edge to her tone.

'She changed, after everything that happened. She cut me out.'

'I don't think she knew how to share it with you.'

'She could have tried. It was awful, seeing her like that. Worse when she started to withdraw from me.'

'She's never really got over it. Maybe this baby will bring the old Tamsin back.'

Jamie looked up, recognising the slightest wobble in her voice. 'Even if it does, it's too late,' he tried to reassure her. 'We can't go back to how it used to be. It's been too long. Too much has changed, for both of us.'

'She's still your wife, Jamie. She's going to have your baby.'

'I can't stop her. I never dreamt she'd get pregnant. It was meant to be near impossible.'

Lucia could only shrug, drinking her own wine too fast. 'Not impossible enough, apparently.'

'I'm sorry.'

She shook her head in frustration. 'This isn't about apologies. A baby shouldn't be something to be sorry for. My best friend has got what she's always wanted – I should be thrilled for her. Not trying to hide my feelings behind a rictus grin because I'm too guilty to not support her through it.'

'Are you saying I should support her?'

'I'm saying you have to at least face up to the fact you'll be a father. Ignoring it, and Tam, won't make it go away.'

'I don't know how else to deal with it!'

Lucia blew out a frustrated breath. 'You made the bed, Jamie. You're going to have to lie in it sooner or later.'

11

Tamsin – Now

Richard leaves soon after the disturbance. He stayed just sixty minutes, exactly the same length as our old appointments, but it felt like hours.

Three years. I know his true motivation for visiting after all this time. He wanted to check that there was no chance I would recover enough to give my own evidence. He came, quite literally, to make sure the comforting old adage still applied – let sleeping dogs lie.

It is not until Richard has bidden me a cheerful farewell, as if we are parting from another therapy session, that I realise how stressed I have become. My muscles ache and my head throbs from the earlier ocular assault.

But I have no opportunity to recover. The occupational therapist arrives immediately afterwards, to stroke my limbs with feathers and silk scarves and velvet swatches to expose me to different textures. I hate these sessions, even in better circumstances. Today, I want nothing to do with her.

At least she hasn't brought my running shoes this time. She has found out my interests, my passions, and she sometimes uses them to try and provoke a reaction I cannot give. She gets Jamie to provide her with my trainers ahead of our sessions, fits them onto my lifeless feet, flexes my ankles as if I am striding and plays me songs with a steady, upbeat tempo, tracks I would have listened to as I pounded the pavements.

All it does is leave an unbearable ache in the pit of my stomach, knowing I may never enjoy my favourite hobby again.

I fight to switch my brain off to her endeavours as she runs today's fabrics over my skin. My mind is still occupied with Richard, but I can't concentrate until this session is over for another week. It annoys me to such extremes that the aura inside my skull becomes disturbed again, bombarding me with waves of bold, disorienting colours like an out-of-control fairground ride.

When it is finally done, I can feel the therapist's frustration that, yet again, she has elicited no response. I, however, am proud to have defeated her. I take whatever victories I can get these days.

There is no time to gather myself before Milena takes over for the late shift and comes to give me a bed-bath with another carer, a regular agency worker named Claudia who always lulls me with her warming St Lucian accent. Together, they wash me like a mother would her baby, like I would have bathed Elise if I'd had the chance.

I cringe even though they are tactful and gentle, making sure my naked form is safe under towels, only ever exposing the minimum amount of skin they need to complete their task. I appreciate their consideration. Compared to the humiliation of shower day, this is almost tolerable.

Milena brushes my hair, smoothing it with her fingers after each pass. I hear her colleague gathering the damp towels, recapping the bath oil and taking the water to pour away in the bathroom.

'She's your favourite, isn't she?'

I hear the smile in Milena's voice as she replies. 'I know I would have liked her, if I'd met her before all this. She must have been a very clever woman.'

'You sound proud of her.'

'She must have been proud of herself. Now she can't feel that. So maybe it will help her if I feel it for her.'

'You get too attached.'

'No.' Milena pauses. 'Not unless I think it is worth it.'

For a few more minutes, they bustle about, completing their tasks.

'What is this in her notes?' Milena asks.

'She was a bit unstable earlier,' Claudia replies. 'Everything settled down after her visitor left.'

'Mr Attwood said he wasn't coming today.'

'It was someone new. Richard somebody. Strange surname.'

I hear Milena take a sharp breath. 'Richard?'

'Do you know him?'

An uncomfortable pause. 'Mr Attwood talked about him. He was Tamsin's client.'

'He didn't seem the type to need a psychiatrist.'

'She was treating him when she had the accident. Was he alone with her?'

'Of course, we don't supervise visitors. He didn't stay long.'

'It's strange to have a new visitor now, after so long.'

'He must have had a reason.'

'Maybe he wanted to check up on her.'

'What does that mean?'

Milena doesn't reply, and I imagine she has shrugged. She turns away from me, to the equipment trolley, and begins to prepare the liquid that sustains me.

'Is everything OK?' Claudia asks uncertainly.

'Yes.' Milena's reply is too quick. 'Sorry. My head is somewhere else this evening.'

'I'll go do room five's obs,' Claudia says. 'You have your dinner with Tamsin. It's chicken curry tonight.'

I hear the familiar sounds of Milena aspirating my feeding tube and checking the syringe measurements before attaching it and raising my bed into the semi-upright position. Her movements don't have her usual rhythm; they seem jerky and tense. She doesn't hum, as she usually does, as she gradually depresses the plunger.

I am unable to feel fullness anymore, but I can detect a tautness in my abdomen after a feed, like the urge to unbutton your jeans after a substantial meal. How I long for real food, to feel the rough crust of sourdough on my tongue again, to savour a creamy brie or a bite into a ripe, juicy tomato.

Milena's phone buzzes and she waits too long after pulling it from her pocket to answer. She speaks in the Slavic language again, moving away from the bed. It definitely isn't Polish. I don't recognise any words. She must have turned towards the French windows she often opens so the breeze can drift over me, for her voice becomes muffled.

It is a short conversation, barely anything said by Milena before a sharp noise as if she has slammed the phone onto a hard surface.

'How many times do I tell her?' She speaks in English, telling me she is addressing me rather than speaking to herself. 'I can't do what she wants. If only it was as easy as she thinks.' She snatches up the book that holds my daily log and scribbles rapidly as she records my feed.

'I make this mistake before. I try to please people. I let them control me.' A sob escapes, a hiccup that she immediately smothers. 'Now I have to accept this life. Running away will only make it worse.'

Is the woman on the phone trying to lure Milena to another country? Another promise of a better life? But Milena has already learned that the grass isn't necessarily greener and, if she has had bad experiences in her past, I can understand why she would be hesitant about another move.

Besides, selfishly, I don't want her to go. I'd be lost without her.

'I will *not* answer next time she calls.' I hear the resolve in her voice. 'You don't need to hear my problems, anyway. Sorry, Tamsin, you have too many of your own.'

I strain to tell her to carry on, that the one thing I can be is a confidante. I want to hear her worries and, just for a few moments, feel like I am myself again. My brain is already engaged, forming the questions I cannot ask.

Milena squeezes my hand. 'You are a good listener,' she says sadly. 'I think you would give me good advice, if you could.'

She wants someone to talk to, and if that someone is a person she thinks is completely unresponsive, at least that is better than keeping it all inside. It must be hard, being so far from home, from her family and friends and all that was familiar to her. Swindon is very different from Warsaw.

Milena keeps hold of my hand for longer than is necessary. 'I wish you could talk to me.'

If only I could tell her how much I wished the same.

Her evening meal is delivered as she tidies up the equipment. I smell rich, tomatoey curry, bright with spices and coconut, and my mouth waters.

Usually, she chats to me as she eats, describing the tastes of the food or telling me about her latest night out in Swindon with her friends, but today she turns on the TV and flicks between channels. She isn't eating much. Her fork scrapes as she moves the food around the plate, but she only raises it to her mouth a couple of times.

She settles on some sort of reality show, and I groan internally, but she is quickly bored and continues to channel hop.

Her clicking of the remote stops abruptly. I hear the clear, moderated tones of a news reporter. He states he is outside the Royal Courts of Justice, at a landmark retrial ordered by the Court of Appeal, and I picture the beautiful Gothic building behind him.

I know it is Richard's case even before the name is mentioned, but Milena's sharp intake of breath is a surprise as the report delivers the day's update, focussing on the two victims and their lives since the attacks. Milena's fork falls onto her plate with a clatter.

'Milena!' Hannah's strident summons echoes from the corridor and I feel Milena's body jump. 'Staff meeting is starting, you're late.'

Milena drops her plate onto my bedside table and hurries out without saying goodbye to me. She is never untidy, never slapdash. She pays attention to details like keeping rooms neat and treating patients like real people.

The news item has distressed her, and my professional mind voices my suspicion even though my mouth cannot.

I am woken by the sound of my door opening. I hadn't been aware I'd fallen asleep, but my energy had been sapped by Richard's visit.

I am groggy with exhaustion, slow to recognise who it is. It seems late. There is a hushed tranquillity that never happens during the day.

'It is me again, Tamsin. Sorry I disturb you.' Milena's voice sounds thick and heavy, like she is getting a cold.

She moves to the foot of my bed, standing unusually still, and I can feel her watching me. It becomes disconcerting as she remains there, motionless and silent. The air feels thick and unyielding, and my own breathing becomes shallower.

'What are you doing in here?' Claudia's voice asks from the doorway. The staff instinctively speak softly after dark, considerate even though they don't believe I have wake and sleep cycles.

'Just checking she's OK before I go home.'

'Are you crying?'

A hard sniff. 'It doesn't matter.'

'What's wrong?' Claudia steps fully into my room, shutting the door. 'Tell me.'

Milena makes a strangled noise, as if she has almost howled, but smothered her own sound.

'They want to let Tamsin die.'

The silence is just long enough to allow me to understand what Milena said, but not for me to process.

'Who do?' Shock strains Claudia's voice. 'What are you talking about?'

'Hannah told me to write up the case notes for Tamsin's file. The notes said Tamsin's family can choose to take her treatment away. She can't survive without it.'

A scream threatens to suffocate me as it swells in my throat. Panic surges, red-hot to ice-cold in seconds.

'But …' Claudia's words fade away hesitantly.

'It's been too long. She had to show improvement. Like she could take a test. So they're giving up on her.' There is anger now in Milena's voice, real fury. I can feel her shaking as she leans over to take my hand. 'They will stop her nutrition and hydration. Then she will die, slowly, like an animal caught in a trap.'

How can this be happening? How can they be prepared to give up on me because a certain time has elapsed? No one ever told me I was against the clock. No one ever thought to mention that I had a finite time granted to me.

What am I supposed to do? I have no way of communicating, to rally against this death warrant. No way of proving I am worthy of continuing to live.

Are they really going to let me die because they believe I am nothing more than a breathing corpse?

'When?' Claudia asks the question I am fighting so hard to shout.

'When Jamie makes the decision. The doctors agree that, after so long, there is no chance of progress. They say it's cruel to keep her going like this.'

Claudia is silent for a long moment. All I can hear is the sounds of their breathing. Milena's is rapid, like she has sprinted.

'What if they're right?' Claudia finally asks. 'We don't let our pets suffer, but we let people. What life does she have, really?'

'She still deserves the chance,' Milena interrupts. 'Everyone is prepared to give up on her. It's so fucking wrong.'

I can tell she is crying again, even before she sniffs hard and drags her sleeve roughly across her skin.

A sense of claustrophobia grips me. Waves of dizziness wash over me, and I can hear blood thrashing in my ears. Pain stabs through my chest and it feels like my throat is being squeezed closed. I am trapped in a well and the water is rising.

What the hell am I going to do?

12

Jamie – Now

Jamie hears Elise scream just after five a.m. Bleary-eyed, he stumbles to her room before she wakes the entire house.

She sits bolt upright in her white wooden bed, stencilled with 'flappy flies' by the artistic Mateo, who has endless patience for the little girl despite his hatred of her father. Her tiny fists clutch her covers to her chin for protection against the demons that invade her sleep.

'It's OK, Els,' Jamie whispers as she freezes, staring in terror at his outline in the door. He strides across the room to tap the dimmable bedside lamp.

He hears a sigh of pure relief huff from Elise's clenched lips.

'Daddy's here, sweetheart.' He sits carefully on the edge of the small bed, sliding his arms around her. She is damp with sweat and trembling violently. 'Everything's fine. You're safe.'

'Mummy shouting for me,' she sobs, clinging to him.

'Lu-Lu, you mean?'

'No!' She shakes her head impatiently, her fingers tightening on his T-shirt. 'Real Mummy. She wants me to stay with her.'

'You don't need to stay with her, sweetheart. Mummy's asleep in the hospital. You see her sometimes, then we come home.'

Elise thinks about this, her sobs gradually settling to soft hiccups. 'Mummy coming home?'

'No. She lives at the hospital.'

'Forever and ever?'

What is he supposed to say in response to questions like these? Isn't there a manual or a script he can read from? 'Maybe,' is all he can think of to say.

Elise thinks again. She is calming now, her tiny chest no longer rising and falling so hard. 'Where's Matty?'

'Mateo's asleep, sweetheart, like you should be. It's really early. Think you can go back to sleep till it's time to get up?' He strokes her silken hair.

Without realising it, she has snuggled down against the pillow again, her arm drawing her soft toy bunny closer.

'Don't like sleeping. Matty knows.'

Jamie wonders if Mateo has his own struggles at night. He would never admit so to him, but he might to innocent Elise. They share a lot, those two.

'Close your eyes. Let's try those deep breaths we practised.'

He demonstrates, exaggerating the swell of his chest and the sound of inhaling through his nose. Elise resists at first with a stubbornness that is unsettlingly familiar from her mother, but eventually she submits and copies him, following his count.

After three rounds, she is fast asleep again and Jamie fights the urge to remain by her side. The play therapist said staying with her would only increase the insecurity, making her believe there really was something to fear.

He tiptoes from the room. There is no point crawling back under the plump, inviting duvet with Lucia. The sun is up and the birds are on the river as they are every morning, chirping their greetings as they bob gracefully with the current.

Jamie pads down to the kitchen, setting the coffee beans to grind before slowly identifying the correct buttons on the ridiculously expensive barista machine Ben had worshipped. His every movement feels like swimming through treacle. His own reflection in the polished chrome avoids making eye contact.

He has to do something to protect his daughter from her dreams. Elise can't go on like this, her sleep broken by her subconscious need to understand what has happened to her mother. How can she grow up with that sort of weight hovering over her each night?

It should feel momentous, he thinks, this realisation of what he has to do. It shouldn't feel like a quiet whisper in his ear; it should smack him in the face and announce its presence.

But there it is, and Jamie knows what his answer for the director at Rushmore will be. And although it brings tears leaping to his eyes, he can't tell if they are of sadness or relief.

'Did you get Els back to sleep?' Lucia's drowsy voice makes him jump.

Jamie quickly knuckles his eyes. 'Sorry, thought I'd got to her before she disturbed anyone.'

'Don't worry, it's not her fault.' She hops onto a stool and takes a deep, appreciative sniff when he delivers a steaming mug of black coffee to her. She is wearing one of his hoodies and it drowns her, making her look impossibly appealing. 'Was she OK?'

'The usual. Shaken up. It kills me seeing her like that.'

'Emotions can't be easy for a young child. They must feel things more intensely than us. That's why they have tantrums, apparently, because they can't communicate it effectively.'

'I never thought of it like that.' Jamie scrubs at his eyes again. 'Am I a shit father?'

As he knew she would, Lucia slides her arms round his neck and pulls him to her. 'Utterly shit,' she says with a teasing grin.

He makes a pathetic attempt at a laugh.

'Jamie, you know you're trying your best. Not every man can cope with being a single dad.'

'I'm not though, am I? A single dad. Not when you've been part of Els' life since day one.'

She smiles at his acknowledgement. 'We're in it together. Besides, I love her like my own.'

'Thanks for being a real mum to her.'

Lucia's chews her bottom lip. 'I'm not trying to replace Tamsin.'

'I never thought you were.'

'Other people do. The mums at nursery.'

'Like you give a shit about what other people think. Without you, Els wouldn't know what it feels like to have a mother. It's not as if Tam can give her what she needs.'

Lucia is quiet for a moment. 'Imagine if Tam does slip away ...' she mumbles. 'What if she *is* aware? What if she knows what's happening ... when the time comes?'

'If Tam was still in there, she'd have found a way to show us by now.'

'But what if she can't? Maybe she tries and her body won't let her. It doesn't matter how clever her brain is if her muscles aren't able to respond.'

'Lucia, please.' Desperation cracks Jamie's voice. 'I can't think about that. I'm sorry, I know it worries you, but if I let myself even consider the possibility ...'

Lucia's body tenses against his and she steps back, wrapping her arms around her middle. 'You sound like you've made up your mind.'

Jamie stares into his mug, unable to look up. 'I haven't stopped thinking about it since Friday.'

'Then why haven't you talked to me about it? You've barely mentioned it over the weekend.'

'You didn't want anything to do with it last time I brought it up,' he points out.

It's the wrong thing to say. He glances up in time to see her face shutting down, and he wants to explain that he didn't know how. That he couldn't find a way to voice the maelstrom of thoughts that tormented him or explain why, each time, he arrived at only one conclusion. But the explanation doesn't come, and Lucia is moving further away from him, putting the barrier of the kitchen worktop between them.

'Have you decided?' She makes herself another coffee, jabbing the buttons too hard, spilling some when she snatches the mug away too early.

'No,' he stammers. He isn't ready to tell her the truth yet. It still feels too new. 'It's just …'

'Jamie, for God's sake, do you want to end Tam's life – yes or no?'

'Don't say it like that!'

'How else can I say it? That's the choice, plain and simple. No matter how we dress it up to make it sound nicer, that's what it comes down to – she carries on living, or she dies.'

Jamie rubs his forehead, her anger, reverberating across the room, preventing him from formulating a sensible reply.

'I want this to end,' is all he can come up with, and he cringes as the words leave his mouth, 'and there's only one way for that to happen.'

'And what about me? What about what I think?'

'Lu, you said it wasn't fair putting that responsibility on you. You said it was my decision.'

'And you said you didn't want to play God.'

'What else am I meant to do? Rushmore won't wait forever. The decision has to be made, one way or another.'

'I don't want her to die, Jamie.'

So definite is that statement, made so abruptly, that Jamie is thrown. He had known Lucia would have her reservations – Tamsin had been her best friend, after all, despite everything – but he hadn't envisaged her to be adamantly against it.

'Tam was always there for me when I needed help. I've already betrayed her with you. I can't do it over this.'

Jamie drags in a breath, holding it until he's sure he isn't going to say something he'll regret. 'And I can't let her continue to lie there year after year,' he says tightly. 'I can't keep dragging Els to Rushmore to pretend her mother knows she's there. I can't live this half-life for the next decade or more.'

'So that's it?' Lucia practically snarls. 'Start planning the funeral? Tell Els to say goodbye and pull the plug?'

'Or we can put her behind glass and make her Snow fucking White if you want! But a prince isn't going to come along and revive her, no matter how long we wait. I want my life with you, Lucia. For as long as Tam's still here, you'll always be my mistress.'

That was the wrong thing to say. Her face goes rigid, her fists clenching. 'That's how you see me?'

'Of course it isn't. But you said it yourself, that's how you feel around the nursery mums!'

'Fuck you, Jamie. If you think I'm a mistress, after everything I've done for you and Elise –'

'Lu-Lu?' a little voice interrupts. Elise tiptoes into the room. Both adults stiffen, clamping their lips together as if they can take back the words they have thrown.

'Hi, baby!' Lucia moves before Jamie can, scooping her up, cuddling her close.

'You should still be in bed, sweetheart,' he tells her, swallowing down his anger at Lucia before she can spot it.

'Can't sleep,' Elise states, squirming free of Lucia's embrace. 'Hungry.'

Lucia hands her a croissant before she can work herself into a tantrum. Elise is instantly distracted pulling apart her favourite breakfast food, sending a shower of pastry flakes everywhere. She wanders off to sit cross-legged on the tiled floor in front of the TV.

Lucia watches the little girl for a long moment. 'I only hope she won't be too messed up by it, later on,' she mutters pointedly.

'That's exactly what I'm trying to protect her from, by doing it now, while she's still young enough to forget.'

'She won't forget her mother, Jamie,' Lucia hisses.

'But she *will* forget the pain.'

'Give her some credit. She's too clever for that. She's got Tam's brain.'

Jamie flinches like he has taken a blow. This is all going wrong. He had wanted a united front, himself and Lucia, making the ultimate decision as a committed couple with a future to look forward to. Without that support, the weight of his responsibility is crushing.

He moves across to her, reaching to take both her hands in his. She tenses, about to pull away.

'I love you, Lu,' he murmurs. 'Elise and I both love you so much.'

Lucia allows him the contact for a moment before tugging herself free and turning to sweep up croissant crumbs from the tiles. 'You should see if the play therapist has any more ideas to help with the nightmares.' It is her way of drawing a line under the row, for now. He can tell by the set of her shoulders and the tightness of her jaw that it isn't over.

'Yeah, I will,' Jamie says quickly, trying to appease her.

He can't afford to upset Lucia. He can't do this on his own, wouldn't be able to keep up the pretence that he has everything under control. He can't let social services know that he has no idea how to raise his daughter – that, since the crash, he has lived in fear of fucking it up just like he fucked up everything else.

Because they don't provide any instructions at antenatal classes about what to do if you're suddenly left to parent your accidental child alone while your wife lies in a hospital bed like Sleeping bloody Beauty.

The midwives briefed him on the signs of meningitis, but not on how to bond with a tiny stranger he was terrified of inadvertently damaging, physically or mentally. They showed him how to sterilise bottles but not how to persuade Elise to stop screaming for long enough to drink them. He was taught what to do if she choked but not how to stuff four frantically wriggling limbs into a baby-grow.

Thank God for Lucia, who had already raised her own child with seemingly effortless competence and apparently had no qualms about doing it again, even when Jamie worked long nights trying to keep both businesses afloat. He had managed to keep Porteños open, with Ben's former sous chef Franco stepping into the breach, a competent and reliable chef who could manage a budget as well as busy services. At least Jamie didn't need to worry about the standard of food.

But there were too many other concerns, even once Porteños was running smoothly and efficiently. Lucia had been the only one he could turn to and it felt so good to have someone to lean on, that he had allowed her to take control.

No, now more than ever, Jamie cannot risk falling out with Lucia. He has far too much to lose.

His counsellor's office is too similar to Tamsin's former premises. The walls are a similar sage green, the furniture comfortably neutral, the artwork benign, all designed not to provoke emotional responses.

Jamie sits opposite the neat, middle-aged woman who greets him with a familiarity that makes him wince. Before all this, he would never have been the type of man to seek therapy. He had only agreed to this in the first place because Elise's social worker had insisted that he couldn't successfully parent a baby if he was mental – though it had been phrased in gentler terms.

He had never expected he would still be coming here after all this time. Each month, he dreads and looks forward to coming here in equal measure, but today, the latter is the dominant feeling. He'll use the 'quiet time' his counsellor ends every session with to rehearse what he will say to Lucia this evening, how he will justify his decision.

'Elise's night terrors are getting worse,' he says before she can speak.

As usual, she doesn't react immediately while she analyses his words.

'Do you discuss the crash at home?'

'Not really.' Not recently, anyway. He and Lucia tiptoe around it as much as they can. 'We're trying to get on with things as normally as possible.'

'So Elise may realise it's become a taboo subject?'

Jamie frowns. 'It's not *taboo*. We just can't spend every day dwelling on it.'

The psychologist raises one eyebrow. 'You've been seeing me a long time, Jamie,' she observes, 'but you haven't spoken to me about the accident once. You exist in a suspended reality, not gaining anything from your relationship with Tamsin. Three years in limbo. That would affect anyone.'

Jamie realises his chin has dropped onto his chest. It takes more effort than he expected to raise it.

'Do you feel guilt?'

'Guilt that I still get to live my life while my wife can't?'

'Maybe. Or something else.'

Jamie wishes he'd requested a male psychologist. Sometimes, this is too much like talking to Tamsin. She had tried her best not to analyse him openly but, on occasion, she had slipped. He had hated the feeling that she could read his innermost thoughts, the ones he would never allow her to glimpse.

'You're living with Tamsin's best friend, effectively as man and wife. She's raising your daughter. Perhaps you feel guilty that you're in that relationship while married to Tamsin. Is that fair to say?'

He can't exactly deny it, so he nods. 'I love Lucia. I have done for over three years.'

There it is, just the tiniest flicker across the impassive face. He has never admitted to her how the affair started. 'You were together before the crash?'

'Tamsin and I weren't in a good place. It had been like that for ages, like there was a gulf between us. She shut me out, made me feel useless. Lucia didn't do that. She made me feel like I wasn't a waste of space.'

'But Tamsin became pregnant.'

'It wasn't supposed to be possible.' He squeezes his hands together. 'It was a massive shock. I didn't want a baby – I already knew my future wasn't with her – but if I'd told her that, she'd have found out about Lucia and me.'

'What about Lucia's husband?'

'He *was* a waste of space. I worried he'd hurt her. He'd lose his temper over nothing, lash out before thinking. She wasn't safe around him, but she couldn't leave him. Her son would have gone with his dad if they'd split, and she couldn't risk that.' Jamie takes a long breath, holding it until his lungs burn. 'I hated him by the end. I wanted him out of our lives.'

'And then he died.' The statement is made calmly, neutrally, but Jamie's head snaps up regardless.

'What are you suggesting?'

'I'm not suggesting anything, Jamie. I only mentioned it to highlight that Ben can't interfere in your life anymore. Why do you think your response was defensive?'

Jamie realises his knees are bouncing, and presses the balls of his feet hard against the floor. He doesn't like the way the conversation has turned. He can feel the therapist's astute eyes on him. He begins to sweat, heat blooming beneath his shirt.

'When I got the call, it was from Tam's phone,' he says, forcing his legs to stay still. 'I was with Lucia, at her house in Kent. Ben knew she was there, so I guess he and Tam were coming for a visit. The police told me to meet them at the hospital, but I had to drive down the same road to get there.'

His mind, without instruction, conjures a scene in slow motion. Jamie abandoning his car in the middle of the road, engine still running, sprinting towards the site of the devastation.

'There was nothing left of the car, just a heap of crumpled metal. I saw the body bag on the verge, and I thought it was waiting for Tam. The police didn't get hold of me in time, and I grabbed it like I was going to prevent them putting her in there. Then I realised it wasn't for her.'

The police had finally hauled him away from Ben's lifeless figure and he had stumbled back towards the road, stammering gibberish, fear gripping him with icy fingers.

'I couldn't get anywhere near her. She was surrounded by all those medics.' Jamie hears his voice becoming sharper. 'The police drove me and Lucia to the Royal London. They wouldn't tell us anything besides confirming that Ben hadn't survived. We were just left to wait, hours staring at the same white walls.'

He doesn't say Ben's drug use had ultimately led to his death. The cocaine had weakened the walls of his blood vessels. He might have survived the internal injuries otherwise, if his own vices hadn't caused a catastrophic bleed that claimed his life before the emergency services arrived.

It eases Jamie's guilt, just slightly, to know Ben was effectively to blame for his own demise.

'You seem very on edge today, if you don't mind me saying so.'

She's right. He is suddenly anxious to divert the therapist away from the subject of Ben.

'We've been given the option to not continue Tam's treatment,' he blurts out.

She considers the sudden revelation, taking her time. 'How do you feel about that?'

'Relieved.' He might as well be honest now he's put himself in this vulnerable position. 'I can see an end, for the first time in three years. We wouldn't be stuck in this never-ending Groundhog Day.'

She says something in reply, but he doesn't hear her. He can't talk anymore, can't focus. His mind has already departed.

At first, he hadn't even realised they were panic attacks. They aren't moments of gasping for breath, chest tightening, extremities tingling; even in the early days, they didn't have any obvious symptoms. They are more like absences, when the world around him slows, sounds become muffled and he is unable to continue a conversation or hold on to a thought.

They can last seconds or minutes, and he has no control over when they end. These attacks leave him as helpless as Tamsin.

Only now, he has the chance to banish them forever. To let his contrition pass along with his wife.

Once she is gone, Jamie will be safe.

13

Tamsin – Now

A tornado has been unleashed in my mind, wreaking havoc. I haven't slept a moment all night, tormented by my inability to prove the truth – that I am still here.

I know I'm getting carried away, catastrophising like I always urged my clients not to do, but I can't stop.

How has it come to this, that my own husband has been granted the power to decide whether I live or die?

I haven't experienced terror like this since the early days of regaining consciousness. Surely Jamie won't do it. He isn't a callous man. Whatever has happened between us, surely he still feels a connection to me. Why else would he trek out here every week?

Besides, he hates having to make decisions. He puts them off for as long as possible, adopting an ostrich's approach to avoidance.

Rushmore is still quiet. The early shift team will be upstairs, gulping down breakfast and coffee during handover from the night staff. I hope Milena is coming on duty. She will realise what hell I am experiencing.

The brain has power and autonomy that no other organ can boast. It works to a different beat from the circulatory or lymphatic systems, and that is why I am in this state of amnesia.

It has deemed the events that led to the car crash are a threat to me. It has decided I cannot be allowed to confront them.

But there is one comfort. Hope is still with me. She is in my ear, reminding me that I have one thing I can do.

Your brain is trying to protect you from the memories, keeping
  you in this state.
If you can remember, it won't need to do that anymore.
It might just let you wake up.

I am disturbed by the arrival of the morning staff. I can hear Hannah's heavy breathing; her movements are sharp and rapid, and she mutters under her breath as she goes about the daily routine.

'All this bloody fuss,' she hisses as she jabs at the buttons to raise my bed. The jerk upright disorientates me momentarily as my blood pressure drops in response to the abrupt change in position, and I have to wait for the dizziness to pass.

'I only said what I think,' Milena snaps. I hadn't realised she is here because she hasn't greeted me. She always greets me.

'You're here to do a job, not cause chaos.'

'I must stand up for my patient! No one else is going to.' I hear a rustle of paper. 'Listen to this. I printed it out from a case study. There's been research into it.'

Milena reads aloud.

'"A subset of PVS individuals have meaningfully functioning minds even as they remain completely unable to engage in another form of volitional communication or behaviour."' Milena struggles with the complex terminology, her pronunciation hesitant, and it steals her impact, much to my frustration. She has clearly understood what the research means, and she has applied it correctly when no one else has, but Hannah will dismiss her as uncomprehending. 'That means she has a chance!'

'It's none of your business. Carry on and I'll have to report you to the director.'

'I'm only trying to do the right thing.'

'The *right* thing is what Tamsin's doctors and next of kin choose!' Hannah thunders. 'Go back to the desk, if you're going to keep pestering me.'

The door slams. I hadn't expected Milena to leave me, but it is better that she takes the opportunity to calm herself. I couldn't bear her to be sacked.

'Bloody ridiculous behaviour,' Hannah growls. 'Acting like a teenager. So unprofessional.'

My indignation swells and I battle to force out some sort of noise in support of Milena.

'Sudden BP spike,' she mumbles, her pen moving against my daily log. 'Unexplained.'

I'll give you a fucking explanation, I shout inside my own head.

Hannah doesn't hang about today. It's like she can't wait to get away from me. Maybe she's already decided I won't be around for much longer, so there's little point in bothering with me now. Or could it be she feels uncomfortable being with someone whose fate lies in the balance? She leaves the door open, and I can feel the draught from the hallway.

'Tamsin!' Milena is back, making me start as she whispers urgently into my ear. 'You have to show them. If not, they will let you die. You have to fight now. Find strength, please.'

Her hand takes mine, gripping fiercely, as if she can pass her own fire to me.

'Show Jamie. Show Lucia. Anyone. If you can hear me, you need to trust me. I believe you're in there, but no one else does. They need to see proof.'

Does Milena know something I don't? Not being able to ask questions or find out more for myself is torture. I can feel my inhalations are shallow and too fast, my pulse a tiny hammer reverberating through my neck and throat.

'I don't want you to die, but no one will listen to me. I can't stop them for you. I am nobody.'

I want to tell her what I see in her, to make her understand she is not a nobody. She has qualities some of the people in my life could only ever aspire to.

'Milena!' Hannah snaps. 'We have other patients, in case you've forgotten.'

Milena must have nodded, for Hannah thumps out of the room with a triumphant *humph* and Milena drops my hand. Exhaustion envelops me in its heavy cloak and I drift away.

When I wake, I know immediately there is someone else in the room. It is no effort to recognise Lucia. Her scent is so familiar to me, from years of sitting close together on sofas as we drank wine and put the world to rights in front of *Dirty Dancing* and Brat Pack films.

It takes me a little longer to realise Lucia has someone with her. I smell custard creams and a child's shampoo and, suddenly, I am calm.

Elise is here to see me.

My heart clenches with gratitude towards Lucia. Did she know my daughter's presence would reassure me, pause the spiralling fears and allow me to collect myself?

'I thought I'd bring her before her birthday,' Lucia tells me. 'I can't believe our little one's turning three.'

Her casual use of 'our' makes me want to grit my teeth. Elise is *mine*, not ours, yet it seems she has become communal in the three years since the day that changed all our lives. How painfully slowly, yet incomprehensively quickly, it has passed.

'I am *two*,' Elise insists stridently.

'Only for one more day, sweetie. Say hello to Mummy. She wants to wish you happy birthday.'

The mattress dips slightly as Elise kneels on it and whispers her shy hello. She always pats my cheek gently as she greets me, as if checking I am definitely real, not a waxwork or a doll. Her touch leaves a soft sensation caressing my skin even after she has moved away.

Happy birthday, my darling. If only I had been aware of your arrival into the world. If only I'd done more to protect you.

'Mummy says hello back,' Lucia tells her. 'Tell her about your birthday party.'

'Zoo.'

'We're having a Mad Hatter's tea party like *Alice in Wonderland*,' Lucia corrects, as much for my benefit as Elise's. 'Daddy's taking you to the zoo at the weekend and you're having your party tonight with pizza and cake and ice cream. And all your friends from nursery are coming.'

'All my friends,' Elise agrees. 'I love *Alice in Wonderland*.'

How I'd have loved to read that childhood classic to her. She crawls about until she chooses her spot beside my feet so she can lean back against the foot of the bed. Her legs stretch out, pressing against mine. 'Matty here?'

'No, sweetie, just Lu-Lu today. I thought you might like to tell Mummy about your bad dreams.'

'No.' I hear the ringing obstinance in Elise's voice, and picture her folding her arms across her chest.

What bad dreams? Is something upsetting my little girl? I can do nothing to help but I'm glad to know. Jamie takes such care to give me a sanitised version of everything. I have to wonder what else he hides from me.

'She's definitely your daughter, stubborn as hell.' Lucia laughs, but I am sure I detect unease in her bright tone.

Elise giggles in response, a sound that sends warmth washing over me.

'You should see her, Tam,' Lucia continues. 'She dressed herself this morning. She looks like a party balloon exploded. Sparkles everywhere. It's adorable.'

Lucia has always lived in technicolour. Her words flow with vibrant description when she chats to me, bringing the one-sided conversation to life in a way Jamie and Dan can never manage.

I wonder if Jamie has told her of his moral dilemma yet. I like to think Lucia will fight for me with the same fierce protectiveness she always demonstrated for her boys, that she now shows for my daughter, but I can't be sure.

'The staff said your vital signs have been a bit of a mess. You OK in there? It's hard to tell. I wish there was some way of you showing us how you're feeling.'

I strain to make some sort of signal. I order my eyelids to flicker, my toes to curl. I try to grunt, to compress my lips.

I can't do anything, no matter how badly I want to show her I am not OK.

'No, Els, we can't go yet, we only just got here. Here, play with your tablet.'

How dull this must be for Elise, staring at my silent, motionless form. No wonder she gets upset sometimes. It really isn't fair on her, expecting her to comprehend the reality of the situation.

'Here, put your headphones on. It's OK, the noises are just Mummy's monitors.'

I wait impatiently for Lucia to resettle her, hearing the tinny sound of her favourite cartoon.

'I needed to come and talk to you, Tam,' Lucia finally says. Her voice is closer than usual. She must have pulled her chair right up to the bed. 'I know you might not hear but I can't leave you in the dark. It's not fair.'

So she's going to be the one who admits it. Has Jamie sent her to do his dirty work for him? He will be desperate to shy away from such a responsibility.

'You've done so much for me.' Lucia takes my hand, squeezing it tight. Her usually warm, dry skin feels damp and chilly. 'And I ...'

Her voice trails off. For once, she doesn't seem to know what to say. Is she trying to tell me that it's been too much for her, raising Elise, helping Jamie, everything she's taken on in my place? *She's* done so much for *us*.

'I've told Jamie I don't want to pull the plug. I said you deserve the chance to get better.'

A surge of relief floods over me. I have another person in my corner.

'But he doesn't think it's fair,' she continues. 'Not for you and not for Elise. She has night terrors. She wakes up screaming for you.'

A fist clenches my heart in an iron grip. My daughter's nightmares are because of me. I am the cause of her distress. They shouldn't have kept it from me. I'm her mother; I have a right to know.

'We should have told you before.' As if she's read my mind, Lucia shifts uncomfortably in her seat. 'Though you've got enough to worry about, right?'

Just add it to the list, I want to tell her. But with the extra concern comes an unexpected motivation. I need to do this for Elise, to show her I'm really in here. I need to give her intelligent mind the evidence it needs to ward off the night terrors. Most of all, I need to prove it will be possible for her to live a normal life with a present mother.

'I've tried my best, Tam,' Lucia murmurs. 'I've done everything to raise Elise as well as you would've done. I know I'm not her mum and I swear I'm not trying to take her from you, but she needs someone to do all the stuff ...'

All the stuff I can't do, I mentally finish for her. I can't deny it, no matter how strongly I want to.

'It's not been easy since the crash,' she goes on. 'Jamie's had to keep us all afloat, helping me to pay off Ben's debts. He had to accept investment into Porteños to save it and he says the investor's turned out to be an absolute pain the arse.'

At least that explains how Jamie's financial situation has improved so dramatically. I'm glad there will be money to comfortably raise Elise, to give her a secure future, especially if I won't be around to see it.

No, I can't think like that. I *have* to be around. I have to be there for my baby.

Lucia is still talking, but I find I am tuning out. Usually, her visits are my favourite. I enjoy her tales of mutual acquaintances, daily trials and tribulations, her cooking disasters. She saves me nuggets of gossip that previously I wouldn't have cared a jot about but now give me a tiny thrill. Today, I find her vacuous, her voice insincere.

She has been a good friend to me, and now she is to Jamie. She helps out with childcare and meals, nursery collection and laundry. She is doing what I can't, taking care of my husband and my daughter. And while I am so jealous of her it hurts, for being able to revel in their love and affection, I am also glad I don't have to worry if the fridge is stocked with fresh fruit and vegetables, or if the bedsheets are regularly changed, or if Elise's nursery clothes are ironed.

Besides, I'd have no right to rage against it, even if I was able to.

I was hardly perfect, before all this.

14

Tamsin – Before

I struggled to make eye contact with Lucia. I could see she was hungover from the Michelin celebration. Her forehead was rigid with a headache, and she continually swallowed against nausea, but she had ushered me in and made elderberry tea while I sat limply on her sofa, my hands instinctively clasped over my abdomen as if shielding the baby.

'What time did you get home?' I asked after she handed me a steaming glass mug.

'God knows. I sent Matty back in an Uber at midnight and we were still going a fair while after that. Not my finest hour as a mother.'

'Sorry for sneaking off so early.'

'Jamie didn't seem in the party mood either.' Lucia sniffed her drink, wrinkling her nose. 'This could do with a splash of brandy. Don't look so mortified that you left early, Tam. I wasn't expecting you to hang around for hours hating every minute. I knew it wouldn't be your scene.'

'It was a bit ...'

'Wanky?' she offered.

'I was thinking ostentatious.'

'You always phrase things more nicely.'

Lucia was in no way inarticulate, but she worked in the sort of environment where the most strident voice won, and she didn't believe in mincing her words.

I sipped the tea, welcoming the tingle as it burned my top lip. I gently rubbed circles around my belly button, trying to detect any hint of a bump. As I waited for her to ask me about Jamie's reaction to my news, I scanned the mess scattered across the coffee table. The contents of Lucia's makeup bag, a couple of charging leads, two empty coffee cups, a pack of playing cards roughly crammed together and a copy of the *Independent*.

Lucia always made a point of avoiding the news. She prided herself on declaring she didn't need to be stressed by the darkness in the world and, although that may have been interpreted as ignorance in other people, Lucia's sunny, sparky personality was enough for her to get away with it as a quirk. She didn't read the papers or listen to the hourly radio updates, and hadn't done for years, so the presence of the newspaper threw me.

She followed my gaze and rolled her eyes. 'There's a piece about Porteños and photos of the party. Ben wants to see them. There's a nice one of us, actually.'

She flips rapidly through the creased pages and shows me a shot of the four of us, wide smiles and raised glasses, our gazes fixed on the camera as if we don't dare to glance at each other. Jamie's hand hovers, torn between resting it on my waist or tucking it into his pocket. Lucia's body is angled towards us, attempting to turn her back on her husband, who is laughing too hard and trying to hug her close to him.

'It's a good picture,' I lied, glancing through the rest of the article out of duty, flipping over to check for any more pictures. My eyes were drawn irresistibly to the big, bold headline on the next page.

Battersea predator demands landmark retrial.

'The tea's not agreeing with me,' I said abruptly. 'I need some water.'

I folded the newspaper in half, hiding the story, dropping it back onto the table as I stood up and crossed to the fridge, riffling unnecessarily to find the bottle of sparkling water that always sat in the door shelf. I took my time, watching ice cubes tumble into the highball glass, carefully pouring the fizzing liquid over them as they crackled in protest, gripping the glass so my scar, which stung like it was freshly scored into my skin, pressed against the coolness. I fought for calm. The fragile life inside me didn't need to deal with spiking blood pressure or a racing heart.

For so long after the encounter that caused the scar, the mere sight of it was enough to trigger flashbacks, but my professional background had given me the tools to manage them, to the point they had become a rare event.

Their return has caught me off guard, unprepared to deal with the sudden and unexpected bolts that snared me and hauled me back into the past. They could be visual, auditory or sensory. No pattern. They were debilitating in their power, and I found I could lose minutes to them without being aware. In my line of work, that was dangerous.

It's bitterly cold but there's no ice on the grass. I'm wrapped up in layers, face buried in a snood, gloves not quite preventing the chill in my fingertips. The sky threatens snow, but the trail beckons as I begin to stretch, waiting for my running mate to join me. The birds chirp from the bare tree branches and dogs bark in the distance. Everything is normal, until the moment that it isn't.

'Have you got any lime?' My voice was too loud, jolting in the quiet room as I wrenched myself out of the flashback.

Lucia turned, her head tilted as she frowned. 'Huh?'

I swallowed several times to rid myself of the enormous lump threatening to block my throat. 'Lemon's giving me heartburn,' I managed to say in a more normal voice.

Lucia obligingly got up and rummaged through the crisper drawers until she found a solitary, slightly browned lime. I managed not to wince as she carelessly chopped it into uneven wedges, not bothering to find a chopping board to protect the marble worktop, leaving the little puddles of juice to sit as she popped one into my glass with her fingers.

I grabbed a cloth from the sink and mopped up quickly, counting the strokes across the counter to soothe myself.

'You're never going to cope with a toddler's sticky fingers wiping smears all over your pristine home.' Lucia seized a bottle of Malbec and returned to the sofa. She patted the cushions to coax me away from cleaning her entire kitchen.

I forced a smile as I joined her, and watched her own smile slide away as she abandoned her tea and poured a glass of wine. She grimaced. 'Jamie didn't take it well, then?'

'He left. I went for a shower, to give him some processing time, and when I came back out, he'd gone and so had his car keys. I haven't seen him since.'

Lucia expelled a long breath, but she wasn't looking at me. 'I'm sorry, Tam.'

I almost knocked over my water glass as the front door banged and a loud voice echoed through the ground floor, making us both jump. Ben was unable to arrive anywhere without announcing his presence.

'Tammy! *Como estas*, beautiful, how are you doing? You have fun last night? Great party, yeah?'

I had lost count of how many times I had told Ben I hated being called Tammy.

Now I noticed the little clues I had previously missed: the regular sniffs, the rubbing of his nose, the inability to remain still. When he rested his hands on the back of the sofa, I saw the tiny tremors.

'Is Jamie at the restaurant?' I asked.

A frown. 'No, I didn't see him since last night.' Ben made a show of looking at his watch, oblivious to my anxiety. 'I have no time. I gotta be back before service. Just shower and I go.'

Ben exaggerated his accent as part of his brand. He had been in the UK for twenty years but he still spoke, even in the privacy of his own home, as if he had only just left Buenos Aires.

'Why you don't know where Jamie is?' he asked me as he turned away, as if it had suddenly occurred to him that my question was strange.

I busied myself pretending to search my handbag for something. 'He must have forgotten to charge his phone again.'

Ben shrugged, not giving a damn, and pounded off upstairs without a backwards glance.

'Lucia! I need my black shirt,' Ben bellowed from the stairs. 'The Armani one.'

We rolled our eyes simultaneously at his need to name-drop. Lucia took a fortifying slug of wine and strode off to attend to the emergency. I moved my abandoned mug of elderberry tea next to her glass. The two liquids were near identical in colour and my fingers itched to reach for the comfort of the wine.

The newspaper lay on the coffee table, demanding my attention. I took a mouthful of water, but it did nothing to cleanse my mouth of the sour taste that lurked, and nausea rolled in agitated waves through the pit of my stomach. I set the glass away from me, cracking my knuckles one by one to give my hands something to do, but I already knew nothing would prevent me picking up the paper.

A violent sex offender, convicted of two separate attacks on women in isolated areas of Battersea Park in 2017, will seek to overturn his convictions as he petitions the Court of Appeal to grant him the chance of a retrial. Richard Mandeville, forty-four, served half of his original sixteen-year sentence before being recently released on licence. A former army captain who was decorated for tours of Kosovo, Iraq and Afghanistan, Mandeville is the fifth Earl of Southvale and a notable landowner across Dorset where his family seat Barmond Hall is located.

Mandeville spends weekdays at his Chelsea apartment in the prestigious Cheyne Gardens, allowing easy access across the river to Battersea Park. The levels of violence used in both assaults left the women with significant injuries.

The officer in charge of the case stated at the time of sentencing: 'These were ferocious attacks that left the victims with significant injuries, as well as immense psychological trauma. We have worked tirelessly to ensure a dangerous offender has been brought to justice and I am satisfied the sentence reflects the severity of the threat Richard Mandeville poses to the public.'

Mandeville pled not guilty to all charges and has been vocal in protesting his innocence since his conviction.

Lucia's footsteps were thumping back downstairs and I hurriedly thrust the paper into my handbag, tearing it as I struggled with the zip. I squeezed my hands rhythmically, making and releasing fists, tapping my feet against the thick carpet until the pins and needles receded.

Lucia dropped down beside me and grabbed her glass. 'Are you OK? You look like you're going to throw up.'

'Is it too soon for morning sickness?' I pulled a face.

'Nope, you're bang on time. I don't envy you that part.' Lucia gave my arm a sympathetic squeeze. 'How will you cope at work? Can you run out on a client to puke?'

'They're not under arrest. I don't have to supervise them at all times.'

Lucia fixed me with a look usually reserved for her son. 'It worries me they'll see you as an easy target.'

'I know what I'm doing.' I forced a smile. 'Everyone tells me I'm very good at my job.'

'It's easy to believe you're safe when really you aren't.'

I cast for an answer, something reassuring and smart, but drew a blank.

'I'd better go track down Jamie,' I finally said. 'He might be at his office.'

'He'll turn up when he's ready. We could go for lunch instead?'

I was already gathering my coat and bag to leave. I couldn't go for lunch. I wanted to be alone.

'I'll message you when I find him.'

As I walked down the street, I didn't need to look back to know Ben was on the terrace, buttoning his Armani shirt, making sure I was definitely gone.

* * *

'I don't think you should keep the baby.'

Jamie's first words as he walked through the door on Sunday morning made me leap to my feet. We faced each other like familiar strangers, neither willing to step closer to the other's personal space.

'Where have you been?' I asked, taking care to keep my voice neutral.

'It doesn't matter.' He was biting off the ends of his words, so they spilled out in a torrent. 'Do you need to know my every move now?'

His paranoia was evident in his inability to be still – tapping his fingers against surfaces, shifting his weight from foot to foot – and the constant darting of his eyes, bloodshot and sore-looking. Tension radiated from him, along with the smell of stale sweat. A sudden question jabbed at me. Was it possible Ben had tempted him to dabble with drugs too? Jamie's was the type of personality to be drawn to an easy escape from reality.

'You're my husband,' I pointed out, forcing calm I didn't feel as I filed that query away for another time. 'I care about you. I only want to know you're safe.'

Jamie raked his hair off his forehead. He hadn't prepared his answers. Maybe he didn't expect me to challenge him.

'You had no right to keep all this from me,' I said. 'Just as Ben has no right to keep it from Lucia.'

'We were trying to protect you!'

'This is the opposite of protecting. It's concealing, Jamie. At worst, it's plain lying.'

He strode across to the kitchen units, grabbing a banana from the fruit bowl. He hated the texture of bananas, and I watched him struggle to swallow the enormous bite he took.

'Why do you want me to get rid of our baby?' I asked as he took another reluctant bite.

'Because I don't think there's enough money for us, let alone a child!'

'I can take care of everything for the baby.'

112

'You don't understand.' Desperation made his eyes gleam unhealthily. 'The bank is threatening to repossess Porteños. My company debts are huge, and that's without Ben siphoning funds from the restaurant every fucking month. If I go bankrupt, your salary will be the only income we have.'

I moved to stand directly in front of him, leaving him unable to escape eye contact. 'How long has the bank given you and how much do you owe?'

His shoulders slumped. 'Six months. Half a mil.'

'Half a million pounds?' I echoed, my voice shrill enough to make myself cringe. 'How is that possible? How can you not have made a profit from your other commercial lets?'

'That was what funded my share in Porteños.' He barked a furious laugh. This was costing him more than money. Jamie had always enjoyed his success, his charmed life where everything seemed within reach. To admit he was so close to losing it all must hurt him badly.

'Jamie, why would you do that?' I pleaded. I needed to understand, not just pretend that I did. 'Why take such a huge risk when your own company was financially secure?'

Jamie turned away, shielding. 'I had a good reason.'

'But you're not going to tell me it.'

'No,' he whispered.

I searched my brain for what his reason could be, what could possibly drive him to gamble everything. There would be a motivation, there was always a motivation, but it was beyond my reach for that moment.

'And this is why you want to deny me the only chance I'll ever get to have a baby?' I moved into his eyeline again, but he determinedly stared at the floor tiles. 'You know what the specialists said. This is my one in a million.'

'Tam, you never expected to become a mother. We accepted that after the surgery.'

I flinched, remembering how desolate I'd felt when waking from that operation eight years ago. Knowing it had saved my life, and abruptly ended my first and, I believed, only pregnancy. I clenched my left hand, feeling the ridge of my scar, digging my nails into it. '*You* accepted it.'

'You seemed OK. You got on with life.'

'I didn't have a choice, I had to carry on! You didn't see what was on the inside. I couldn't let you.' My palm had found its way, uninstructed, to my abdomen, defending the tiny foetus. 'It was easier to let you think I'd come to terms with it.'

He jerked as if I had slapped him, half-turning away from me to avoid having to acknowledge his error of judgement. He had thought everything was fine because that was what I had wanted him to think. It would have done no good for us both to mourn. Jamie didn't like to dwell on his feelings; his lack of emotional literacy was uncomfortable for both of us.

I stepped away, allowing him his space, but my tone was strong enough to make him look at me.

'I'm keeping this baby.'

15

Tamsin – Now

I wait impatiently for Jamie to arrive. Today is the third anniversary of the day my life was torn apart, but I am not interested in myself. I am hoping Jamie will tell me about Elise's birthday party, the first one she's had. I want to hear about her cake, if she managed to blow out three candles as a chorus of eager voices sang a tuneless happy birthday to her. I want to picture her tearing the wrapping paper from her presents, exclaiming at her spoils. At least I can pretend that I was part of it and, if it is the last birthday I know about, I want to savour every moment of it.

And once I have lived vicariously through him, even for a few brief minutes, I hope I will have the strength to address my second problem. I want to know if Jamie is going to admit to me the choice he has been presented with. If he is going to discuss the options, make me feel like I still matter to him, that I am still his wife.

Milena is administering my peg feed, double-checking each stage, making sure she is getting everything right. I imagine it is a bowl of my favourite ramen being sent gradually down the flexible tube connected directly to my stomach. I can taste the rich, salty miso broth, the slippery noodles, the tender pork belly and fresh crunch of blanched vegetables.

The door opens, ruining my mental meal.

'Hi, Jamie,' Milena says quietly.

'How's it going?' Jamie asks, too casually. I listen to him shrugging off his coat, placing a book onto my bedside table, settling himself in the chair on the opposite side to Milena.

There is a long pause before Jamie speaks. 'You've heard the latest, then.'

'Have you talked to Tamsin about it?'

'No.' Jamie sounds bewildered.

'She has a right to know.'

'Even if she can hear us, her brain won't be able to process it.'

'I don't agree.'

Jamie huffs a frustrated breath. 'OK, Milena, you believe what you want and so will I. I don't want an argument. There's been enough of those already.'

A pause. The atmosphere tightens, a sudden tension radiating between them.

I hear Milena pick up my chart, her pen scratching against the paper, giving herself an unnecessary chore to avoid looking at Jamie. She leaves the room, but returns within moments.

'Tamsin had another visitor on Monday.' She passes something to Jamie with a rustle of pages. The visitor log, I predict.

Jamie takes a little too long scanning the information. 'Richard Mandeville came to Rushmore?' he raps out. 'Were you here? Did you see him?'

'No, I was off duty. Hannah met him.'

'What the hell did he want?'

Now I am badly confused. I had never mentioned Richard Mandeville to Jamie during his time as my client, deliberately so. I was always strict with confidentiality. They have never been acquainted. Has Dan said something about the retrial? It would be unlike Jamie to pay attention to anything Dan had to say.

'Milena, why have you got the visitors' book?' Hannah demands, her voice distant as if she is calling from the hallway.

'She thought I'd want to know that Tam had a new visitor,' Jamie defends Milena.

I can hear Hannah's unimpressed huff clearly. 'While I'm here, Mr Shaw, I wanted to let you know Tamsin was unstable for a while over the weekend. Her pulse and blood pressure rose quite significantly.'

A pause while Jamie digests the onslaught of information.

'What does that mean?'

'It could be distress. Tamsin might be experiencing pain.'

'I think she responded to the visitor,' Milena cuts in sharply.

I can picture Hannah rolling her eyes. 'She's never responded to a visitor before. Was she close to Mr Mandeville? They used to work together, he said.'

I can almost hear the ticking of Jamie's brain. 'I don't know him.'

I know when Jamie is lying. His voice gets a semitone higher and, although others won't recognise that tell, surely they will spot his habit of running his hands through his hair and rubbing his nose.

'Has she responded like that since?' Jamie asks after a beat too long.

'No.' Hannah is getting impatient with the questions. 'Not since her levels returned to normal.'

Jamie takes my hand as Hannah departs for more urgent business. He squeezes it harder than usual, as if trying to stir something in me.

'Can I ask you a question?' Milena asks carefully.

I can tell from Jamie's tension that he wants to say no, that he doesn't want to talk to her anymore, but he likes Milena; she has helped him navigate most of his stilted Rushmore visits.

She takes his silence as acquiescence. 'Jamie, did you ever wonder if it wasn't an accident?'

I sense him sit more upright. 'What are you talking about?' he asks with unusual sharpness.

Milena hesitates for a little too long and I am sure she is avoiding eye contact. 'The men she worked with. What if one of them went too far?'

Jamie's tone is firm. 'That's unlikely. Tam was extremely professional. She wouldn't let any client cross the line.'

'She might not have known. Those sorts of men are clever, they manipulate.'

'She was cleverer than any of them. Tam would never have compromised herself.'

'Sometimes you don't realise, until it's too late.' A distinct note of sadness seeps into Milena's voice. 'I know how badly people can hurt you if you let your guard down.'

'Milena, it *was* an accident. The police examined the car remains, checked the road, tested Tam for drugs and alcohol. They didn't find anything to explain what caused the crash.'

'That means there was no proof it was an accident.'

'Or that it wasn't. Why the hell are you suddenly asking these questions now? It's hardly the time to start digging into the past.'

'Mr Attwood was telling me more about their crimes. They harmed other women, so why not Tamsin?'

My skin has gone clammy, hot and cold shocks rushing through me. I would be trembling all over if I was able to, but the sensation is the same on the inside and it is as if my very neurones are shuddering. Every sound becomes amplified as hypersensitivity kicks in, fight or flight responses preparing themselves even though I cannot perform either.

No one has ever questioned the crash before within my hearing. Both Jamie and Dan have spoken of the police investigation previously, how no evidence had been found to suggest it was anything other than a tragic accident, and I had accepted that, keeping my tunnel vision on relearning to use my brain and my senses. It hits me how naïve I had been, to have never debated the authenticity of the police findings until Milena began to query it.

I should have died that day. My chances of survival were minuscule, I know that from all the discussions that have happened over my prone body in the years since. If someone had planned it, they would have been confident of my demise.

Milena is right. It has been treated as an accident because there was no evidence to contrary. But people know how to prevent evidence being created. People who already have experience in lies and secrets. I have been so stupid, so intent on my fight to return to a waking state, that I have ignored what has been staring me in the face.

Jamie's sigh is forceful. 'Unless you've got any proof, I'd leave this well alone, if I were you.'

His dismissal stings me as well as Milena. He is so quick to disregard her concern, as if it is of no consequence to him if the crash had been deliberate. Do I matter that little to him?

He shifts in his chair, unable to be still. He squeezes my hand again and I detect the tiniest tremor in his grip.

'Tam? Can you hear me? Can you feel this?' He is swallowing too often. Is that anxiety tightening his throat?

I have no control over my vital signs. They remain stable, the monitors calm and regular. I am not responding to his stimulus and I don't know why. Surely, I should react to the man I shared my life with, even if it's purely physiological, the dopamine and norepinephrine surges.

Nothing.

Richard Mandeville's presence was enough to send me off the charts, but my own husband can't even evoke a rising pulse.

How can I ever prove to Jamie that I am not ready to die?

'This is pointless.' Jamie releases my hand and I hear his back thud against his chair.

'It's not,' Milena argues. 'You have to keep trying, you can't give up on her.'

'It's not fair to her, not if she's suffering.'

'She isn't suffering.'

'You don't know that. None of us do.'

'Maybe you're just looking for the easy way out, Jamie. It will be a simpler life for you, yes, if Tamsin isn't here anymore.'

'Don't talk bollocks,' he snaps, and there is real anger radiating from him.

Milena doesn't flinch. 'She is inconvenient to you. She takes your time, your money. You want your life back. She stops you from being free, doesn't she?'

'Milena! Just fucking stop it, will you? I don't need this shit!'

Milena's name is barked from the corridor, Hannah demanding that she leave my room immediately.

'Sorry about this, Mr Shaw.' It's a hollow apology, born of fear of repercussions rather than genuine regret. 'She's not herself at the moment.'

'I didn't mean to upset her.' Jamie stammers. He has not seen this side of Milena before.

I can picture Milena whipping round as his words follow her out.

'You chose Rushmore for a reason, Jamie,' she states. 'You said it was safe here. You can't change your mind now and destroy people's lives.'

There is the gasp of a sob trying to be concealed, followed by footsteps rapidly beating a retreat. Jamie sits in stunned silence, allowing me a chance to gather my racing thoughts.

I have never had cause to wonder why Jamie had chosen Rushmore as my care facility when it was so far from London. Now, my brain begins to pick away at the rationale. What did Milena mean by Rushmore being safe?

Safe for who?

My husband slumps in his chair, blowing out a long breath. 'Jesus,' he mutters, his fingers making scratchy sounds as they scrub through his hair.

After a while, he shakes himself and picks up the book he had deposited on my bedside table.

'"My father's family name being Pirrip, and my Christian name Philip" ...' he begins, slipping into an easy, melodic rhythm which tells me he has been reading regularly to our daughter. In the early days, he had struggled with pacing and inflection, no doubt feeling a fool for reading aloud to a woman who happily polished off three books a week and whose tastes were the polar opposite of his own.

Great Expectations is my favourite book, an old friend I would turn to often. Despite my confusion at Jamie and Milena's inter-action, I find myself drawn in, the opening scene spooling through my mind as I sketch a mental image of that lonely, wild marsh Dickens brought to life so effortlessly.

His words guide my memory to the drive to Kent, a trip I had made regularly on free weekends, to Ben and Lucia's second home, buried deep in the land that *Great Expectations* made familiar to me before I ever saw it for myself. It was easy to believe in myths and spirits amid the unique beauty of that wild and untamed place, to hear their rough whispers in your ear, as if they lurked just beneath the opaque surfaces of the marshes' brackish water.

I knew those isolated roads well. I treated them with respect, took no risks. I would not have gambled the life of the baby inside me, that day in October, by flying around blind bends.

I stretch out my mind's fingers, reaching as far as I can into the shadows, searching for anything to grasp that might give me a clue. If I can just show Jamie a glimmer, the tiniest hint of aware-ness.

But all I can find are the memories I already have, and I can't summon the strength to dig for more.

They are already painful enough.

16

Jamie – Now

Jamie feels like a coward, creeping into the house with the hope Lucia will already be in bed. The sound of the TV in the next room tells him she's waited up for him. As he quietly locks the front door, his second phone pings. He doesn't need to wonder who it is at this hour.

Monthly figures. Next Thursday, is all the message says. It comes from a withheld number, like always – a number that will change again in a couple of weeks.

Jamie obediently types an acknowledgement, his head beginning to throb at the prospect of sitting down with his investor for their regular dissection of Porteños.

'Are you going to stand in the hallway all night?' Lucia's voice makes him jump.

'Sorry,' he mutters, left with no choice but to move into the kitchen-cum-living room. He goes straight to the fridge, grabbing a cold Peroni.

'How was it?' Across the other side of the room, Lucia's eyes don't move from the TV. She is leaning forward, her arms wrapped around herself, as if fascinated by what is on screen.

Jamie glimpses one of the *Mission: Impossible* series. Lucia always complains about his love of action films, refusing to watch them with him. He suspects she had flicked on the first available channel when she had heard his arrival, to give herself a reason not to look at him.

'Milena knows. She thinks I'm a complete bastard if I let Tam go.'

Lucia says nothing, her expression unreadable. He almost tells her about Tamsin's strange reaction to her new visitor, but catches himself just in time. That is yet another explanation he doesn't want to get into.

'Want a beer?' he offers instead.

'No.' Lucia stretches her arms towards the ceiling and points the remote to turn off the TV. 'I'm shattered. Think I'll go to bed.'

He knows she wants him to tell her to stay and talk, but he takes the easy escape. 'I won't be long.'

'No rush,' she tells him as she leaves the room.

Jamie gulps the crisp Peroni like a drowning man and immediately opens another bottle. The alcohol hits quickly, slowing his pounding pulse. He picks at the label, creating a pile of soggy paper as he puzzles out how he can build bridges with Lucia, what olive branch he can offer.

A sharp hiss comes from the doorway and a mouthful of beer goes down the wrong way. Mateo smirks as Jamie splutters. It seems he is about to spin on his heel and walk out, but then he stalks across to the counter and grabs the remains of Elise's unicorn birthday cake.

Jamie stays quiet, watching him snatch at the clingfilm before hacking himself a slice. He demolishes it in a few mouthfuls and cuts another piece. This time he peels off the pink icing in strips and eats it slowly.

'Aren't you going to bed?' he demands of Jamie.

Neither of his current options are particularly appealing, so Jamie settles for removing himself to the other end of the room, perching on the edge of the furthest sofa arm.

'I know what you're up to,' Mateo says.

'I'm having a drink at the end of a long and shit day.'

'You're going to pull the plug on Tam. I've heard you and Mum talking.'

Jamie's grip tightens on his bottle. 'You can't tell Elise. I need to explain it carefully to her, when the time's right.'

'Explain that you're killing her mum?'

'I'm not having this discussion with you, Mateo. It's my business.'

'And it was my business when my dad was scared you were going to bump him off.'

Jamie accidentally bangs the bottle mouth against his teeth and recoils. 'What the hell are you talking about?'

'You threatened to kill Dad.'

'I did not!' He is aware he sounds like an outraged teenager, but he can't prevent the denial flying from his lips.

'He told me. He said you wanted Porteños for yourself.'

'I wanted to *save* Porteños, to make sure neither of us ended up ruined.'

'And you said you couldn't save it as long as my dad was around.'

'I actually said I couldn't keep it afloat while he was determined to sink it. You don't know the whole story, Mateo. You don't know what your dad was like.'

'He was a brilliant chef. If the restaurant was in trouble, it wasn't his fault.'

'It was entirely his fault!' Jamie's voice rises with his temper.

'You were interfering in how Dad ran his business.'

Jamie slams his empty bottle onto the coffee table. 'We shouldn't talk about this. I'm going to end up telling you things you don't need to know.'

He hauls himself to his feet, prepared to lose face, prepared to walk away from Mateo, who is still gripping the chef's knife he had used to slice the cake like he intends to hurl it across the room.

'What is going on?' Lucia demands, hurrying into the room. Neither of them had heard her come down. 'You'll wake Elise!'

Mateo rounds on his mother. 'Ask him! He's the one lying to everyone.'

Jamie waits for Lucia to calm her son, but realises she is instead looking to him for an explanation.

'All I said was Ben didn't always tell the truth,' he blusters.

'He wanted Dad dead!' Mateo snarls. 'But you won't believe me, will you? You'll side with *him*, like always.'

Lucia looks from one to the other. Jamie draws himself up to his full height, planting his hands on his hips, the aggrieved party. Mateo taps an aggravated tattoo with the knife against the worktop, his chest rising and falling sharply.

'Matty, you can't go around throwing accusations like that.' Lucia's eyes narrow, but Jamie can't tell if that's aimed at Mateo or himself. 'I understand you don't like Jamie living here, but you won't get rid of him by behaving like this.'

Mateo shoves the remains of the cake back into the corner of the worktop, not bothering to wrap it up. 'It was Dad who said it, not me! He can't speak for himself now, can he?'

'If your father did say something, he didn't mean it. He was paranoid that everyone was out to get him, even me.'

'He told me Jamie threatened to kill him.'

'That won't have happened. Why would Jamie want to harm him?'

'Loads of reasons! Because he wanted control of Porteños. Because Dad was in the way of him being with you.'

Lucia is calm, holding out placating palms. 'First, Jamie never wanted a share in Porteños. He invested because I asked him to.'

Jamie watches Mateo hold his breath, clenching his fists, and sees he is finally listening.

'Secondly, we didn't need a death to be together. We could have just split up our marriages.'

'Dad wouldn't have agreed to it. He loved you too much.'

'If he loved me, he wouldn't have treated me the way he did. That's why I ended up with Jamie, because I couldn't take any more. I'm sorry to say bad things about your dad, but he wasn't a saint and there were plenty of times when you disliked him too.'

'No one's perfect, not even your precious Jamie. Dad knew what he was planning. That's why he told me, in case something ever happened to him.'

'It's been three years, Matty. Why are you dragging this up now?'

Mateo's cheeks flush. 'Everything will change when Tam dies. Jamie will never be out of our lives, cos you won't be his hidden bit on the side anymore.'

Jamie doesn't dare say a word in his own defence. He barely dares breathe in case he draws Mateo's attention back to himself.

He sees Lucia's nostrils flare, watches her eyes widen.

'Bit on the side?' she snaps. 'Who the hell do you think you are, calling me that?'

'You cheated with your best friend's husband!'

'Only after I couldn't take any more! I was faithful to your father for our entire marriage, until Jamie.' Lucia's voice wobbles. 'Do you really want to do this?'

'For once, yes, I want the fucking truth!'

'You want me to tell you that your father had more affairs than holidays? That he was hooked on cocaine? That he was so deep in debt he had no chance of getting out of it? That we'd have lost the houses, the restaurant, absolutely everything, if it hadn't been for Jamie?'

Lucia is panting but Mateo's breathing is barely audible, as if he is taking tiny sips of air.

'You're a bitch,' Mateo growls.

The sound of a slap echoes sharply around the room.

'Oh, God, I'm sorry,' Lucia whispers, reaching for her son, trying to draw him to her and take it all back. 'I didn't mean it. I'm so sorry. Matty …'

A noise erupts from Mateo, a sound of raw pain and, for a moment, Jamie thinks he will strike her in retaliation.

'Jamie,' she says, 'please go upstairs and let me deal with this.'

He pauses, torn between staying to defend her and seizing the reprieve. But he chooses discretion over valour. He takes his leave and pads up to Elise's room, relieved to find she has slept through the disturbance.

He is under the duvet by the time Lucia eventually comes upstairs, scrolling mindlessly through his phone in an attempt to distract himself. His chest feels tight, a burning knot behind his sternum, and his head pounds.

'I'm not going to visit Tam tomorrow,' she says, almost as if she is talking to herself, facing away from him as she tidies her dressing table. 'I can't sit there and witter away, pretending everything's OK. I'll take Matty out, try and get him to talk to me. I shouldn't have told him those things. I didn't mean to be so harsh.'

'Did you manage to calm him down at all?' Jamie asks carefully.

Lucia twitches her shoulders. 'He won't listen to me. Says I'm just trying to protect you.'

'I don't understand where it's come from.'

'In his head, he was sure Tam would wake up and you'd go back to her. Now he's realising that's not going to happen, and he's desperate to find another reason to prevent us having a future together.'

She gets into bed but doesn't snuggle into him like she usually does. Jamie frowns, making his headache stab sharply.

'Lu ... you don't actually believe him, do you?'

Lucia sighs, rubbing her eyes. 'No, of course I don't.'

Relief seeps into Jamie's tense muscles, until Lucia looks across at him, serious-faced.

'But other people might.'

17

Tamsin – Before

'What do you know about my original convictions?'

I doodled in the margin of my notepad to give me the opportunity to look away from Richard. My clients were usually the ones to avoid eye contact, but Richard had a direct gaze I found difficult to meet for long.

My interest was piqued by his use of the word 'original', as if he was already assured those convictions would be quashed. His impatience was palpable as I took my time considering the question.

'I know you were very vocal about your innocence when you took the stand.'

'And what does that tell you?' His voice was light, but I heard the challenge.

'That you were worried the prosecution had enough evidence to convince the jury, so you decided attack was the best form of defence.'

His eyes narrowed. 'Did you think I'd capitulate?'

'I'm not sure that's in your nature, Richard,' I replied carefully, resisting the urge to lay a protective hand over my abdomen.

He gave a single nod, as if satisfied by my response. 'I'd only been questioned for five minutes before I realised it would be a waste of time. I could see the jury's expressions. They'd already made up their minds.'

'Was there any DNA?' I knew the answer, but I wanted to hear it from him. He shook his head. 'But there *was* forensic evidence?'

'Minimal.'

'You anticipated being found not guilty,' I stated. 'You were incensed the jury didn't believe you. The conviction statistics for rape are so appallingly low, and you were certain you'd walk out of court a free man.'

He didn't like my resolute use of that unpalatable word – *rape* – any more than he liked my dissection of his expectations. His entire body stiffened and his lips thinned. 'I believed my barrister's assurances.'

'Perhaps your barrister thought you were guilty.'

I had crossed the line, deliberately baited him, and although I had wanted to observe his reaction, it still startled me. Richard was out of his seat and pacing the room. I found myself standing, stepping closer to the safety of the panic strip running along the wall. But I didn't hit it. Because I couldn't.

The flashback struck hard. I was powerless to prevent it, my mind already locked in its fight or flight battle against Richard's reaction, and it overcame me with ease. I was gone, far from my office, back to that bitterly cold day as I stretched to begin my run.

I haven't noticed the man approach but as I turn away from the tree trunk I've been using as a counterbalance, he is behind me. Eyes flash from the gap in the black balaclava, dangerous eyes full of threat.

I take an abrupt, instinctive step back, inadvertently trapping myself against the tree. Those eyes never flicker as I drag air into my suddenly constricted lungs, ready to scream.

'Don't.' The single word is uttered softly, but with absolute authority.

I catch the breath before it leaves my throat, remaining completely motionless. I couldn't move even if I wanted to.

'What do you want?' I whisper, matching his volume.
Then I glimpse the knife.
'No!'

A shriek from the street outside pulled me back, jolting me enough for the flashback to clear. Laughter rang out, two teenage girls in school uniform, playfully fighting over a takeaway box from a chicken shop. Their normality, their vitality, was enough to chase away the lingering threat.

I looked to Richard, who had stopped pacing and was watching me with an expression I couldn't quite read.

'It's hard to discuss these sorts of things,' I said, clearing my throat.

'Very.' He looked down, focussing on his shoes, grounding himself.

I took several deep breaths and, when my legs felt strong enough to support me, I stepped away from the panic alarm and returned to my seat. My hands shook but it was only noticeable to me if I kept them clasped on my lap.

'Part of this therapy will involve me asking questions you won't like.'

'I accept that has to happen. It's just …'

'You'd prefer never to speak about it again.'

He stilled. 'Exactly.' My sensitivity had taken the edge off his agitation. He was feeling a tentative connection with me, an understanding he hadn't predicted. This was the first time I had been in full control; subordinate was not an easy position for him.

'Sit down, please.'

He did as I asked before he had even realised it, and looked surprised to find himself back in his seat.

'You moved to the security alarm,' he said. 'I didn't mean to make you feel threatened.'

'Self-preservation,' I replied lightly, inwardly impressed that he had noticed.

'I wouldn't hurt you. I apologise for making you think I might.'

I tipped my head to acknowledge the apology. 'It's part of the job.'

His eyes darken to the colour of rain-soaked pebbles. 'Clients have hurt you?'

'A couple have lashed out. Nothing serious.' I paused, debating whether to elaborate. 'One became a bit … obsessed. Again, not uncommon.'

'I can understand why.' Richard reacted to his apparently impulsive comment by smacking himself in the forehead with the heel of his hand. 'Again, sorry, that was out of order. I need to remember you're my shrink, not a date.'

So, he found me attractive. He wasn't the first and wouldn't be the last, despite my attempts to appear exceptionally ordinary at work. He had been more subtle than some and he didn't appear to be embarrassed by his slip, more annoyed at showing his hand.

'Is it difficult to form new relationships now?'

'No.' The familiar twitch of his lips. 'What's difficult is weeding out the women who are only interested in money and titles.'

'Your convictions don't worry them?'

'You'd be surprised how motivated some are.'

'And uninitiated by Google searches, apparently,' I said tartly.

He grinned at my tone. 'I googled you.'

'Why doesn't that surprise me.' I kept my voice steady, even though it had taken me aback, and crossed my arms over my midriff. 'Did you find any skeletons?'

'There was a nice photo of you at a function. You were wearing a stunning emerald silk dress. Zimmermann, I think.'

I arched an eyebrow. 'Impressive fashion knowledge.'

'Who was the man in the photo? Very tall, dark hair, looked like he would rather be anywhere else.'

I was amused. 'Dan Attwood? Your probation executive?'

'Christ, was it really? He scrubs up better than expected. I've only met him a few times.'

'He's keeping close tabs on your treatment,' I felt compelled to say.

'Is he?' There was amusement in his voice. 'I must tell my probation officer to say hello to him. Are you two close?'

'We're old friends.'

'Thought as much.'

'What do you mean?'

'In the picture. The way he looked at you.'

I fought the compulsion to retreat to my desktop computer, search the image for myself. I remember the function, the Royal College of Psychiatrists' annual awards ceremony. It hadn't been a comfortable evening.

'Why did you google me, Richard?' I asked.

'I like to be fully conversant. A hangover from the military.' He held up his palms. 'Nothing untoward, Dr Shaw. The information the probation service provided about you was rather limited.'

'What exactly did you want to know?'

He held my gaze, letting me know he had heard me, but didn't answer. I needed to close the topic. I had begun to sweat, and my head was buzzing like a swarm of insects had invaded my brain. He would notice if I didn't divert him.

I nudged the session's printed worksheet towards him, as if I didn't care whether he looked or not. He took it, reading the exercises with his usual efficiency.

'Have you ever done any of these yourself?' He indicated the page.

'A few, years ago, when I was training.'

'You could try now.'

'This one's designed for a set demographic.' I cringed inwardly. I sounded like a textbook. 'Not one I'm a part of.'

'You could interpret.' He read the first task out to me. '"Consider your personal values and how they influence your reactions to the following situations".'

'The situations are ones you may have encountered, not ones I am likely to have been involved in.'

'What about this situation, here and now?' He spread

his hands to indicate around my office. 'How did your personal values influence your reaction to my faux pas just now?'

He used the term without irony, with affectation, but I couldn't prevent a grin.

'My personal values compel me to laugh at anyone who uses the term *faux pas*.'

There was a momentary pause, just long enough for me to wonder if I'd misjudged, before he burst into laughter. Mirth softened his face, making him look a decade younger, and I could too easily see him as the playboy, the life and soul of a party, a man who drew others effortlessly to him.

At that moment, what I couldn't imagine was him beating a woman to within an inch of her life, abusing her, robbing her of the security she had always taken for granted. I couldn't, even as I tried to focus on the inescapable truth of his crimes.

Richard's smile was broad. 'Who'd have thought, a shrink with a sense of humour.'

I shrugged, deflecting. 'Some of us are even capable of independent thought. We don't all see Oedipus or Freud in every scenario.'

'That's a disappointment.'

He was flirting and I knew it. He wanted to know if he'd gone too far, letting me know he was attracted to me. He was testing me.

I should have stopped it there and then. I should have drawn the line, as a professional and as a woman. I should have reminded him what we were there to achieve.

I should absolutely not have felt a tiny, but undeniable, flicker of triumph.

I needed a few moments to collect myself after Richard left. I was too warm and flung open the window, letting in the biting wind. My pulse danced to an unpredictable tempo, a maelstrom churning in my belly as I replayed the conversation.

What was I doing? I had never, in the five years I'd had this contract, let a client breach my defences. They were too important.

Richard Mandeville was different. It wasn't the title, the money, the status; such things were unusual in my client base but of little consequence. Even the elite were not exempt from depravity.

It wasn't his protestation of innocence, either. Sex offenders didn't always deny their crimes – in fact, some were boastful of their self-described dominance – but I'd come across enough who did to never doubt the legitimacy of their convictions.

No, there was something else.

My office door opened so abruptly, the papers on my desk scattered from the draught. Dan strode in. Security knew him well enough to wave him through unannounced and I bit back irritation at being caught off guard.

'You're supposed to text after every Mandeville appointment.'

'And you're supposed to knock before barging into someone's office,' I snapped.

'I was worried!'

'I haven't heard a word from you since you drove off weeks ago. I assumed that deal didn't stand anymore.' I stood to meet him, not prepared to let him tower over me in my chair. My feet took me behind the desk, putting a physical barrier between us.

Dan was sharp enough to recognise why I had removed myself from his personal space. He folded himself into the seat Richard had recently vacated.

'You got here bloody quickly,' I said. 'The appointment only finished ten minutes ago.'

'I was in the area. Can I shut the window? It's freezing in here.'

'No, I'm boiling, leave it open,' I said, mostly to be contrary. 'You're never *in the area*.'

'How are you?' he asked as if he hadn't heard me.

'Nauseous.'

'What the hell has Mandeville been saying?'

'Because of morning sickness, Dan, for God's sake.'

'Oh. Right. Sorry.'

I waited for him to ask the question I could see burning his lips, but instead he busied himself rubbing an invisible speck of dirt from the sleeve of his leather jacket

'Jamie must be pleased,' he finally said.

'He's not. He doesn't think I should keep the baby.' I hadn't intended to tell Dan the details but, somehow, they were spilling out before I could control them, as if my body needed to purge. 'Apparently, we're in serious financial difficulty that I knew nothing about. Jamie has invested in Benicio Aguero's restaurant and it's failing badly.'

Dan's eyebrows jumped. 'The *Cocina Loca* restaurant?'

'Christ, tell me you didn't watch that shit.'

'It was funny,' he said defensively. 'That guy's a lunatic. Why the hell would Jamie want to get involved with him?'

'He's my best friend's husband,' I sighed. 'We live round the corner from them. We've known them for years.'

'Shit.'

'Exactly. So Jamie is using that as a reason not to have the baby. Times are too unstable. We might have to survive off my wages if he goes bust.'

Dan's shoulders visibly tensed and he shoved his chair back, striding over to the window and banging it closed. I was still uncomfortably warm, but this time I said nothing.

He returned to his seat, leaning forward over his knees. 'Are you a hundred per cent sure the baby can't be mine? I'd support it, you know I would.'

I should have known that question would come, but I was still unprepared for it. I busied myself straightening each item on my desk, aligning everything precisely, weighing up the pros and cons of each potential reply.

Finally, I made my choice.

'I've worked out the dates. It's possible.'

'Did we use protection?'

135

'I don't know!' I snapped, even though I did.

'Aren't you on the pill or something?'

'It generally isn't necessary when you've been told you're infertile.' I wanted him to stop asking questions and, in my experience, men usually shut up quickly when fertility issues were mentioned.

'Is Jamie going to push for an abortion?'

I stared at him. 'I'm not his property.'

'I didn't mean it like that.'

'There's a lot going on. Jamie wouldn't be a bad father.'

'Nor would I.'

'But you're not my husband.'

'If the baby's mine, it doesn't matter which one of us you're married to.' Dan audibly grinds his teeth. 'I want a DNA test after the birth.'

'It might be obvious without one.' Dan, dark-haired and fair-skinned, couldn't be more different from Jamie's blond locks and olive tones.

Dan's lips thinned and he stood, then strode to the door, his business apparently concluded.

'Nothing is obvious with you, Tam,' was his parting shot.

18

Jamie – Before

Last year, Ben had impulsively spent half a million pounds on a period farmhouse on the Kent marshes. It was meant to be a second home to escape the pressure of fame. Jamie had been furious about yet another loan taken out against the restaurant.

It turned out, however, to be a blessing in disguise. Ben had soon discovered he hated being out in the countryside after so many years in busy cities. The sounds and the silences unsettled him, and he had declared the house to be full of troubling spirits.

'I can hear the ghosts there,' he had pronounced to Jamie. 'Always whispering to me. Never leave me alone, even when I sleep.'

'That's your paranoia, not the paranormal,' Jamie had retorted.

Ben had solemnly shaken his handsome head. '*Fantasma*, my friend.'

Now he refused to go near the place, and it had become Jamie and Lucia's little nest. Jamie had come to love the low ceilings and original beams, the open fire and the twisty, narrow staircase up to the cosy bedrooms.

Usually, they only went once a week, but, ever since Tamsin had dropped her bombshell, Jamie had been using it as his hide-out whenever he wasn't at work.

Yet another mess he couldn't get himself out of.

Lucia arrived just as he was about to drive back to London. He was slumped on the sofa, his lukewarm cup of tea on the coffee table, barely touched. She bit into his abandoned ham sandwich, regarding him carefully. He noticed she didn't rush to kiss him like she usually did.

'Did you feel anything when you saw the scan pictures?'

'An impending sense of doom.'

'Jamie,' she warned.

He gritted his teeth. 'I didn't feel anything. How can I, for a baby I don't want with a wife I don't love?'

'Don't do that. Don't act like you don't still care about Tam.'

'Lucia, what do you want from me?' he demanded, gripping a handful of his hair before realising he was in danger of causing a bald patch and shoving his fists into his pockets.

'I don't know!' she cried. 'I wish I did! There's no fucking self-help guide to a situation like this.'

They stared at each other for a long moment before Lucia's tears finally fell and Jamie wrapped her in his arms. They clung to each other, not knowing what to say.

Until a noise outside made them spring apart. It was the unmistakeable crunch of tyres on gravel.

'What the fuck?' Lucia hissed, dashing to the little side window. 'It's Ben.'

'What's he doing here?'

Panic bloomed, neither of them sure what to do. Jamie grabbed his coat and scrambled for any other belongings in plain sight.

'Go out the back door. Quickly!'

Jamie rushed from the room, down the hallway and into the kitchen, but Lucia yelped his name before he could unlock the door.

'No! Ben's coming round the back!' She ran to grab his arm, dragging him out of the kitchen. 'Hide in the bathroom.'

'He might want the loo!'

Lucia looked around frantically as if expecting a solution to leap out at her. Jamie's eyes fell on the door to the understairs cupboard in the hallway.

It was a tight fit, but he managed to squeeze in next to the vacuum cleaner and the bulky winter coats hanging from hooks. He clicked the latch shut softly, holding his breath as he heard the back door's unoiled hinges groan in the kitchen.

'What the hell are you doing, Ben?' Lucia snapped, as if his arrival had only just surprised her. 'You scared the shit out of me, sneaking in like that.'

'I didn't know you'd be here!' Jamie could hear the nervous energy emanating from Ben, his state of mind as much as the chemicals. 'I'm meeting a guy off Marketplace to sell him the paintings.'

Jamie ground his teeth. Lucia had inherited the oil landscapes that hung in the hallway. She was very attached to her grand-mother's legacy.

'We're not selling Granny's pictures!' Lucia cried. 'I love them. As if you're offloading them to a random on Facebook bloody Marketplace.'

'We're not waiting. I need money now.'

Jamie could picture their standoff, both of them with hands on hips, refusing to yield.

'Why are you here, anyway?' Ben dangled the question like a challenge.

Lucia rose to meet it. 'You're so paranoid it's almost funny.'

'I think I need to be paranoid, when my wife is keeping secrets from me?'

'That's rich coming from you. It's fine for *you* to go where you want, do what you want, do *who* you want behind my back, but I have to disclose every detail of my life to you, without question.'

Jamie was getting increasingly uncomfortable, both emotion-ally and physically, as he tried to remain motionless, stooped against the cupboard's low ceiling. An umbrella was poking into the small of his back and his calf was cramping from trying not to stand on a bag of Christmas tree baubles. The dust hovering in the disturbed air made him want to sneeze.

'You never understand,' Ben declared.

'Don't you dare!' Lucia cried. There was the sound of a brief struggle, followed by the unmistakable ring of a stinging slap.

Ben gave a yelp. 'You crazy bitch!'

'Just get out, Ben! Leave the fucking artwork alone. Go and pretend you're the boss of your kitchen.'

'At least in the kitchen they love me.'

'Love to laugh at you, you mean! They have no respect for you.'

'My wife has no respect for me.'

'If only I could find something *to* respect.'

A snarl burst from Ben and Jamie held his breath, waiting to hear the damning sound of a blow.

Instead, the glass in the back door rattled alarmingly as it was slammed shut.

Jamie scrambled out of the cupboard. Lucia was shaking, her eyes swimming with tears, but he suspected it was anger rather than fear. His fingers skimmed gently across her face, checking for any marks.

'He didn't hurt me.' Lucia sighed.

Jamie stretched his aching spine, rubbing at the bruise the umbrella's point had left. 'He suspects something's up.'

'He'll have forgotten all about it by tomorrow.'

She wasn't wrong. Lately Ben had been unable to concentrate on anything for long, not even kitchen tickets or recipe components.

'Thank fuck I was here to save the paintings. I can't trust him with anything these days. What else is he going to try and sell without asking me?'

Jamie had been wondering the same thing. If Ben was desperate enough to start stripping the restaurant for pocket money, the customers would be quick to notice. They made the pilgrimage to Canary Wharf from their usual West London haunts, favouring Porteños for the opulent atmosphere as much as the food. They would spot bare walls and missing chandeliers. Rumours would start circulating. People would know the empire was crumbling, and Jamie's reputation would soon follow.

Sweat beaded on the back of his neck just thinking about it.

'I need to get back to London.' He pulled Lucia to him, hugging her close. 'Will you be OK?'

'Don't worry about me. I'm used to dealing with Ben's shit. He'll go and find one of his girlfriends, take it out on them.'

'I still don't understand why he stays, when he has so many affairs?'

Another shrug. 'Like I told you, I'm like the houses, part of the package. And it'll look bad on the next season if he ends up divorced, shagging a twenty-year-old apprentice chef. Argentines are all about family.'

'This whole mess is like a reality show,' Jamie sighed. 'I keep expecting to see a camera.'

'It would be easier if it was a TV programme. At least then we could switch it off when it got too much.'

Jamie dug in his pocket for his car keys. Usually he would sweep the house, checking he hadn't left anything behind, but today he just wanted to leave.

'When will I see you?' he asked.

Lucia raked wild tendrils of hair off her forehead. 'Let's just breathe for a while. I need to be there for Tam. I don't think I can do both.'

Jamie flinched, sliding his eyes away from hers.

'We need to find a solution to this, once and for all,' he said as he left.

'Where you been?' Ben cried, appearing in the office doorway. His accent was back in place now he was in the public domain again. 'I keep calling you!'

Jamie pulled his phone out of his suit jacket as if puzzled. 'On silent. Sorry. What's up?'

Ben shut the door but didn't sit, striding up and down in front of the desk. 'I called the producers again.'

An icy shudder ran through Jamie without warning, someone walking over his grave. He tensed, waiting for the blow that was certainly coming.

'The assistant said they were busy. They were never too busy for me before.'

'What else did the assistant say?' Jamie asked quietly, ignoring Ben's agitated pacing.

'That the budget has been cut. What the fuck? I made them millions and they can't even return the favour!'

'Tell me what that means,' Jamie just prevented himself from shouting.

Ben's foot connected with the wastepaper basket, sending it flying across the small room. 'The show is cancelled. There is no season two.'

Even though he had known it was coming, the damning confirmation winded Jamie. He let his head drop into his hands, his eyes burned by tears of rage that he hurriedly knuckled away.

Why would the producers want to put themselves through the stress of another series, after all Ben's wild behaviour? During the first filming he had thrown a knife across the kitchen and broken a camera by slapping it out of his way in a fit of temper. The viewers had loved it, but the crew had rapidly become fed up and threatened to quit. Ben's increasing demands for higher fees had only made the tension worse.

'Fuck them,' Ben spat. 'I don't need those bastards.'

'We *absolutely* needed that production fee,' Jamie ground out. 'It would be halfway towards getting us out of this bloody mess.'

'I'm gonna get some money. There is some valuable stuff at the Kent house. Antique furniture and paintings and shit. I'll sell it.'

'For God's sake, Ben, there's no point! It won't be enough.' He span his laptop round to face his co-owner. 'We can barely meet the kitchen bills. You need to let Franco deal with the suppliers from now on. The costs are astronomical.'

Ben's face darkened at the suggestion his sous chef would do a better job than him. 'You have to pay for the best. I know what I need to cook Michelin-standard food! You can't understand this!'

'Franco cooks exactly the same food as you.'

'Not like me! Not with the passion. My dishes are *mine.*'

'Keep going like you are and this restaurant won't be yours. You don't have the money for Wagyu beef and Tuscan truffles! You'll lose everything.'

Ben was glancing repeatedly towards the door. 'Whatever, Jamie. I have to meet someone.'

'Just call him your dealer, for fuck's sake.'

'It's not your business.'

'It's exactly my business. Fifty per cent of it, remember?'

'I'll make the money back. It's gonna be fine.'

Fury roared in Jamie's chest as Ben reached once again for the door handle. 'It won't be *fine*! It's too late for that! When are you going to open your eyes and see the mess you've made?'

Ben opened his mouth to throw back a retort, but nothing came out. He gripped at his sweat-dampened curls, an expression of pure agony creeping across his features.

'I can't fail,' he eventually croaked, 'or everyone will know I'm a fraud. I'm no superstar chef. It's not real. It's just acting.'

That unexpected statement, delivered so factually, stalled Jamie's anger. 'Ben, you're a good chef.' Even in the circumstances, he couldn't deny that, as much as he wanted to. 'You've got the stars, no one can deny that. You wouldn't have earned them without talent.'

'Not enough. Why you think I have to give the kitchen what they want? They keep quiet and they help me look good. I'm an imposter.'

So he was plying the staff with free cocaine to keep them onside. Yet another explanation as to why his debts were so high.

'It's your brain telling you that. Tam's treated people with imposter syndrome. It's like some type of anxiety, she said.'

Ben snorted. 'In my culture, no such thing.'

'The coke will make it worse.'

'It's the only thing that makes it better. I can't make myself come to work without it.'

Jamie heaved a defeated sigh, rubbing his chest against the deep ache that had lodged behind his sternum. It had become a constant discomfort without him noticing and now it plagued him day and night, burning away, slowly consuming him.

But worse than the pain was the knowledge that it would not go away, not for as long as Benicio Aguero and his demons were part of the equation.

19

Tamsin – Now

Dan announces his arrival softly, as he always does, saying my name to alert me. Even so, I am so deeply entrenched in my own thoughts that I startle.

As if he senses this, he makes sure to touch my hand before he moves the chair closer to my bedside, leaning his elbows on the mattress as usual.

This is another change to the schedule, a Thursday visit, and I hope he has come to tell me more about Richard Mandeville's retrial.

'Sorry I'm ballsing up your routine again,' Dan says. 'I have to fit everything around this fucking court case for the next God-knows-how-many weeks. It already feels like it's been going on forever.'

He settles himself more comfortably and I hear him sip something effervescent, his fingers making dints in the can as he drinks. I catch the caramel scent of Coca-Cola and crave the feeling of bubbles bursting on my tongue, although I never liked sugary sodas before the accident. On second thought, a good vintage of Laurent-Perrier would be more to my taste.

'I'm knackered.' He stretches audibly, his leather jacket creaking. He rarely bothers to take it off when he arrives, as if he is ready to stride off and attend to an urgent matter at a moment's notice. 'We've still not found another psychiatrist we're happy with. The latest one charged a fortune and did fuck all. Where did you hide all the decent ones?'

My fellows should be grateful they have managed to swerve the task of reassessing Richard Mandeville. His is not a psyche that any professional should wade into unprepared. I was fully prepared, yet even I was no match for him, and he knew it.

'I think he's taking the piss, myself,' Dan continues. Richard will certainly have enjoyed toying with my replacements, a cat teasing the mouse. 'He knew we'd request a more recent analysis but, as usual, he's objecting. I swear he's doing it simply to fuck with us.'

It will have incensed Richard, a stranger raking over old ground he was certain had been buried for good. It had been hard enough for him the first time, with someone he had come to know well.

But he will not have laid his cards on the table. Those deepest parts of himself, that he concealed behind a ready wit and straightforward gaze, will have remained shielded from my colleagues. They will have pushed him, needled him, to draw them into the light, but they won't have succeeded, although he will have allowed them to believe they had.

'They all confirmed he's sane, but none of them were prepared to say they thought he was still a danger to the public.'

Frustration burns through my veins like battery acid.

I recall the sensations that had overwhelmed me during Richard's visit to Rushmore. The helplessness of my situation, the power he had over me.

Richard Mandeville commands such danger that it should be impossible to miss it, yet I know from experience that it is all too easily done.

'Surely someone can see through him,' Dan says through gritted teeth. 'They've all fallen for his charms, even with all their qualifications and accolades. Their reports have read like fucking love notes.'

Or Dan has interpreted them as such. Perhaps the jury will be more objective, understand that without evidence, not even a shrink can provide definitive analysis of anyone's state of mind. We are not clairvoyants.

'I got a proper grilling last week from his barrister. They're claiming the terms of his probation were unjust.'

Were they? It was clear from the very beginning how Dan felt about Richard Mandeville, and he made no attempt to hide it behind professionalism. His prejudices could easily have influenced the decisions he made when the board had first granted Richard's freedom. But whatever methods he undoubtedly used to try and block Richard's entry into our programme, Dan is not ready to admit to them.

'He had the biggest smirk on his face while I was being accused of unprofessional standards.' Dan sounds genuinely affronted. He is convinced he was justified.

He mutters to himself for a few moments, words that are not meant for me, and I don't try to interpret them. I wonder if Dan knows how meticulously Richard will have planned this. A retrial is a risk, bringing him back into the public eye, resurrecting old ghosts that had been allowed to rest. He will only have entered into it with a strong degree of certainty that the judge would rule in his favour.

Dan has misjudged the situation by treating it as an act of petulance. For Richard Mandeville, this is an act of redemption.

My pulse has quickened at that thought. I can feel the rapid beat thudding against my skin. Once again, my body has responded to Richard.

'I'll put the TV on for you,' Dan says, decisive once again, back in control of himself. 'The news will be starting. I hope you can hear, Tam. You'll want to know about this.'

The familiar theme tune sounds, before the sober tones of the newsreader. Richard is the lead item.

'The Right Honourable Richard Mandeville directed his press officer to give a brief interview after leaving the Royal Courts of

Justice today, as his historic retrial continues. The earl's representative told reporters he was going against the advice of his legal team, but that he had nothing to hide. A statement was also read on the earl's behalf, explaining how the long wait to pursue justice has affected him.'

Dan snorts sharply, but I refuse to let him distract me. It isn't Richard's voice that speaks next, but I can easily imagine the words from his mouth, and my pulse pounds harder.

'"I lost eight years of my life to a tiny cell, for crimes I did not commit."' The representative's speech flows with confidence, an absolute certainty that Richard's words are true. I picture the gathered journalists drinking it all in.

'"I have suffered every day since I was convicted. I have been tormented. I no longer sleep more than a few hours a night. My hands shake for no reason. I am startled by sudden noises or loud shouts. I wake up screaming, convinced I am back behind bars. I am a shadow of the man I once was."'

'Convenient that he showed absolutely none of these symptoms during his sessions with you,' Dan growls.

Richard is playing his part admirably, and I am certain his audience is compelled, but Dan is right. None of it is true.

'The bastard will charm the jury just like he does the media. I can see it happening. All he has to do is look in their direction and they're all smiles. They like him. They can't be trusted to be objective.'

'"I have been forced to put my faith in the justice system for the second time,"' Richard's representative continues. '"It betrayed me once before, and I am terrified it will do so again. I can only hope that, this time, the truth will out."'

The shot cuts back to the studio, and the anchor continues to talk about the trial. Dan speaks over him.

'The one thing he seems troubled about is you,' Dan says. 'He reacts each time you or the crash is mentioned in court. He's got a tell. The jury haven't noticed, but I bet you spotted it straight off. He pinches his philtrum whenever he's uncomfortable.'

That revelation throws me. I cannot remember ever noticing that subconscious signal of unease. I don't like it. It means I missed something. The tunnel vision had blinkered me yet again.

'He doesn't like hearing your evidence being read out,' Dan insists. 'He was digging his nails into his skin when we used your diary notes.'

He turns his attention back to the news anchor, but I am no longer listening. I am still trawling the recesses of my mind for any recollection of Richard's tell.

The door opens. I can tell it is Milena by the lightness of her footsteps. She must be starting her shift and coming to say hello to me first, as usual.

But she stops abruptly, as if taken aback to see Dan.

Dan mutes the TV. 'Hi, Milena. I'll be out of your way soon. I can never predict what day I'll be free to visit at the moment.'

'Is that your trial, on the news?' Milena asks shakily. She sounds like she has a cold coming on.

'Yeah, it wasn't a good day today,' Dan says grimly, hitting the volume button again. The presenter is wrapping up the headline item.

'You don't think you'll win?'

'At the moment, no, I don't.'

'You're angry.'

'More frustrated. I don't like what I'm seeing in court.'

'What happens if he wins?'

'He'd be a free man. He wouldn't be monitored, no one would check up on him. If he wanted to reoffend, there would be nothing to stop him.'

'And you think he will do it again,' Milena states.

Dan's teeth are gritted. 'I'm certain he will.'

I hear a sound I can't identify at first, a rapid tapping, like a moth bouncing off a hot light bulb. Finally, I realise it is Milena's fingertips beating a rapid tattoo against her thigh, trying to calm herself.

Is she afraid of Dan, a large man radiating frustration, or is it the prospect of a convicted abuser going free?

I don't have time to find out. She strides out of the room without another word.

20

Tamsin – Now

'What's up with her?' Dan wonders aloud.

He makes no move to follow Milena and find out. Instead, he switches off the TV and sits in contemplative silence. In my head, I urge him to go after my carer, ask her what is wrong.

Milena hasn't been herself in recent days. She jumps at every unfamiliar noise and her English has slipped, as if she can't concentrate as easily on translating the words in her head. Even the tone of her voice has changed, lower-pitched, quieter, like she is trying to blend into the background.

We sit in silence for a few minutes. Dan doesn't find talking to me a challenge but, unlike Jamie, he has always been as comfortable with quiet as I am. I sense his eyes roaming over me, checking for any changes, any degeneration. His thumb and index finger lightly circle my wrist, measuring to see if the circumference has reduced again.

'I have a confession, before I go.' He speaks suddenly, making me jump. He lowers his voice tactfully. 'I ordered a DNA test.'

I flush hot and cold. After three years without a test, I'd thought he had decided against it.

'I wasn't sure how I'd ever be able to get a sample from Elise. Then I thought there might be some of her things at your old apartment.'

My *old apartment*. I can't dwell on his apparent certainty that I will never return there, that I'll never go home. I'm too consumed by fear. I have enough dangers to contend with already, without Dan's refusal to let go, of me, of Elise.

'I asked Jamie if I could go through your office stuff,' he says, 'to see if there was anything we'd overlooked for the Mandeville trial. It's all at Apollo Point, in your wardrobes. Jamie stores Elise's baby stuff in there too. He'd kept a clipping from her first haircut, her first hand and footprints, but they were no good. Then I saw he'd saved her umbilical stump.'

My racing thoughts pause momentarily. I would never have expected Jamie to keep the last evidence of Elise's attachment to me. Maybe he thought there'd be some medical reason for keeping it if I never regained consciousness.

'I haven't sent it off yet.' A short laugh. Dan is oblivious to my inner turmoil. 'Too scared of the result. If she is Jamie's, then that's it. Not that he's ever doubted it, has he, Tam?'

My heart begins to pound again, an urgent rhythm as dread takes its icy grip. What game is Dan playing? Is he planning to tell Jamie about our night together, infuse doubt into his mind about Elise's parentage? He doesn't realise that would give Jamie even more motivation to bring my life to an end. Why would Jamie want to keep supporting a wife who had betrayed him?

I can hear that tense exchange playing out in my mind. Dan baiting Jamie, Jamie hurling denials and insults, until one of them snaps.

I see them fight, their fists flying in a film projected onto the inside of my eyelids. I see Jamie in a police cell. I see Elise being taken away by a faceless stranger, sobbing for her father, for Lucia, for me.

The thought of that perilous conversation, the irreversible damage it could do, sends a strange sensation coursing through me. So fixated am I on the potential disaster that I fail to recognise it at first, but then I'm sure it's happening. Minute tremors shimmering through my limbs.

An alarm blares beside me. Dan has pressed the call button.

'Her monitors!' he says sharply to whoever answers it.

Rapid footsteps to my bedside. Dan's grip on my hand is painful and he has shot to his feet. I hear the rustle of pages from my notes, as someone compares my base readings.

Milena's voice calls for Hannah. The uncertainty in her tone makes Dan panic and squeeze my fingers so hard I want to cry out. He seems to realise what he is doing and his hold loosens, although he doesn't let go. His palm has become clammy.

Hannah's heavy feet cross the carpet and I picture her scrutinising the monitors, snatching my notes from Milena to log the latest statistics.

'Is she OK?' Dan demands.

'This has been happening on occasion recently. Tamsin is showing signs of responding.'

Dan's tone is a combination of confusion, fear and hope. 'You mean she's waking up properly?'

'She's reacting to something. Possibly the beginning of an infection. We haven't narrowed it down yet.'

'But that's good!'

'Not usually. Not in patients like this. I'm sorry to be direct but we find it often means their body is starting to shut down. This is the first sign their system isn't coping.'

I hear Dan's chin catching rapidly against his jacket collar and know he is shaking his head. 'There's no evidence of that.'

Hannah has already moved away, impatient to escape the conversation. 'I need to carry on with my rounds. Milena will answer any other questions you have.'

Dan finally sits down again, gently laying my hand back on the mattress.

'Hannah might be wrong. Maybe she's coming back to us,' There is such anguish in his words that I feel sorry for him. I don't feel like I'm coming back, not when I can't even twitch a finger or make a sound.

'I'm not sure what it means,' Milena says, apologetically. 'I haven't seen this before, not like Hannah. I don't think Tamsin is suffering, but I can't prove it.'

Her fingers land on my wrist as she feels for my pulse.

'Mr Attwood, there's something you need to know.' Milena is whispering, and I can tell she is glancing around for eavesdroppers by the changing direction of her voice. 'Tamsin might not be here for much longer, whatever is happening to her.'

More glances around. 'I'm not supposed to say anything. It's confidential information, but Jamie won't tell you and that's not fair. He's deciding whether it's time to withdraw Tamsin's treatment and let her die.'

I sense Dan's body go rigid and he holds his breath for a long moment. 'As if that prick should have the *fucking* power to choose whether she carries on living.'

Fury whips from him, the aggression in his words directed towards Milena as the nearest person, who lets out a tiny sound of fear. Dan jumps to his feet, and I picture him holding out his hands in apology.

'Sorry, Milena, sorry. I didn't mean that to be aimed at you.'

Milena's breathing is rapid. I'm sure now that she has known male violence; only survivors react this strongly to a man's belligerence.

'I would never hurt you,' Dan assures her, and those words are so familiar to me from Richard Mandeville's lips. 'It was the shock.'

'I shouldn't have told you.'

'I would have found out another way. Things that serious can't be kept secret for long.'

'Please don't tell anyone I said anything.'

'I won't, I promise.' I can physically feel Dan's struggle to quell his temper. 'Thank you, Milena. I appreciate what you've done.'

He paces the room after she leaves. I listen to his unsteady breaths, the occasional gasp as his emotions nearly overwhelm him. I will him to get a grip.

'I can't believe he gets to play God with your life,' he snarls, striding back over to me. 'What the hell gives him that right?'

This isn't the time to debate the power of next of kin. Dan has no say in that. My only chance is if he can focus on Jamie's dilemma and how he could influence it.

'How can he sit here, pretending to be a loving husband, after how he's behaved?' Dan's obsessive side is now firmly in charge and, as much as I am frustrated by it, his wording gives me pause for thought.

What is Jamie pretending?

'I didn't want to upset you, Tam, in case you can hear us. It didn't seem fair when there's nothing you can do about it.'

Do about what? What the hell is he talking about?

'Jamie is with Lucia now. You should see Apollo Point. It's abandoned – Jamie hasn't lived there for a long time. I doubt Elise has ever lived there. They're all at Lucia's house, as a family.'

My breath stalls in my throat and I feel like I'm choking. I can't seem to force the air down to my lungs, a fish thrown clear of its water. A flash illuminates my mind with the intensity of a nuclear bomb.

Jamie and Lucia.

That is why Dan referred to Apollo Point as my *old* apartment. They all knew, all this time, except for me.

'He hasn't worn his wedding ring since you left ICU,' Dan continues, his words rushed, as if he can't wait to score another point against Jamie.

Of course he would have noticed such a tiny detail, as would I, once upon a time. What a fool I have been. How could I have missed the signs, especially something as obvious as Jamie's wedding ring? All the times he has held my hand and I never thought about the absence of metal against my skin.

'He doesn't advertise it. I doubt anyone here knows. But they've got a life together, Tam. I watched him walk round to

Lucia's house, when I went to collect your things from the apartment. Maybe he wants more now.'

Another nail thuds dully into my waiting coffin. If Jamie wants to be legitimately with Lucia, maybe even marry her, I am the hurdle standing in his way.

Dan looms over the mattress, as if looking for a reaction on my face. His fingers tap an impatient beat against my bed, sending vibrations running through me. The odd pulsing runs down both legs again, a sudden compulsion to clench my muscles. Just for a second, it feels possible.

I try to wriggle my toes, but it's too late.

The feeling has passed, and I can't be sure it ever really existed.

21

Tamsin – Before

I couldn't go to my twelve-week scan alone. There was only one person I felt able to turn to, and it seemed Lucia had been keeping track of the dates.

'Isn't Jamie going with you?' was her first question.

'He doesn't know about it. We've barely spoken since I told him I'm keeping the baby. I try, but it's easier for him to deny I'm pregnant. He's blocking me out.'

'Of course he is,' Lucia muttered, and I felt the tension ebb away from my clenched jaw. Lucia understood and it eased the sting of my humiliation. 'I'll come with you.'

'You don't have to, if you're busy …' I hated how needy I sounded.

'Tam.' Her tone brooked no argument. 'You've been there for me, when I've needed you. You never let me down.'

'Yes, but …'

'This isn't a small deal. You've waited years for this. You can't see your baby for the first time without someone to hold your hand. I'm coming.'

The moment we walked into the scan room, I realised how right my friend had been. My knees turned to jelly, and a wave of dizziness surged over me.

I slid on to the examination bed and rolled up my top. My body flashed hot and cold, and I didn't know if I would pass out or vomit.

'Have you been pregnant before?' the technician asked as she tucked blue paper towels into my waistband.

Lucia's grip on my hand tightened.

'Yes,' I said to the ceiling. 'Eight years ago.'

I closed my eyes as a sob built in my throat.

'It was an ectopic pregnancy,' Lucia explained quietly, when it became clear I couldn't speak. 'The surgeon had to remove the ovary.'

'I'm sorry.' The technician gave me a muted smile. 'That's a rare complication, an ovarian ectopic.'

'I was told I was unlikely to be able to get pregnant again,' I managed to say. 'Because of the damage.'

'Your chances would have been quite low, but not impossible. As you've proven. You must be so pleased.'

I squeezed Lucia's hand back.

'Let's have a look and see your baby.'

The gel was cold against my skin and the instrument felt like it was pressing too hard into my abdomen.

'There we go.'

The screen was turned to allow me to see but, for a never-ending moment, I was too scared to look. Lucia let out a little squeak and, finally, I plucked up the courage to turn my head.

I saw the tiny, perfect fingers and toes. I saw the outline of a button nose and pursed lips. The legs looked long and strong, curled up tight.

'Good heartbeat,' came the report from the technician. 'Everything looks fine.'

Lucia was crying, attempting to discreetly wipe the tears away.

'I can't believe it,' I whispered to her.

She nodded rapidly, her gaze still glued to the screen.

'Are you sure the baby's OK?' I looked to the technician, needing the reassurance I was usually able to provide myself.

'I'm sure. There's nothing you need to be concerned about.'

I wanted to howl in sheer relief, but I couldn't let myself show such emotion in front of a stranger. We left with an envelope containing two pictures of the new life that had become my consuming focus.

Safely in Lucia's car, I burst into tears, equal measures of relief, shame, exultation and fear. Lucia held me silently, letting me release every pent-up feeling.

'Jamie still doesn't want the baby,' I mumbled into her shoulder. 'I don't think he wants me either.'

'I don't know what to tell you, Tam.'

'I can do this without him.' I sat back, swiping my cheeks with a tissue, rearranging my hair to hide the fact I was bluffing. 'I don't need him.'

I wasn't sure who I was trying to convince – Lucia or myself. I did need Jamie. I couldn't imagine raising a child without him. I couldn't imagine living my life without him. I'd made mistakes, too many mistakes, but my marriage wasn't one of them.

'Is that what you want to do?'

I swiftly conjured a scenario in my mind. It came from the weak plot of a nineties rom-com, one that reflected absolutely nothing about how I really felt, but it sounded plausible.

'If I've no other choice, I will. We can sell the apartment, split the profit. I'll be able to get a mortgage on a little house for the baby and me.'

'Tam, you're waffling nonsense now.'

She was right. I blew my nose and focussed on breathing until I'd got a tentative grip on myself.

'Jamie doesn't seem about to change his mind.' That was one fear I needed to voice, and I thought I saw relief in Lucia's expression, that I'd finally let her in.

'Will you show him the scan?'

'Not unless he asks to see it. I'm hardly going to put it on the fridge.' I didn't believe in fate, but I absolutely would not tempt it. I would take no chances until this pregnancy safely reached full term.

Lucia started the engine but didn't pull away. Her hands gripped the steering wheel a little too hard as she focussed on the quiet street ahead.

'Did you know the producers have pulled out of the new series?'

'I had no idea.' That would have been a bitter blow to both Jamie and Ben, precious income snatched away from them. 'I thought it was almost guaranteed.'

'God knows what went wrong. Ben won't tell me. He only comes home to sleep and that's just for a few hours. He snaps whenever I ask him a question.'

'He must be feeling the pressure,' I said, careful not to say too much.

Lucia checked her mirrors but still didn't put the car in gear. 'Tam, you would tell me if you knew something was wrong, wouldn't you?'

'You know I would.' I took another tissue to clean up my smudged eyeliner as best I could, taking my time about methodically dabbing away the remnants of my tears. 'And you'd do the same for me?'

'Of course I would.'

Lucia finally drove away. We both stared straight ahead, afraid to look at each other.

Afraid to recognise each other's lies.

As soon as I opened our apartment door, I realised Jamie was home. I didn't need to see him to know – his presence was tangible to me – and sure enough, when I stepped inside, his shoes were on the rack, his car keys on the hook.

I found him on the balcony, leaning over the rail despite the light drizzle. It was barely afternoon, but he held a tumbler of amber liquid loosely in his fingers, careless of it falling.

'Jamie?'

He started visibly, spinning to face me. 'You're home early.'

'I had a hospital appointment. Where have you been?'

'Working,' he mumbled. Exhaustion was written across his face – pale skin, red sclera, deep lines carved into his forehead – or was it the result of something else?

I wanted to believe him, so I chose to accept his explanation. My brain fired questions, but I resisted voicing them even as I analysed him for any telltale signs of cocaine use.

'I missed you.' I rested my palm on the gentle swell low in my belly. 'We both did.'

He averted his eyes. 'What's in the envelope?'

I held it out to him, giving him little option but to take it. He stood upright and finally turned to me. He tugged the photos loose, staring at them as if he had no idea what they were.

'The baby's healthy, growing well. Lucia came with me.'

He looked up sharply. 'Have you talked to her about our ... situation?'

'I had to tell someone.'

'I asked you not to!'

'I've talked to her about us, Jamie, not the Porteños problem.'

He didn't look convinced that either issue should be discussed. I watched him slide the scans back into the envelope, carefully refolding the flap. Rather than hand it back to me, he placed it on the glass drinks table between us.

'I've been thinking about how we could help Ben,' I said carefully, 'rather than putting him under more pressure. Lucia told me about the TV series.'

A muscle jumped in Jamie's jaw. 'He's not the one under pressure, I am.'

'He must have reasons,' I continued, determined. 'People's lives don't just collapse like this. Ben must have an underlying problem and, until he faces that, he won't be able to recover.'

'You're talking like a shrink again.'

'I could find him a counsellor.'

'I don't want you to get involved in any of this.'

'You're my husband, of course I'm involved. This affects me as much as you.' I took a step closer, resting my hands on either side of his waist. 'I love you. I want us to come through this together.'

'You wouldn't be saying that if you weren't pregnant. If there was no baby, you'd have got the hell out of here before I ruined your life too.'

'Do you really think that little of me?' It hadn't occurred to me before that Jamie had any reason to doubt my feelings for him, and it stung.

I felt his muscles tense, knew he wanted to step back, but I kept my hold just firm enough to keep him still.

He dropped his chin to his chest. 'You can't solve this, Tamsin.'

'Everything has a solution.'

Jamie's lips compressed. I had inadvertently slipped back into professional mode.

'The best solution is not to bring a child into this fucking mess,' he spat over his shoulder as he strode back inside.

22

Tamsin – Before

'Tell me about your army career.'

I waited quietly, apparently unconcerned whether Richard chose to reply or not, shading in a margin of my notebook. I pressed the pen against the ridge of my scar, sending a tiny shock through the damaged skin. It seemed to shoot straight to my womb, and it felt like the baby was absorbing the sensation, to protect me from it.

But it was already taking hold, forcing me into another flashback. *The chill of the air raises goosebumps all over my body. My nostrils are filled with the smell of damp earth and hot blood. I can feel the pulsating throb of my palm, the slick of precious red rivulets running up my forearm, dripping to the cold earth. I can see the flash of the wicked blade, stained, gripped in a gloved hand.*

I managed to shake myself free before it overtook me. I followed the familiar technique – find something I could see, could touch, could smell. My neat, tidy desk. The velvety fabric of my chair soothing the phantom burning of the scar. The uplifting scent of J'adore on my pulse points.

Richard hadn't noticed. He was still deep in thought, seeking my motive, trying to work out what angle I was coming from. By now, we'd had a number of sessions and, slowly, the enigma of Richard Mandeville was being revealed. Or so I thought. He presented like no other client before, which terrified me as much as it intrigued me.

'No one's asked me about that for a long time.'

I pressed my feet into the floor, swallowing the lump in my throat. When I finally spoke, I was relieved to hear I sounded normal. 'Any particular reason?'

'It's easier to pretend not to notice what's occurring in the rest of the world. People prefer to concentrate on the comforts of home.'

I raised my eyes to his. 'You're very perceptive.'

'Thank you,' he grinned, with a modest tilt of his head in acknowledgement. 'I could say the same about you.'

'It's my job to be.'

'Are you so different outside of work?'

I was compelled to consider yet another unexpected question. I couldn't risk giving an impulsive answer. 'I'd like to think I am.'

'In what way?'

'More open. Less intense.'

He smiled. 'I'd like to see that. Though I reckon you still analyse everything. Your brain never switches off, does it?'

'No,' I agreed, pretending I hadn't heard his first comment. 'That's one thing that never changes, no matter the situation.'

'Do you think you're always right about people, the judgements you make about them?'

'No one is always right. Besides, I try not to judge anyone. I form opinions based on evidence. But opinions are fallible.'

'As if yours don't carry significant weight.'

'With the probation service?'

'Least of all.'

'Is that what you're concerned about, that I give a positive report of you?'

His lips quirked. 'No. That doesn't really bother me. Your personal opinion of me, that's more important.'

I returned my attention to the notebook in front of me, scoring my pen across the page. Drawing a line.

'So, your military career?'

Richard shrugged, accepting my diversion. 'Mostly unremarkable. Kandahar got a bit hairy, but I was lucky.'

'You were decorated in Kosovo, your record said.'

'I pulled some people out of a burning shelter.' He said it matter-of-factly. 'A girl and her little brother were trapped. I went in and got them.'

'You were brave to put yourself at risk.'

'Someone had to.' He shook his head. 'It was difficult, peacekeeping. It was hard not to take sides. I don't like standing by and watching.'

'How long were you in Kosovo?'

'Two years. It's a beautiful country, though most Brits would never think it.'

'Have you been back since?'

'Several times. I wanted to see what the place was like without war. I feel a strange attachment to it.'

'But not to the Middle East?'

His lips quirked again. 'You get tired of the dust. It gets everywhere. Even between your teeth, like a gritty moules marinière. Grim.'

I couldn't help but grin at his simile. 'Bet the seafood menu choices were lacking too.'

He laughed easily, comfortable with poking fun at himself. 'I'm a walking cliché of the upper classes, aren't I?'

'Oh God, yes. I've never heard anyone mention mussels and Kandahar in the same sentence.'

We were straying into unplanned territory, I recognised, just in time. I needed to return to the task in hand. Richard had sat back, confident that he had once again controlled today's discussion, but I had my cards ready. Before his arrival, I had arranged the room differently from normal, so my chair was against the wall with the panic strip. He had noticed, of course he had, but he hadn't commented.

On the low table between us, I laid out photographs of two women, both tall, blonde and slim. Attractive, professional women whose lives had been torn apart. Their haunted eyes were identical even though their expressions varied. One defiant, chin raised, lips pursed. The other like the proverbial deer in the headlights.

He sat back, a knee-jerk reaction. He wouldn't look at the pictures, tilting his head so he looked past them, fixing his eyes on the art hanging on the far wall.

'Bryony Davies. Inga Petrauskaite.'

'I know who they are.'

'They came to court, didn't they? Did you see them?'

'Yes.' He closed his eyes momentarily. 'Why do you need to show me their photos?'

'How do you feel when you look at them?'

'Sick, if you must know.'

'Inga was the most badly injured. She really fought back.'

'Yet they didn't find my DNA under her fingernails.'

'They didn't find anyone's DNA under her fingernails; she was wearing gloves.'

'You've done your research.' Richard's voice was like ice.

'Bryony tried to kill herself several times in the months following her attack.' I touched the first photograph. 'She was sectioned under the Mental Health Act. She may never return to work.'

'You're telling me this as if I haven't already heard it in court. I know how those women suffered, but it *wasn't me* who hurt them.'

I carefully gathered the photos and slid them back into their folder. Their job was done; it would be counterproductive to overplay their impact.

'A lot of clients experience denial.'

'This isn't denial.' His voice was forceful but not aggressive. He made eye contact and my stomach contracted sharply, as if the baby was shying away from him. 'I'm not delusional.'

'No, delusional people don't form rational arguments.'

'I'll take that as a compliment.'

I didn't give him further chance to recover before I placed two more photos on the table. These were group shots. In one, several men in military fatigues and blue helmets, strong-jawed and broad-shouldered, stood stiffly on a snowy, muddy road bordered by bombed-out houses. Alongside them, two women in civilian clothes gazed at the camera with eyes that were at once afraid and defiant. Richard was at the edge of the small group, his weapon slung casually across his chest, although one hand remained close to the trigger, ready.

In the second, the same two women but a different group of men, only Richard remaining from the previous shot. They were in a darkened bar, holding shot glasses aloft to the camera. This time, everyone was relaxed and laughing, their uniform jackets unbuttoned and heads bare.

'Where did you get these?' Richard rasped, picking each one up in turn. 'These are my property.'

'The police sent them. Your former unit supplied them with some copies during the investigation. You're familiar with these?'

'I remember them being taken. It was near Christmas, in Kosovo.'

'Who are the women?'

He tapped the face of one, her beguiling dark eyes huge in her sculpted face. 'Katya. She was my translator. I forget the other's name.'

'And how do these photos make you feel?'

'Nostalgic,' he murmured. He held the pictures a moment longer, drinking in the details with a hint of a smile. 'I haven't looked at these for years. Some memories, I tell you.'

'Please do tell me.'

A tiny shake of his head. 'Not this time, Dr Shaw. Those are just for me.'

He returned the photos to me and watched me put them away. His eyes found their way back to mine.

'I'm aware this is a strange question,' he said, 'but have you ever known war?'

'Only in my own mind,' I murmured, without thinking.

I froze, cursing myself for such a careless slip in my professional mask, waiting for him to seize the advantage, but he only nodded thoughtfully.

'I'm the same. Even when I wasn't in a conflict zone, I was still fighting inside my head.'

'You've no diagnoses,' I felt compelled to say. I had checked his file to be sure.

'It's not PTSD or anything like that. I wasn't traumatised. I was angry.'

'What were you angry about?'

'The futility of it all. It felt so pointless, being part of the UN. I was just another pawn, even with my rank.'

He shook his head rapidly, throwing up his hands. His back thudded against the chair as he pushed himself away from the edge of his seat.

'You understand me, Tamsin. No one in the army ever did, though they claimed to.'

The professional voice in my head told me to redirect him, to remain Dr Shaw, but maybe we had reached a stage where such formalities no longer mattered. He had breached defences and boundaries I would never have allowed to be compromised in the past. Perhaps he had earned the right to treat me as his equal.

'I like to think I do,' I said carefully.

Finally, his body loosened, the tension in his jaw ebbing away. I allowed him silent recovery time, watching as he glanced around the room. His focus was wavering.

'I like your artwork,' he said quietly, indicating the frames on the far wall that had previously held his attention. They were photos of various landscapes I had chosen as conversation starters for reluctant clients. Richard hadn't so much as glanced at them until this session.

'Thank you. I like being reminded of the natural world, away from city life.'

'This one's my favourite.' He pointed to a woodland scene, fledglings about to fly their nest for the first time. 'Delicate creatures, aren't they? Vulnerable.'

I found his choice of adjectives strange enough to make a note of them. 'I think of them as carefree.'

'No creature is carefree. There are too many threats in the world.'

'Have you ever been carefree?'

His eyes told me he knew we were back to business. 'As a child, maybe. It was a pretty idyllic upbringing. How about yourself?'

Despite my better judgement, I felt compelled to answer. 'Not that I ever remember. I've always taken life rather seriously.'

'I can see that. You have an intensity, like you always give your full effort to whatever you're doing. You feel pressure, don't you? To do well in life?'

'A drive, rather than pressure.'

'We're not so different, you and I.'

'I'm not sure if I agree with that, Richard.'

A smile flickers in his eyes, although his mouth remains neutral. 'I like how you say my name.'

I didn't know what to say to that, and I took too long trying to find an answer.

'You don't like being caught off guard, do you?' Richard chuckled.

That time, I was able to look him directly in the eye, the reply coming easily.

'I hate it.'

23

Jamie – Now

Jamie stares at Dan Attwood's number as it flashes up on his phone screen. What the hell does he want now? The man is obsessed.

The phone goes silent, displaying a missed call notification, before starting to buzz again, insistently.

'For fuck's sake,' Jamie hisses as he smacks the answer icon with his middle finger.

'Were you going to tell me about Tamsin's treatment potentially being stopped?' Dan demands, without waiting for a hello.

For a moment that drags on for too long, Jamie has no idea what to say. 'How the hell did you find that out?' he finally blusters.

'I went snooping, if you must know. Are you there now, at Rushmore?'

'No, I couldn't make visiting this morning. I had meetings.'

'If you were, you'd see it's all in her notes at the end of her bed.'

Jamie grits his teeth. 'It's a family matter. I'll give you a chance to say goodbye.'

'Magnanimous of you. What about Elise?'

'It's Elise I'm thinking of! Do you expect her to spend the next twenty years visiting a breathing mannequin?'

'She deserves the chance to have her mother.'

'She doesn't *have* her mother! And what the hell is my daughter to do with you?'

'You want Tam out of the way, so you and Lucia are free to be together, don't you?'

Jamie opens his mouth but can't find the words. He knew it had been a mistake to let Dan into the apartment. 'What –?'

'Don't waste your time bullshitting me. Apollo Point was like a museum. You've been living with Lucia for a long time, mate.'

'I'm not your fucking mate. And so what if I'm with Lucia? Who cares?'

'Were you with her before the crash?' Dan's voice changes, as if he has switched into professional mode, and Jamie is immediately wary of the interrogative tone.

'As if I'm going to answer that,' he retorts.

'Then I'll take it as a yes. Bit convenient, don't you think?'

'What are you banging on about?'

'That your wife was involved in a near-deadly car crash at a time when you wanted out of your marriage?'

Jamie barks an incredulous laugh, as if sweat isn't beading on his forehead. 'You're mad. You can't seriously think I'd harm Tam just to be with Lucia.'

'You're considering harming her now, for that exact same reason.'

His reasoning is so eerily similar to Mateo's accusations that suddenly, Jamie has no idea what he can say that will be a plausible denial. Dan has backed him into a corner.

'Will you fuck off?' is the best he can manage. 'My relationship with Lucia is no more your business than my daughter or Tamsin's care is.'

There is an intake of breath that suggests Dan is wrestling with his temper. 'I don't want Tamsin to die.'

'Look, Dan, I get that you're in love with my wife. No, don't deny it. I know why Tam was the only one good enough for your little project.'

'Tamsin was the best in her field.' Dan's voice cracks. 'She could achieve outcomes no other psychiatrist could. How can you let her go?'

Jamie stumbles as he tries to snatch at a reasonable explanation. 'Because she's already left us. That body is *not* Tamsin. She's been gone for three years and it's time to move on.'

'Why can't you open yourself up to the possibility that she could heal?'

'I've got to get back to work.' Jamie needs to end this conversation. Dan cannot be allowed to plant doubt in his mind, any more than he can be permitted to hurl wild accusations. 'I'll be in touch when it's time.'

He hangs up without letting Dan speak again. He stares at the blank phone screen, trying to analyse what has been discussed, but his brain races in a panicked carousel of guilt and fear.

He had intended to wait until he got to Rushmore that evening to inform the director of his decision, but the urge to get on with it is too strong. Dan Attwood has only succeeded in convincing Jamie that he is making the right choice. He wants the man out of their lives, before he can dig up any more of Jamie's secrets.

Jamie taps the icon for Rushmore, asks to be put through to the director's office. She keeps him waiting long enough for fear to set in again. He isn't sure what he was expecting her reaction to be, but her neutral acceptance, as if they are discussing a change in visiting hours rather than life or death, throws him.

'And when do you wish to withdraw Tamsin's support?'

He hasn't set a date in his mind. He had half-expected her to check a schedule, to ensure no one else was due to die the same day or it wouldn't clash with the window cleaner.

'Tam's fortieth birthday is a week today,' he says, surprising himself with his decisiveness. 'It seems right to do it then.'

'Friday 16th October. I've made a note, Mr Shaw. Would you like to discuss the practical arrangements when you visit?'

'Practical arrangements?'

'Who will be present, any music or readings, the undertakers ...'

He starts to retort that it isn't a funeral, then he realises that is exactly what it will be.

'I haven't thought about all that yet,' he stumbles. 'I'll let you know. I can't make morning visiting today, so I'll be there this evening.'

He ends the call swiftly, no doubt leaving the director unconvinced that he's capable of making any decisions, let alone ones of this magnitude.

There is no real reason for him to have chosen to skip this morning's visit. He may well have evaded going at all, but for Dan bloody Attwood bringing Elise into it. He can't deprive his daughter of her last few chances to spend time with her mother, as much as he wants to shield her from everything Rushmore represents.

A week today suddenly seems very soon.

Jamie arrives home to find Elise drawing, a pastime she never tires of. She seems to have an instinctive ability to capture a scene and even Jamie can usually tell what Elise is attempting to depict.

Entirely focussed on her project, Elise blinks as if emerging from a trance. 'Hi, Daddy.'

'Hi, sweetheart. It's time to go and see Mummy.' Jamie keeps his gaze on her, uncomfortably aware that Mateo is sprawled on the sofa mere feet away, watching a film. Lucia keeps a careful eye on them all from the kitchen as she wipes down the worktops.

'Say goodbye to Mummy, you mean,' Mateo mutters, just loud enough to be heard.

Elise glances up, her brow furrowed, and Jamie finds himself holding his breath. He knows he should intervene, protect his daughter from such a damning statement, but he is afraid of making it worse.

'Matty!' Lucia cries.

The fire in Mateo's eyes dies as his brain catches up with his mouth. He climbs off the sofa, crossing to sink to his haunches in front of Elise, ignoring Jamie completely.

'Sorry, Els,' he murmurs. 'Didn't mean it. You know I love you, right?'

'Love you too,' Elise murmurs back, matching his tone. She holds her arms out to the teenager, and he pulls her into a brief, gentle hug. 'Can we draw?'

Mateo glances at his mother out of the corner of his eye, reading her reaction. 'I'll draw with you when you get home,' he says softly, redirecting Elise back to her picture before striding out of the room.

'I'm sorry,' Lucia whispers. 'That was an awful thing for him to say.'

Jamie pinches the bridge of his nose, checking his daughter isn't listening. 'He's not wrong, though. I rang and told the director earlier. We're going to do it on Tam's birthday.'

Lucia flinches as if he has slapped her.

'Lu, you knew I had to tell Rushmore sooner or later.'

'But her birthday? That feels so wrong.'

'It'll make it one less date for Els to observe in the future.'

'A neat and tidy ending, then?' Lucia snaps.

'When did you want to do it?' He manages to keep his frustration tamped down.

'I didn't want to do it at all! Least of all on her fortieth.'

'She won't exactly recognise the significance of the date. Were you going to take a cake and champagne?'

'Don't, Jamie,' she warns, through gritted teeth. 'Don't try and make me out to be the unreasonable one.'

'You're the one making it an argument.'

'I'm facing saying goodbye to my best friend, in case you've forgotten.'

'And I'm saying goodbye my daughter's mother,' he reminds her. 'This isn't going to be much of a fresh start for us as a family if we keep going like this.'

He doesn't give her chance to respond, moving across to his daughter before Lucia can react. 'C'mon, Els, we've got to go see Mummy.'

'Why?'

'Because …' He realises he has no idea how to answer that question. Should he lie, tell his daughter he believes Tamsin appreciates their presence, knows they are by her side?

After all, what's one more lie when he is already juggling so many?

24

Jamie – Before

By the following week, Jamie couldn't put off looking at the figures any longer. He hid himself away in the Porteños office to see exactly how bad things were. It took three attempts to understand and, even then, he had to check again to be sure he wasn't missing something.

His hand was shaking as he grabbed the desk phone and rang down to the kitchen. 'Is Ben there?'

'He's here,' Franco confirmed, 'but I don't think you want to talk to him at the moment.'

Jamie squeezed his eyes closed. 'Did you see the orders for this week?'

'Ben said he didn't need them checking.'

'Because he didn't want anyone to know he's ordered caviar that costs more than your weekly wage!' Jamie almost bellowed, his volume rising abruptly. 'Why the fuck does an Argentine restaurant need fucking caviar?'

'I don't know what to tell you, Jamie. They're his ideas, not mine.'

'Tell him to get his arse up here.'

'Not a good idea, mate. He's high as a kite. Give him an hour to come down a bit – you won't get any sense out of him.'

Jamie slammed the phone down. The fury coursing through his veins was like molten lava, and it was scaring him a little. Had Ben appeared in the doorway at that moment, Jamie didn't trust he would be able to keep a grip on himself.

He dropped his head into his hands, his breath hot against his palms.

The door opened.

'Why you bitching to Franco about me?' Ben demanded.

The sheer audacity of the man would almost have been laughable in different circumstances. As it was, Jamie's throat was so constricted by anger that he could barely breathe.

'What the hell is wrong with you?' he roared. 'I told you to let Franco do the orders!'

'My food, my orders,' Ben hurled back.

'And what happens when we can't pay the bills you're running up? Because that's where we are, Ben. We can't pay.' Jamie stabbed at the computer screen with his index finger. 'What do you see? Red. Everywhere is fucking red.'

Ben's eyes swept over the screen but only for a second, not long enough to absorb any of the information. As usual, ignorance was bliss, and what he didn't see, he didn't have to think about.

'Look at it!' Jamie slammed his hand onto the desk. 'You've made this mess. You can't pretend it isn't happening!'

'Numbers mean nothing to me.'

'Then understand the words I'm saying! Start seeing what you're doing to us!'

'Fuck off, Jamie. I don't have to do what you say. You're not my boss.'

Ben turned on his heel, about to storm off in a fit of wounded pride. And something deep within Jamie snapped. He physically felt it give, an elastic band stretched too far, and, before he knew it, he was launching himself across the office.

His hands grabbed Ben's collar, spinning him round, driving him up against the wall. Ben's back thudded hard against the plasterboard, and he just managed to twitch his head to avoid Jamie's punch. It left a dent in the surface and stinging grazes across Jamie's knuckles.

Jamie's fingers were at his throat, gripping, squeezing. He was taller than Ben, stronger, fuelled by a rage that had been contained for far too long.

Ben's face was turning red as he battled to free himself. The two men locked eyes. Jamie was leaning all his weight forward, his arms like steel. Ben began to rasp painfully, his fingernails scraping uselessly at Jamie's bleeding knuckles, his legs kicking out frantically, but Jamie didn't feel it. For the first time in forever, inside his head was silent, almost peaceful.

But he saw himself reflected in the terror of Ben's eyes. He saw the snarl contorting his face and he didn't recognise who he was, who he had become.

He let go.

Ben slid down the wall to land with a thump, clutching at his throat, coughing pitifully. Jamie didn't wait to see what he would do. He strode down the stairs and into the expansive dining room, not pausing to check what belongings he had left behind, focussed only on escape. Before he crossed a line that he couldn't come back from.

'Hey!' Ben's voice was too loud, and Jamie winced as several customers' heads turned to look at them. 'Don't run away from me!'

Jamie ignored him, making for the exit. He could hear Ben pounding after him but looking back would only make it worse.

He stalled in mid-step as desperate fingers seized his arm.

'Get off me,' he hissed, fighting to pull free without making it obvious to the entire restaurant.

'You don't leave!' Ben's accent was thick once again and he had recovered enough to play the victim. 'You stay and listen to me.'

The monster in Jamie's chest threatened to erupt again.

'We can talk upstairs,' he ground out through gritted teeth.

'No, we talk here, so people can see you threaten me.'

Jamie span so quickly Ben was knocked off balance. He grabbed Ben's arm and hustled him between the tables like a TV cop marching a suspect into custody. He made it as far as the corridor at the back that ran down to the kitchen before Ben planted his feet, refusing to be moved any further.

'What, you gonna strangle me again?' The fingertip marks were still livid white against the flushed skin of his neck.

Jamie clenched his fists despite the sting of his torn knuckles 'I shouldn't have done that. I lost my temper.'

'You want me dead, Jamie, I know!'

'Are you out of your mind? Christ, this is more than paranoia. It's the coke that'll end you, not me!'

'I never trusted you!'

'You trusted me enough to take my money. Funny that, isn't it?' Jamie made himself step back, aware of how badly he was shaking.

He glanced sharply around them. One of the closest tables outside the corridor had paused with their cutlery in mid-air, clearly listening. Another was continuing their conversation just a little too obviously, their laughter forced, their motions choreographed. A third was occupied by a solo customer who had his back to them. He had barely touched his steak and was leisurely sipping his wine while glancing around the restaurant as if interested in the artwork, and it was his languid actions that caught Jamie's attention.

'If that's a fucking critic, I really will end you,' he snarled in Ben's ear. 'Will you get in the kitchen before every customer finds out we're about to go under.'

Ben spat something in his own language before marching through the swinging doors. Feeling the eyes of the diners burning into his back, Jamie strode after him, coming to a stop in the vestibule where crockery and linen were stored. It was telling that not one of the workers showed the slightest curiosity in what they were doing, even as plates were ferried past them.

'This can't go on. I can't do this shit anymore. I'm done, Ben. Let it all go bust. It's not worth saving.'

That was enough to shock Ben into silence. Whatever he had been expecting, defeat wasn't it.

Jamie scrubbed his hands over his face, horrified to find he was close to tears.

'Excuse me for interrupting you.'

Jamie almost leapt out of his skin. Directly behind him was the customer who had been eating alone. He had a hesitant voice that matched his very stiff dark suit. With hair severely gelled back and poor posture, a stoop to his upper back, Jamie pegged him as a banker out for a quick lunch rather than the food critic he had feared. No threat after all.

Jamie cleared his throat. 'Is everything alright, sir?'

'Are you the owner?'

'Co-owner, yes.' He coughed again, straightening up, smoothing down his shirt. 'Jamie Shaw. Can I help you with something?'

'It might be the other way round, actually.' He extended his hand and Jamie felt he had no choice but to shake. The grip felt limp, and Jamie tried to convey his own authority through his firmer grip.

'I am Benicio Aguero, the *owner*,' Ben emphasised, seizing the man's hand.

'Pleased to meet you both. I couldn't help but overhear your conversation.'

Jamie winced. 'You must have misheard us,' he said shortly. 'Everything's fine. Thank you for your concern.'

'Perhaps we could speak somewhere for a moment? You may be interested in what I have to say.'

Mortified at this intrusion, Jamie began to turn away, but Ben and his impulsive idiocy were already leading the stranger upstairs, babbling away about the pampas and gaucho culture.

It was too much of a risk to leave them alone. Jamie had no option but to follow them, seating himself firmly behind the desk before Ben could take the chair. Reluctantly, he indicated for the visitor to sit.

'Allow me to explain. I make my money through investing. I have a fair amount of capital at my disposal.'

Jamie sensed Ben perk up at the mere mention of money, and silently willed him to keep his mouth shut. 'What does that matter to us?'

'My preferred investments are in struggling companies, to get them back on their feet.'

'And what business is it of yours if we are struggling?'

'That's why I came to talk to you. It's exactly my business, so to speak.'

Jamie stared at the man, his mind flying in circles, trying to make sense of the conversation. The stranger held out a card, looking pleased when Jamie took it.

'It's simply something to think about. An option, if you need one. I've saved a good few failing companies and I'm sure I could help you out of the situation I overheard you arguing about.'

Jamie had no idea what to say in response. Ben reached over and grabbed the card to read. The visitor smiled, rose and tipped his head in genial farewell. The door closed softly behind him, and Jamie listened to his footsteps meandering downstairs.

Jamie neatly relieved Ben of the card before he could stash it in his pocket. He studied the details as he attempted to replay what had just happened. Ben was wittering away about miracles, his voice high and fast with excitement.

Jamie was not naïve enough to believe in godsends but, for the first time in many long, dark months, he thought he might have glimpsed a faint ray of hope.

25

Tamsin – Now

To my surprise, Dan is back again. It is Friday, Jamie's visiting day, but he didn't show up this morning. Perhaps I'm already slipping from his mind, even less of a priority than I already was. Or he's choosing to withdraw, saving himself from a protracted goodbye.

Dan is different today. He bristles with energy, unable to keep still for long. When he speaks, enthusiasm lightens his voice.

'I can't stay long, I've got to be at the office today while I'm not needed in court, but I had to come and tell you. I think we're on to something!'

Hope sparks in me. Could he have found a way to stop them withdrawing my treatment?

'Your notes said you'd analysed Mandeville's military career as part of the background work. I wonder if you ever talked about the Amnesty International investigation.'

A sour taste floods my mouth. Dan's fixation is purely on Richard. He isn't here to save me. I am being left to my fate, and the blow of that realisation leaves me winded.

'He told you about his time in the Balkans. You wrote pages about it. How it affected him.'

In spite of myself, I am curious. I remember the session when we had talked about Richard's army days, but I knew nothing about any Amnesty International investigation.

'Mandeville served in Kosovo for several years. There's been a report published on the abuse and trafficking of Kosovar women during the conflict by service personnel. The sick bastards used civil war victims for their own kicks.' Dan's voice tightens to the point of hoarseness. 'The judge is deciding whether we can include it.'

My rage dissipates as my interest grows. War crimes, sickening as they are, occur simply because there is little to prevent them. In ravaged communities, the weak are defenceless against those seeking to exploit. Richard Mandeville is the type of man who would be irresistibly drawn to such atrocities. But if Richard was involved, how could one report prove it?

'I know,' Dan says, as if he can read my thoughts. 'We can't link Mandeville to it directly. There were thousands of peacekeepers serving there. But you know as well as I do, attacks like the ones he was convicted of are never an offender's first crimes.'

That is true. Depravity does not come from nowhere. It builds over time as the offender becomes more confident, embraces his darkest flaws.

'It's possible his first attacks were on Kosovar women. If that's where it all started for him, we might be able to establish a connection under cross-examination. He won't be expecting us to have investigated this far back.'

Dan has brought a copy of the report. Printed, not on his phone. I imagine the papers are covered in his tight, small hand-writing, trying to highlight passages that serve his agenda. He flicks through it, reading out some quotes to me. Tales of the horror women have suffered at the hands of men sent to a war zone to protect them.

It's awful, of course it is, to think of vulnerable people seeking safety, only to find the opposite, but I can't picture those terrified faces. Instead, I see Richard in his military fatigues, striding through the flames of a derelict basement, shielding two children from the inferno that threatened to claim them.

We are interrupted by the door opening before Dan can say any more. Daisies and clean linen – Hannah and Milena.

'Sorry to interrupt.' Hannah doesn't sound remotely apologetic. 'Time for pressure-sore turn.'

Dan immediately excuses himself, as he always does whenever the staff have to perform any intervention. He hates to watch me being handled.

'Mr Attwood's here a lot recently,' Hannah observes. 'There's always an influx of visitors trying to make up for lost time when they know the end's near.'

Fury burns within me. Hannah has already decided I'm done for. I have been dismissed as casually as an agency carer who didn't meet her standards. She can't leave my room fast enough once the turn has been completed.

I'm just a body to her now.

Elise is quiet as she comes into the room, but I catch her biscuit scent and imagine her holding hands with Jamie, squeezing his fingers for reassurance. The change of schedule throws me. I do not want Jamie here. And definitely not at the same time as Dan, with the threat of the DNA test hanging over us.

Elise climbs onto my bed by herself, planting her soft kiss on my cheek. I remember when she came to visit soon after the coma, how her cries made my breasts ache and her little snuffles enveloped my heart in warmth. Lucia would build a safe nest of pillows and lay her down beside me, close enough so I could feel her body heat and her velvety skin against mine. She had felt wholly mine, even though she maybe never would be.

Now, she is becoming her own person. I hear Jamie in some of her phrases, sense Lucia in her actions. But I am her brain. She thinks like me. She analyses, she questions, she explores, even at this tender age.

I once explained to Jamie the feeling of having forty open tabs working simultaneously in your head, all processing information and data. He had no idea what I meant; he dealt with one thing at once. Elise understands. It happens to her too.

'Hannah told me your vital signs had changed again yesterday, Tam,' Jamie says, surprising me.

It is rare he speaks to me as if we are having a conversation. He will deliver news to me like he is talking to an inanimate object. He doesn't seem to know how to speak naturally, even after all this time.

'Can you do it now? Can you do it for me?'

I want to tell him this isn't about him and, even if it was, I can't control my responses; they just happen. If I react to other people but not him, doesn't that give him an inkling it might be his fault? I'm not the only one in this marriage whose heart beats faster for someone else.

He sits in expectant silence for a long minute, as if I am some kind of circus animal, ready to perform tricks on command. Then I hear his soft sigh.

'What would we do, if you ever did come out of it?' he asks, and I realise he is speaking to himself again, as if I'm not here. He really doesn't believe that I am.

When he says *we*, he means him and Lucia. They will have discussed me, probably lying in bed together. I picture them in each other's arms, her head on his bare chest, and a hot flush of betrayal washes over me.

Elise reaches to take my hand and I wonder if she understands what her father is saying.

'Would you come home?' he wonders aloud. 'Would you walk and talk again? Go back to work? You'd want to raise Els. Maybe without me.'

I couldn't do that to him. Whatever has happened between us, he has done his best for the child he never wanted. I respect him for that, for stepping up to the plate when Elise could very well have been left with no one to look after her.

Even the thought of that makes my stomach clench and nausea swell. If I do leave my daughter behind, at least I know she'll be well cared for, and that gives me a little comfort.

'I'm talking about the impossible,' Jamie says softly, reassuring himself that none of this will ever happen. That nothing will stop him from moving on with Lucia. Or leaving me behind.

Two sets of footsteps in the doorway distract me. My heart sinks as I hear the creak of Dan's leather jacket, and I sense Jamie's tension ramp up another gear.

'Shall I take Elise for some ice cream?' Milena asks, moving into the room. The artificial lightness in her tone tells me she is aware of the atmosphere.

Jamie sits in the chair closest to my head, a tactical move. 'Thanks, Milena.'

I picture her extending her hand to my daughter. 'I saw some in the kitchen. I think it was strawberry.'

Elise needs no persuading and trots off immediately while Dan continues to hover on the threshold.

'I thought you weren't visiting today,' he says. It isn't an apology but at least it isn't a confrontation either.

'And I thought I told you I'd let you know when the time comes to say your goodbyes.'

How nice, I think, that they have discussed my death with each other rather than with me.

'I'm not here about that,' Dan says. He comes closer but doesn't sit. 'Besides, what do you care if I want to spend more time with Tam?'

'She's my wife.' Jamie leans forward to rest his hand on mine, a display of possession.

'Is she? In reality, is she actually your wife?'

I don't like Dan's tone. He is taunting Jamie, trying to gain the upper hand, and I know what a powerful card he has left to show. I hold my breath.

'What's that supposed to mean?' Jamie growls.

'I just find it funny that you can be possessive over Tamsin when you have Lucia waiting for you at home.'

'For fuck's sake –' Jamie takes a grip on my hand, as if he is trying again to provoke a reaction. My body ignores him.

'But does it really matter?' Dan continues, deliberately mild. 'So much has changed in three years. You never expected to have to raise Elise. You wanted Tam to terminate the pregnancy. Yes, she told me, don't bother denying it.'

I sense Dan is working up to the ultimate blow. This is the only way he can deal with the threat of my death, by lashing out, and he is going to use the best weapon he has.

He's going to tell Jamie about the DNA test and, once that bomb has exploded, there will be no way back for me.

I picture Jamie, rage contorting his features, and I know his kneejerk reaction will be to feel utterly betrayed, in spite of his own sins. It will be my end. And I can do absolutely nothing to stop it.

Horror grips my throat with a pressure more intense that I've experienced before. I gasp for air, expanding my lungs as far as they can go.

'Fuck!' Dan inhales sharply, unconsciously copying my action. 'Is she OK?'

His baiting of Jamie is instantly forgotten. He grabs my other hand, and I don't know if he is trying to calm me or urging me on. I can feel their eyes fixed on me as I gasp again, trying with every part of my being to make a noise of protest.

'Did you hear that?' Dan cries. 'She groaned! You said she couldn't make any noises!'

'Maybe some air got trapped in her throat or something.' Jamie sounds almost afraid.

Triumph soars. I did it. I grunted. It was almost nothing, barely audible, and I wasn't even sure it had really happened until Dan confirmed it.

'Tam, do it again!' he urges.

I swell my lungs again to try and repeat the sound. Then I

realise what I would see if I did manage to force my eyes open. Jamie and Dan will be standing over me, and we will all be trying to hide our guilt, and I am not sure if I'm strong enough to face that.

Now I am as fearful as Jamie and the pressure in my chest is dying away.

'Go and find Hannah,' Jamie instructs Dan. 'Tell her what happened so they can make a note of it.'

I expect Dan to resist, but I must have really shocked him, for his long strides thump out of the room without argument. I am aware of Jamie leaning close, examining me for any more signs of life.

'Tam?' he asks, a new urgency in his voice. 'Squeeze my hand if you can hear me.'

I try, but it's no good. I recognise that tone; he is close to tears, but I can't bring myself to care, not after what he's done. Not now I know what he's planning to do to me.

'Lucia and I,' he whispers. 'It wasn't meant to be love.'

My heart begins to pound. Jamie has realised his future is in jeopardy. If I come back, he may lose everything he has built since I ceased to fully exist. Now he feels the urge to explain himself, to confess what he has hidden from me for so long, just in case I try to snatch it away from him.

'I fucked up, I know I did. I hated myself for betraying you like that. I tried to stop but Lu made everything feel better and I wanted to have just a little bit of happiness.'

And you couldn't have gone looking for that on Hinge, rather than with my best friend? I strain to shout.

'I didn't want a stranger,' Jamie says, like he knows exactly what I'm thinking. 'Lucia was just there at the right, or the wrong, time. I swore it would never happen again, but I couldn't stop thinking about how it made me feel. God, Tam, why am I telling you all this?'

He is telling me because my sudden ability to produce noise has spooked him. He is scared I will wake up and ruin his plan.

'I kept telling myself it was just sex,' he says. 'No ties. Sex is just human nature, isn't it, just physical? It's not like love, like emotional cheating. That always seems worse, doesn't it?'

I note his repeated use of the word *just* as he tries to downplay the betrayal, minimise his own guilt. Lucia had been a good friend, the extrovert to my introvert, the champagne to my gin. I had trusted her as much as I could ever trust anyone, and I had done my best to protect her from the threats of the world I had inhabited.

'You'd become a stranger to me. You were either at your office or at the gym. You didn't talk to me. I felt like I wasn't wanted anymore.'

Pain lances my chest. Jamie isn't referring to the last couple of years. He's talking about our life *before*.

He was cheating on me before the crash ever happened. My best friend was sleeping with my husband while I was still present.

This is the last straw. Nothing else can hurt as much as this does. If I could cry, scalding tears would be streaming down my face. But all I can do is lie here, my face expressionless, while Jamie comforts himself.

Everything has been a lie. And I missed it. This supposedly brilliant brain of mine couldn't spot what was right in front of me.

'I pray you can't hear us, Tam,' Jamie murmurs.

For the first time, I wished I couldn't either.

26

Tamsin – Before

'Are we delving into the past again today?' Richard asked tartly. He had arrived for his next session with a somewhat sceptical attitude, after ending our last on a sour note.

'I get the feeling you don't like referring to it.'

'The recent past, no. I would rather never speak of it again. Distant memories are different.'

'Your childhood, for example?'

His eyes danced, apparently pleased I had conformed to his expectations.

'Now we're getting into the real psychological deep dive. Are you waiting for me to tell you about being shipped off to boarding school before I was old enough to tie my own shoelaces? Of cold showers and cruel prefects and how they've affected me all my life?'

'If that's what you want to tell me,' I said, deliberately neutral. He splayed his legs as he sprawled more comfortably in his seat, his body language open and unguarded, doing his best to assure me there was nothing he needed to conceal.

'I hate to disappoint, but I have no such tales for you. It was the sort of childhood I would live again and again, given the chance. I never seem to remember it raining. Always bright sunshine across rolling fields. I was out from dawn to dusk. The cook would pack a bag for me stuffed full of homemade sausage rolls and pork pies, and Victoria sponge and apples from our orchard. I had a piebald cob, Jasper, and I'd share the apples with him and the pies with the Labradors.'

He painted a pretty picture. I wondered how many times he'd told this story before. 'You've read too many Blyton novels.'

A broad smile creased his face. 'It's true, all of it. Idyllic. It really was. I didn't board till I went to Eton; there was a decent prep school across the valley. I was free, in every sense of the word. Even my mother's determination to make me a gentleman wasn't *that* bad.'

'Did you do well at school?'

'I neither excelled nor failed. Let's just say I did enough. School was for sport and camaraderie, but I put pen to paper when required.'

'You knew you were destined for the army, anyway.'

'That course had been mapped out since birth. Every Earl of Southvale has served in the forces. We needed something to interrupt our leisure.'

'You went to Sandhurst at eighteen?'

'I was nearly twenty. I had a gap year first, backpacking round Asia.'

I was momentarily wrong-footed. I had read his file cover to cover, and no gap year had ever been mentioned. 'I didn't know that.'

'You don't like being in the dark about anything, do you?' he grinned. 'Look how you've tensed.'

I looked down to find my hands gripping the arms of my chair. I immediately released my hold, narrowly preventing myself from folding my arms defensively across my chest. He watched with overt amusement.

'It's not particularly relevant anyway. I did the usual – India, Nepal, down into Thailand, Vietnam, Cambodia, then across to Indonesia and Philippines.'

'You must have always been on the move,' I observed.

'There was a lot to see, and not much time.'

'You didn't find anywhere you wanted to settle for a while?'

'I preferred to keep going. It didn't suit me being in one place for too long.'

'I'd have been tempted to stay forever,' I said vaguely, to conceal my analysis of potential reasons for him to have country-hopped so rapidly, sweeping through places renowned for poverty, where desperate people could be coerced into doing desperate things. None of the conclusions I scribbled down in my notebook were positive ones.

'One can't escape reality, Dr Shaw. You should know that better than most.'

I gave myself a mental shake, forcing my attention back to the conversation before he became suspicious. 'So you came back for Sandhurst and graduated as a second lieutenant. Where was your first posting?'

'Basra. That was an eye-opener. Men were expecting me to lead them, and I didn't feel ready to. It was a harsh wake-up call that my days, and theirs, were numbered if I didn't get my act together.'

'You must have seen some awful things.'

'That's war, Dr Shaw.'

I noted how regularly he was using my title, when he usually made a point of avoiding it. He didn't want us to be equals today. He wanted to show he was deferring to me.

'When we spoke in our last session, you said you don't feel any trauma from your army experiences.'

He tilted his head. 'I said I don't suffer from any PTSD-type symptoms. Trauma is another matter.'

He had bested me, and I was furious with myself. I was slipping, distracted by the pregnancy and Jamie, and that put me in unstable territory, a grey area I wasn't used to dealing with.

'Define trauma,' I challenged him, kicking myself immediately for being antagonistic. I wasn't there to bait him; that would only make him shut down, and it would betray the trust he had vested in me.

'For me, it would be an experience that continues to affect the person even years after the event.'

'And how does it affect you?'

'Mood, mostly. At night, not during the day. I wake feeling like something is eating me from the inside. It's insidious. I can't define it. It's not rage or distress. Something else.'

'How do you deal with it?'

'I exercise. Obsessively, in some ways. Once I'm exhausted, it seems to slip away, or at least hides itself well enough that I'm no longer aware of it.'

'That's healthier than how a lot of people cope.'

'Soldiers are a different breed. They learn to keep their issues private.'

'Sometimes that's worse. It means they never access help.' I place emphasis on the latter sentence and note his eyes flick to meet mine momentarily before he shrugs.

'It also means they don't put it upon society.'

'Surely that's what society is there for.'

He smirked. 'Society is there for its own self-preservation. You see that every day, Tamsin.'

I couldn't prevent my eyes rising from my notes at his deliberate use of my first name.

'The society I work with is quite different.'

'Is it really, though? You work with men desperate to keep their situations private.'

'Like you, Richard?' I challenged.

His eyes flashed, the sharpest steel. 'I'm *not* like them.'

I don't reply. I sit quietly, circling my pen across the page before me, giving him chance to regulate himself. It takes longer than usual.

'Do you have a low opinion of me?' he finally asked.

'Not at all.'

'But others do. Should I be working to change that?'

'Aren't you already doing that, by pursuing your appeal?'

'Not quickly enough,' he said grimly.

His impatience took a stranglehold on the room and, for the first time, I considered ending the session early. I didn't feel comfortable with this version of Richard Mandeville.

'You've tensed again,' he said. 'I'm unnerving you, aren't I?'

I looked up to confirm he was baiting me, but his expression seemed to be genuine.

'Yes,' I said simply. 'You are.'

'I apologise. I hadn't realised. Let's talk about something else. I'll tell you about the first time my father took me hunting and I ended up in a gorse hedge with the fox.'

He began to spin his tale, his hands flying to illustrate his words, genial and beguiling once again.

I let him talk. I let him think he was the one in control.

I arrived exactly as lunch service began, settling myself at a window table of Aqua Shard to enjoy the stunning view the thirty-first floor offered. It was a good fifteen minutes before Lucia threw herself down opposite me in a harried mess of handbag, coat, scarf and laptop case that all ended up scattered around her. 'Sorry, sorry, I got held up.'

'Not the end of the world.' I poured her water from the carafe between us and watched as she gulped it down, spilling drops down her white top without noticing. Her lateness had given me a chance to gather myself, to secure all the things I didn't want her to know and force them deep enough that they wouldn't be glimpsed. 'Busy day?'

'Frantic. Ben wanted to talk about some investor he says he's found for Porteños, but it sounded like absolute crap, and I was in too much of a rush to soothe his ego, so he kicked off.' She rolled her eyes. 'Smashed glass all over the kitchen floor right before I needed to leave for work. Prick.'

'Are you OK?' I scanned her bare arms for any signs of cuts.

'He didn't throw it at me, he wouldn't be that stupid.'

One day he will be, I thought. 'What's this about an investor?'

'Not sure. As usual, Ben didn't make much sense. Who would invest in a business that's falling apart? It must be a scam or something dodgy. Thank fuck Jamie isn't stupid enough to fall for it.'

'I'll ask Jamie, see what he knows about it. If I ever see him. He's making avoiding me a fine art.'

I had barely set eyes on my husband in recent weeks. We had become strangers in the night, meeting only in bed, to lie side-by-side, not touching, both pretending to be asleep until we eventually drifted off. He waited to come home until he was sure I wouldn't be up. I had stopped pursuing him; it was only driving him further away. He hadn't so much as mentioned the pregnancy, despite the undeniable evidence of my bump now swelling rapidly.

Instead, I had set my mind to another mission. Nurturing the life growing inside me; a regime of daily yoga or Pilates, gentle runs, a diet rich in iron and protein and morning smoothies packed with green vegetables that I pretended weren't disgusting. Work was a useful fixation, grounding me, keeping my mind alert when it begged to obsess over Jamie.

For the first time, I saw him not as my husband, as the father of my child. I saw him as a man on the edge of losing control of his life.

'I'm sorry, Tam.' Lucia didn't seem to know what else to say.

'Not your fault.'

She kept her eyes on the menu, scrutinising her choices before sighing and ordering a Caesar salad. She usually hated parmesan.

'Is this getting to you?' I asked gently. 'All the problems with Ben? You haven't been yourself.'

'I'm fine,' she says, too brightly.

'You don't seem fine. You seem on edge and about to burst into tears.'

'You don't have to be my shrink, you know. We can simply have lunch and talk about shopping or how delectable Pedro Pascal is or anything at all that won't get too deep.'

'That's a distraction, not a solution.'

'Tam.' Her grin was so forced it made the corners of her mouth crease. 'I'd like to talk about something that won't make me cry in the middle of the Shard, OK?'

She wasn't ready to talk. Never an easy thing, admitting one's marriage was falling apart. I wondered if she had finally recognised Ben's drug use. But it wasn't for me to tell her the truth. Not because of Jamie's decree to keep Lucia out of the mess he and Ben had created, but because it would damage a friendship I deeply valued.

'Have you got your psycho client today?' she asked.

It was my turn to tense, reaching for water that I didn't need. 'He's already had his appointment this morning. And he's not a psycho. Sociopathic maybe, but not psychopathic.'

'Same difference. He's still dangerous. And I'm still scared for you.'

'It's all under control, I promise.'

'You may think it is. But I've seen you react differently to this one than you have to other clients.'

A mouthful of water went down the wrong way and I coughed sharply. 'What's that supposed to mean?'

'You've got an energy about you. Like something's driving you.'

'The pregnancy is driving me.' I wiped my mouth. 'I need to get his programme finished before the baby comes, and that's a little more stressful than I'd like.'

'Nothing more than that?' She eyed me suspiciously.

I smiled at the waitress as she delivered our food and asked whether we needed more drinks.

'No, that's all.' I caught Lucia's eye as I replied to the waitress, answering both their questions at once.

Lucia nodded and forked a piece of lettuce into her mouth, apparently satisfied I was telling the truth.

And I was, in a way.

I just hadn't told her all of it yet.

27

Jamie – Now

Jamie moves across to the French windows in Tamsin's room. Angling his body away from her bed, he stares out over the neat gardens, trying to calm the roaring beast that has taken residence inside his chest.

Dan returns quickly with Hannah. Can the guy not take a hint and leave? Jamie spins to glare at him and, on a childish impulse, weighs up his chances in a fight against the towering ex-rower.

Fortunately, the chances of Hannah allowing fisticuffs to disrupt her schedule are slim. Jamie returns to Tamsin's bedside as Hannah rushes over to scrutinise the monitors, making a great show of thoroughness, before seizing the clipboard of notes and scribbling irritably.

'What the hell's happening?' Jamie demands as Dan hovers behind Hannah, trying to see what she is doing. 'Why did Tam make that noise?'

'I've seen this before in vegetative cases,' Hannah says, still writing. 'It happens when a patient's body begins to prepare to shut down. Their lungs start to degenerate, and their breathing can sound like grunts at times. We've suspected Tamsin has an infection somewhere and these reactions we're seeing suggest that's correct.'

'So she's not waking up?' Dan asks before Jamie can.

'No.' Hannah replies with such certainty that the two men instinctively exchange glances, to gauge each other's reaction. 'I'm afraid it's likely to be the opposite.'

Dan draws a sharp breath, slamming his fist onto the equipment tray, causing the peg feed components to bounce. Jamie scrunches his eyes shut and counts to ten. A disorientating mix of relief and guilt floods through him and that familiar belt squeezes around his sternum again. He can't take much more of this.

'Thank you, Hannah,' he manages to say, glancing up at her.

If she finds his response odd, she doesn't show it. Dan earns a glare for having disrupted the organisation of her equipment tray with his outburst.

'Shout me if anything else happens,' Hannah says half-heartedly as she departs.

Silence sits heavily for several moments as they both digest what she has told them, until Jamie clears his throat pointedly and gets to his feet.

'Can you leave now? I'd like some time with Tam.'

'I need my report,' Dan mutters, avoiding eye contact now they are alone. 'That's why I came in the first place.'

He indicates a sheaf of papers on Tamsin's bedside table.

Both men reach for it at the same time, but Jamie is closest, and he wants to know what is so important. He flicks through the pages, noting the section titles, the highlighted passages, but only a few words actually penetrate his brain. His fingers tighten on the paper as his attention finally focuses and he takes in the information.

'Did you bring this to read to her?'

'It's relevant to our client's court case,' Dan replies tightly.

'Tam prefers Dickens.' Jamie forces sarcasm into his tone, tossing the report back across the bed as if it is of no consequence to him. 'How is Amnesty International relevant?'

'It suggests our man may have been a threat to women long before he committed the attacks he was convicted of.'

Jamie's nostrils flare. 'I didn't know Tam dealt with people who committed war crimes.'

'Didn't you ever ask her about work?' It seems to be a genuine question, but Jamie is still affronted.

'She never wanted to talk about it. Said she left the job at the office. So I stopped asking.'

'Maybe she thought you didn't care.'

That time, the dig is clear, and Jamie raises his chin.

'You know he's visited Tam, don't you? Your man came here.'

Dan's expression betrays that he didn't know that and, even though it is pointless, Jamie seizes his chance at one-upmanship.

'Aren't you meant to be his probation director? Shouldn't you know what he gets up to?'

'That's his probation *officer's* job, and he's not on tag. He checks in once a week, that's it. We don't follow him around.' Dan shifts his weight awkwardly. 'Why didn't you call and tell me he'd been here?'

'Why, can you stop him visiting?' Jamie tosses back.

'No.' Dan spits out the single word. 'None of his terms restrict him from seeing Tamsin.'

'Then change the terms. If he's a threat to women, he shouldn't be allowed near her.'

'It doesn't work like that. I need to have grounds to make that sort of demand. There has to be evidence.'

'What if I don't want him around my –' Jamie catches himself. 'Around Tam?'

'There's nothing I can do officially. Besides, no one will have the opportunity to visit for much longer, will they?'

Jamie has to hold his breath to prevent himself from erupting. Dan knows exactly how to needle him.

'Bye, Tam,' Dan says softly, laying his big palm momentarily on the top of her head. 'I'll see you soon.'

Guilt nips at Jamie. He avoids watching the other man's action, acutely aware that, unless Dan visits again before Friday, he may not see Tamsin again.

This may have been his last farewell.

28

Jamie – Before

'I've done it!' Ben declared over the phone.

Safe in the privacy of his own office in the Docklands, Jamie almost gave in to the urge to drop to the carpet and curl into the foetal position.

'What do you mean, you've done it?' He hardly dared ask.

'That guy. With the card. I called him.'

'I told you not to do that!'

'Why wouldn't I? We need money. He has it. Easy, right?'

'No, Ben, it's not easy,' Jamie spat. 'We know nothing about him. A stranger comes offering you sweets, you don't take his hand and skip off with him.'

Ben didn't seem to grasp the allegory.

'We can't sit around and wait. He has plenty of other businesses wanting his investment.'

Jamie couldn't help but marvel at how competent Ben's English was when he dropped the accent. 'You don't know that. He can tell you anything and you'll believe it.'

'It's all agreed.'

Jamie's grip on his phone tightened. '*Agreed*? Tell me you haven't signed anything.'

Ben muttered something in his own language. 'He needs your signature too.'

'What the fuck have you done?' Jamie hissed, standing so fast his desk chair toppled over.

The only reply he got was three beeps. Ben had put the phone down.

They met in an anonymous pub in Marylebone. The clientele was a mix of tourists and couples looking for a meal deal. No one would remember the two men, deliberately dressed down in jeans and trainers, sitting quietly in the furthest booth, sipping pints of IPA.

'I apologise for my partner,' Jamie said. 'He's … impulsive.'

'So I noticed. It was hard to get him to shut up for long enough to get a word of my own in.'

'Welcome to my world,' Jamie muttered into his glass.

He took a long, slow draught, allowing himself time to study the man before him. There was little resemblance to the quiet, nonthreatening customer who had first approached Jamie at Porteños. He sat with his shoulders back, chest thrown out, one arm draped across the empty chair next to him. He looked relaxed and at ease with himself, as if this meeting was of little import to him.

In contrast, Jamie was so wound up his muscles were twitching. He couldn't stop raking his fingers through his hair with his free hand.

'Are you alright?'

'Bit stressed.' Jamie rubbed his forehead. 'Sorry, I don't have much time to chat.'

'You must be interested, Mr Shaw, otherwise you wouldn't be here.'

'I'm here because Ben claimed he'd already reached an agreement with you.'

The other man smiled. 'Let's just say he was very enthusiastic, but I don't fancy doing business with someone who seems so unpredictable.'

Jamie raised an eyebrow, reassured by this perceptiveness. There was a ringing confidence in the man's words, as if he was used to being in charge. 'So he hasn't signed anything?'

'He has, but it's useless without your approval. As he'd have realised if he'd bothered to read it properly.'

'Why is my signature the important one? We have equal ownership in Porteños.'

Another smile. 'Because you are the businessman. You understand the reality of your situation and you know what will happen if you don't find a solution.'

'And you're the solution?'

'Potentially. I've been on the lookout for a decent project, and this seems a good opportunity for us both. I've had a look through your filing history.' He took a drink. 'Why don't you tell me about your portfolio, including why you're haemorrhaging money.'

Jamie had been flattered at his use of the term *portfolio*, but compressed his lips at the words that followed.

'Ben … he's my friend … well, technically his wife is my wife's best friend. I wanted to help them out of trouble.'

'And that's why you co-own his restaurant?'

Jamie didn't want to explain. The last thing he wanted to admit was his poor judgement. The other man waited patiently.

'I made mistakes,' Jamie eventually said. 'I thought it was a sound investment. It proved to be the opposite.'

'You used money from your own company to invest, I suppose?'

Jamie nodded, focusing on a pool of condensation on the table. 'Then the profits never materialised. The restaurant has got deeper and deeper in debt. It can't pay its rent, so I can't pay the mortgage on the building. I've moved money around as much as I can, but it's not enough. You've seen the figures.'

A contemplative silence that lasted long enough for Jamie to become uneasy. As much as he didn't want to do this, he had precisely zero alternatives. Realistically, this stranger was his only chance.

'My investment would be enough to get the restaurant out of the red. Your own company should recover once it's not having to support Porteños.' The other man pauses to drink again, unhurried. 'Once the restaurant was stable, I'd take back my investment, plus a bonus, then a share of the profits for the next year. After that, my input is generally done.'

'That simple?'

'Usually, yes.'

They both sipped their pints. Jamie found he was warming to this idea, and to the other man. There was a solidity to him that hadn't been apparent during their first encounter, a self-assurance that Jamie liked. He seemed to know exactly what he was talking about, and the prospect of having someone to share the load was already appealing.

'Have you seen *Pretty Woman?*'

Jamie frowned. 'Yeah?'

'I kind of do what Richard Gere does. I have to warn you, you won't like the amount of involvement I demand. No one ever does. I'll want monthly breakdowns in income and outgoings. Expenses will need to be run through me. And I'll provide the staffing.'

'The staff?' Jamie echoed in confusion.

'Not the chefs, your friend can deal with that. But the waitresses, the kitchen staff, they'll come via me. Those are my terms.'

'Are you a partner in a recruitment agency too?' Jamie was bewildered by this last condition.

A soft laugh. 'Something like that. Another business interest, one I've had for a few years. They'll be decent staff, I assure you.'

'I'll just be happy to be able to pay their wages.'

'They'll be employed by you and your co-owner, but I'll be responsible for them.' A slim file was produced and handed across the table. 'These are my company's accounts. Take them away, have a look through. If you decide you're interested, we'll discuss terms.'

Jamie took the paperwork. 'Will I need to involve Ben in this decision?'

A grin. 'If I were you, I'd keep his involvement to the minimum.'

The man stood, stretching casually with a satisfied yawn. He extended a large hand and Jamie stood to take it, feeling only strength in his grip this time. They held eye contact, just for a moment, and the power in that steady gaze was enough to convince Jamie he was making the right decision.

'It was a pleasure speaking with you, Mr Shaw.'

'Likewise. And please, call me Jamie.'

The man flashed a warm smile as he gathered his coat and turned to leave, glancing back momentarily over his broad shoulder.

'Only if you call me Richard.'

29

Tamsin – Now

It is five endless days before anyone else visits. Five days trapped in my own head, and it's not as if I have any outlet for my vexation. I can't kick a chair or thump a pillow or raise my voice to people.

I can only stew over the grim – if baseless – prognosis Hannah bestowed on me, and over how readily Jamie and Dan took her words as gospel. Before my eyes, streams of neon colour flash in the darkness like a fireworks display. My agitation is in full view, but only for me to witness.

When Jamie eventually arrives for his Wednesday visit, I hear the light tap of little footsteps following his heavier treads and a welcome calm suffuses me. I barely had the chance to acknowledge my daughter at her last visit, before Jamie and Dan took centre stage. I must soak in every moment of her company while I still can.

Surely this won't the last time I'll hear her voice.

'Mummy sleeping,' she whispers, her breath tickling my ear, and I fight to tell her that I am here, listening to her.

She stays with her head pressed close against mine, close enough for me to feel her steady heartbeat. She holds her breath, listening carefully.

'No, Mummy awake, not sleeping,' she reports, as if she has heard me. If only Hannah had such perceptiveness, I think tartly. My daughter hasn't dismissed me so easily. I struggle to make another grunt, to reward Elise's faith in me, but nothing happens.

'Mummy's eyes are closed, sweetheart,' Jamie says gently. 'Look. She's not awake.'

'She *is*.' I recognise the note of stubbornness in her voice, identical to my own, and hope swells my heart.

'I don't think that's quite right, Els,' Jamie persists. 'We wouldn't want that for Mummy. It would mean she was stuck inside. That would be really sad.'

Elise is quiet for a moment, thinking. 'Really sad,' she eventually agrees. Her hand finds mine and squeezes hard. She is trying to reassure me. What I wouldn't give to squeeze her little hand back.

'If that was true, do you think Mummy would be better going to sleep forever?'

A shock of ice runs through my veins. Is Jamie actually asking our daughter her opinion on whether I should live or die?

'Forever?'

'It would mean we wouldn't come here to visit her anymore. We wouldn't see Mummy again, but she'd be safe. She'd be warm and comfortable and happy. She wouldn't have to lie in this bed all day, every day. She'd be free.'

He's laying it on too thick and I wonder if my daughter will notice. 'Free Mummy,' Elise mumbles thoughtfully. She is quiet for a moment. 'Why?'

'Mummy might not want to stay here in her bed forever, sweetheart. You wouldn't want to stay in your bedroom all day, every day, would you?'

Hope seeps away from me. Elise strokes my arm, but I can feel her hesitation now. She sits herself against the headboard, leaning lightly against my side. I strain to move a finger, just one, to caress her skin. I try to breathe more deeply, so she can feel it.

'We've had to make a big choice, Els,' Jamie tells her, keeping his words simple. 'It was very hard.'

There's no reply, but I can feel how hard Elise is listening to him. I can imagine her furrowed brow and her pursed lips as she concentrates.

'It's time to let Mummy go to sleep forever. The day after tomorrow, we're going to come and say goodbye to her for the last time. We're going to tell her we love her and that everything will be OK. Then she won't be scared, and she'll know what will happen.'

Two days.

Two fucking *days*?

That's all the time he's deigned to grant me? That's all I'm worth?

Once they switch off my life support, there's no knowing how long I'll have left. My body could go into shock and shut down within minutes. Or it might take days – a slow and cruel death by dehydration.

How the hell am I supposed to accept that in a matter of hours, instead of turning forty, I could be turning in a grave?

I fight to scream at him, beg him for longer, just one more chance to scale my impossible mountain.

'And then Mummy's gone?' Elise whispers.

'Yes, babe, she'll be gone. And we'll be sad because we'll miss her, but we will know that Mummy's free and not hurting.'

'Happy Mummy?'

'She'll be happy not to be stuck in this hospital anymore. And we'll be happy for her, won't we?'

Elise is murmuring under her breath, repeating some of Jamie's words as she processes the enormity of the conversation. Her hand comes to rest on my chest, and I wonder if she has felt my heart rate speed up.

This really is the end. My execution date is written, and the fact it is on my birthday – a day that should be about growth and hopes for the future – only makes the pain hit harder.

I hear the gentle rustle of a book's pages but the last thing I'm interested in is *Great Expectations*. I am consumed by my immeasurable task.

How will I ever find a way to convince Jamie that I am worth the gift of life?

'Jamie?'

Jamie's reading stops abruptly. I realise Milena is here, and I wonder if she heard anything of Jamie and Elise's conversation.

'I've done enough talking today, Milena.' His voice is raspy.

He fidgets in his chair, waiting for her to speak again. He reaches to take my hand, but I sense it is for show, rather than to comfort either of us.

Something fundamental has changed between Jamie and Milena. There is no more teasing, no more of the light patter that he used to start with her in order to avoid talking to me.

'Why so soon?' she asks. So she did hear him.

'Why prolong it?'

Milena hesitates and I know she is looking at me. I attempt to twitch, to grunt, anything that will confirm her belief, but once again, there is nothing.

'She can't hear us,' Jamie says bluntly. 'Tam's not here, Milena. We all need to start accepting that before we say goodbye to her.'

He might accept it, but I won't. I'll keep battling until I hear the alarms shrill from my monitors. And even then, I won't go easily.

Their voices are silent for several moments and I listen to Jamie flicking through pages, wondering if he can skip ahead.

'I think I should leave,' Milena says.

'You don't have to. We won't stay much longer.'

'No, I mean leave Rushmore. I think it's time to move on.'

My heart thuds. Milena has cared for me since the day I came to Rushmore. I can't bear to lose her. I'm too afraid to do this alone.

'Why would you leave?' Jamie is finally paying attention, mystified. 'I thought you liked it here.'

'You know why.'

'Where will you go?'

'I think I should go home.'

'Is that a good idea?'

Milena snorts a laugh that belies no humour. 'Nothing is a good idea right now.'

'Then stay.'

'I can't. Not now.'

'Do you need money?'

'No, Jamie, you've done enough for me already. I need to sort travel documents, then I can go.'

I don't see what is driving her to leave Rushmore so abruptly. Could it be the prospect of my death, or is there more to it? And what did she mean when she said Jamie has already done enough for her? Perhaps he's helped her out when she's struggled on her low income.

'You don't need to run away. There's no reason to leave, even if Tam is gone.'

'There's every reason. It's not safe anymore.'

They fall silent and I picture them making eye contact over me. I cannot begin to understand what is happening between them, and the loose ends make me swell with frustration. There are so many links I cannot connect, too many questions I cannot ask.

One thing, however, is perfectly clear.

I am fast running out of time.

30

Tamsin – Before

'What's our topic today?' Richard asked as he settled himself in his usual seat.

I had watched him from the window, unhurriedly smoking a slim cigar before his appointment. The aroma still clung to him, leather and parchment and spicy cedar wood.

That day, it was enough to trigger a flashback. They were becoming insidious, seizing on any little occurrence as an excuse to erupt, and I was no closer to getting a grip of them.

I gripped the arms of my chair but it was too late. I was gone.

The man seems to tower over me. I can physically feel his stare, his assessment of me, even though he hasn't touched me. He is so close I can smell him – perspiration, leather, musk – and the heat of his body burns like a furnace. He remains perfectly still, his eyes the only part of him that moves, along with the deep, steady rise and fall of his chest beneath his black waterproof.

He raises a finger to his lips in a shushing motion, and I glimpse the latex gloves. Every instinct is screaming at me to run but no part of my body is responding. Our gazes are locked together, and I can't even blink against the sweat dripping into my eyes.

'Dr Shaw?' Richard asked mildly, as if he didn't think I'd heard him.

I was present again, but the sweat was real, drops of perspiration scattered across my brow. I could still feel the heat of the man.

I reached for my water and downed it.

'Are you ill?' Richard leapt to his feet, refilling my glass from the bottle that sat on the table between us.

I gulped at the fresh glass, tapping my feet until my pulse submitted to the same beat.

'No,' I said. 'I'm fine.'

He sat down again, observing me closely, and I took my time sipping the rest of the water until I could swallow normally. When I spoke again, I sounded like my usual self.

'I'd like to talk about your sentence.'

'I suspected that might be coming up soon.' A tone of discontent, intended for me to notice.

'I understand you'd rather not be reminded of prison, but it's necessary,' I said calmly.

'May I ask why? To lay old ghosts to rest?'

'To appreciate why you wouldn't want to return.'

He pursed his lips. 'You think I'd ever find myself in that place again?'

'This programme is specifically designed to prevent reoffending.'

'I haven't offended in the first place! I assure you, there's little chance of me making that mistake now.' He was getting angry, insulted that I had ignored all his declarations of innocence. His body had tensed, and his words were bitten off sharply.

'Richard, I have a job to do,' I said, taking care to keep my voice even, sitting very still, looking at him but not making eye contact. I focused on the dimple in the centre of his chin. 'You are very different from any client I've had so far on this scheme, and I've already done work with you that I wouldn't have undertaken with others, but at the end of your treatment I will still have to present evidence to the probation service that you will not be a risk to others. The only way I can supply acceptable evidence is to follow the programme.'

His nostrils flared but he didn't interrupt.

'I am not making judgements on your innocence, or otherwise. My role is to be Switzerland.'

He leaned back in his seat, regarding me for a minute. 'You want to know about prison? I met men in there who knew only violence. They'd seen nothing of the world beyond their own small circles. They were offended by the easy life I had led, the opportunities I'd had. It made me re-evaluate rather quickly.'

'Weren't you classed as a vulnerable prisoner?'

'In Wandsworth, yes. I was remanded to Pentonville on an ordinary wing, and I didn't fancy six years of that kind of daily battle. So, when the transfer to Wandsworth was arranged, I asked to be put on the VPU. It wasn't particularly pleasant – I didn't like being grouped with child molesters – but it was better than the alternative.'

'You say "arranged" …'

He shrugged. 'I had a connection rather high up in the justice system, who in turn knew people rather high up in the prison service. Old favours were cashed in, and agreements were reached that Pentonville wasn't the right place for me to serve my sentence.'

No surprises there – I took care not to roll my eyes. 'And what was the worst part of prison, for you?'

'Being stuck inside twenty-two hours a day,' he replied without hesitation. 'The lack of natural light. No fresh air. No trees. All I wanted to do was walk for miles and miles through the country-side or along the Jurassic coast. Just me and a couple of spaniels.'

'You led an outdoorsy lifestyle before your arrest.'

'I was rarely in. I never watched TV or played video games; couldn't stand spending hours staring at a screen. In Dorset, I'd be shooting or riding or fishing in my downtime. In London I went out every night to bars and restaurants, and I ran every morning.'

'Through Battersea Park?' I asked.

His eyes narrowed. 'Sometimes. Why do you ask?'

'The women were attacked there.'

'I know that.' He didn't add any further retort, already looking for my next move.

I waited, recognising how his face had shut down immediately. Either a protective instinct, or denial.

'If you're wondering whether my exercising in Battersea Park formed part of the prosecution's case, yes, it did. Because obviously other men don't run there or own homes which overlook the park or live alone.' Sarcasm momentarily roughens his tone.

'You didn't have alibis? No girlfriends staying over?'

'I wasn't ready to settle down back then,' he said stiffly. 'Plenty of girlfriends but none I let stay over. I liked my own space.'

'I imagine you like it even more now, after eight years in a five-by-five cell.'

He smiled, genial once again. 'I love my apartment. I inherited it from my father, but it looks a lot better than it did in his time. I redecorated, enlarged the windows.'

'It must be quite a view from them.'

The smile vanished. 'You think I should shy away from looking at the park?'

'I would struggle with its associations.'

'If I was guilty, so would I.'

The challenge hung in the air, but I refused to respond to it, looking back steadily at him until he was the one to glance away. I watched his chest swell as he took a deep breath.

'I have a question for you.'

I recognised the now-familiar attempt to redirect me and allowed irony to enter my tone. 'Don't you always?'

'This one's a little different. I was wondering if I could take your number. I'd like to ask you to lunch.'

That simple statement robbed me momentarily of the ability to speak. Of everything I could have anticipated from Richard, such a brazen proposal was not on the list.

'We can't do that, Richard,' I finally said, my lips numb.

'I mean later, when I'm no longer your client. I'd like to see you again, on a non-professional basis.'

A thousand replies reverberated through my brain, panic lending wings to each one until I couldn't separate them.

'There are ethics, guidelines.'

'Guidelines,' he emphasised. 'Not rules.'

This wasn't a time for semantics. 'Why would you want to take me to lunch?' I almost whispered, as if fearing being overheard.

'I feel we've connected and, to be honest, it's the last thing I expected to happen when I agreed to meet with a psychiatrist. It's caught me off guard.'

He wasn't the only one.

'You're a very special person, Tamsin. I suspect you don't realise just how extraordinary your abilities are. I've never met someone with your depth, your capabilities.'

I was aware of what he was trying to do. Persuasion would follow the flattery, and this was a man who was used to women falling at his feet. I had not yet seen how he dealt with rejection, but my instincts had already told me the answer, and I didn't want to push him into that danger zone.

'I'd lose my job, Richard, you have to understand that. I can't see you socially. We can't remain in contact after our work is done.'

'But what if we ran into each other in a bar?' He posed the question as hypothetical, even though I knew it wasn't. 'You wouldn't join me for a drink?'

I deliberately laid my palm across my bump. 'I couldn't. I'm sorry.'

A shadow crossed his face, just momentarily, but I spotted it before he smiled and shrugged, making a show of ruefulness.

'Not to worry. Can't blame me for trying.' He sat back, stretching his arms above his head as if shaking off the tension. 'We'll say no more about it.'

I knew he was lying and the temptation to challenge him was strong, but I restrained myself. It would do no good to rattle him yet.

The time for that was not far away, but I had more work to do first.

As I completed the day's paperwork, my phone pinged with a text, and I reached for it in the hope it would be Jamie.

Dan: *I'm heading to Lito's, come meet me?*

I reflexively started to type a refusal, but something made me stop. After the discomfort of Richard's proposition, I didn't want to be alone. I felt on edge, jittery, even though Richard had been good as his word for the remainder of the session, acting like nothing had happened.

Finally, I accepted Dan's invitation. For old time's sake, I told myself.

Before I buttoned up my coat, I stared into the full-length mirror affixed to the back of my office door. Checking the blinds were closed, I pulled my polo neck up to my bra, turning to every angle to examine the gentle curve of my belly.

Since the first scan, I had been assessing my body like this daily. In my bedroom, fresh from the shower, my eyes would rove greedily over the ladder of muscles running down my abdomen, looking for any signs of them softening.

But even by week sixteen, I'd just looked like I'd indulged in a larger meal than usual that day. I started eating more, calorie-counting in a way I'd never had to before, but my reliable metabolism was still firing on all cylinders and eating up the extra energy.

It was exhausting and frustrating in equal measure.

I drove to Lito's rather than battle the Tube, arriving to find Dan already crunching his way through a basket of prawn crackers. My mouth watered involuntarily at the intoxicating smells of garlic, ginger and lemongrass that filled the air.

'How are you?' he asked.

Exhausted. Aching. Regularly on the verge of tears. 'Fine, thanks,' I said brightly.

I ordered a host of starters rather than a main: calorie-rich chicken satay, fish cakes fried in peanut oil, sticky ribs glistening with sauce, a mountain of rice noodles packed with stir-fried vegetables to go with it all. Dan's face was a picture; he had never seen me attempt to eat so much.

'The baby needs to grow more,' I explained as I broke crackers in half and scooped up sweet chilli sauce. 'They've said I'm too thin. My body isn't providing enough nourishment for her.'

'You're five months now, aren't you? Twenty-one weeks?'

'You've been keeping track.'

'Of course I have. You're barely showing.'

'I know.' I smoothed my jumper. 'I'm glad, really. It still feels my little secret.'

'You must have had the second scan now. Did you find out the sex?'

I considered saying I hadn't, but did it make so much difference, if Dan knew? 'A girl.'

His eyes softened. 'A girl,' he repeated. 'And everything's OK?'

'Apart from being a bit small, she's developing normally. I had the amniocentesis, just to be sure. Everything came back fine.'

Dan nodded, as if convincing himself. 'And how's it going with Mandeville?'

'You've read my reports. It's going well.'

'He's engaging.'

'Very much so. I think he's getting a lot out of it, certainly more than he expected to.'

'You sound pleased.'

'I am. I expected him to be a difficult client, but he's been nothing but cooperative. He's quite interested in the whole process.'

Dan snorted.

'He's not a stupid man, Dan. Don't make the mistake of thinking he's some thick aristo.'

'He's a predator.'

I took my time eating a fishcake. 'Have you heard anything about his appeal process?'

'Only that it's moving at lightning speed. It's causing a bit of tension around my office.'

'So he might actually be granted a retrial.'

'When it comes to Mandeville, I think anything's possible. He's got fingers in every pie going.'

'What would happen if he was found innocent?'

'Uproar. No doubt he'd sue. It would be the biggest travesty in the UK justice system for decades. I dread to think what the inquiry would be like.' He shook his head sharply. 'I can't think about that happening.'

He wolfed down half of his Pad Thai before he spoke again.

'I feel like you've been avoiding me.'

'I'm trying to get all my clients through the programme before the baby comes. I haven't much time, or much energy, for socialising.'

'I haven't done anything wrong?'

'No, Dan.' I gave him the reassurance he needed, barely managing not to wince when I saw how eagerly he grasped it.

It was unfair on him. I knew it was, and I acknowledged the guilt I felt for that. Dan was a pawn, an unintentional one. He happened to have been in the right place at the right time.

I shouldn't have got him drunk that night, after the awards dinner. He asked for singles, and I provided doubles. I shouldn't have gone back to his hotel room and stripped him naked as he sprawled, hopeless in the grip of whisky and wine.

But I was ruled by desire, driven by obsession, and I couldn't prevent myself. I was compelled to do it. It wasn't Dan's fault it had happened.

I had made it impossible to avoid.

31

Tamsin – Before

'I have something to show you.'

Richard held out a Manila file, the papers inside meticulously arranged. I glanced through them, noting the official headers, as Richard watched me carefully. I suspected he already knew the contents by heart.

'I've been granted my initial appeal hearing.'

'How the hell did you manage that so quickly?'

He tried, and failed, to conceal a grin. 'Connections, shall we say.'

'A peerage has many advantages.'

'I'm not a patient man. I've wasted enough time, Dr Shaw. Now is the time for action.'

'Spoken like a true soldier,' I said lightly, to defuse the fire that had ignited in his flint-grey eyes.

I returned the file to him, watching him tidy it back into the correct order, aligning the pages precisely. He placed it squarely on the table between us, adjusting it when it didn't sit quite right.

'Is there any point continuing with the programme?' he asked.

His abruptness was uncharacteristic, and I sat back in my seat, creating more space between us. He noticed.

'My reports will be used at your appeal hearing, and at any retrial that may be granted. It's best to keep going. You'll need all the evidence you can get.'

He shrugged. For the first time, he looked bored, uninterested in me and the process we were going through. It often happened as clients reached the latter stages of the programme. The end was in sight, and they became eager to escape from this weekly scrutiny into their psyche.

I had expected Richard to be different. He hadn't hated coming here, not like so many others. He had resented some of my questions, but that was only to be expected.

He seemed to have actually enjoyed my company, and I had come to look forward to our verbal sparring. He had tested me in a way that hadn't happened for years, forcing me to prepare for each session to ensure he didn't best me.

'We're going to talk about women today,' I told him, as if offering an observation about the weather.

He tensed. 'Women in general, or women of my acquaintance?'

'In general.'

'Rather an odd topic, Dr Shaw.'

'Not if you think about why we're here.'

'You mean why we're *meant* to be here. Our meetings have taken a rather different course from what was prescribed.'

I couldn't disagree with him there. 'We've meandered at times, yes, but this is an intended focus. What are your feelings towards women?'

'I'm finding this question rather hard to grasp. It changes depending on the situation. I feel differently about my mother and sister, for example, than I do about you. In turn, I feel differently about you than I do about my cleaner. Same goes for a woman I might buy a drink for versus one I may intend to marry.'

'Very concise. Do you find women appealing?' I kept my tone steady, giving no hint of the trap I was laying for him.

'Obviously not all of them.'

'Do they irritate you?' It was a leading question, but one I felt justified to ask.

'Some female habits do, yes. I'm not a fan of gossip or backbiting.'

'That's quite a generalisation.'

'You'd understand if you moved in the same social circles as me,' he laughed. 'Don't glare at me like that. It wasn't a sexist comment.'

I begged to differ, but I let it go for the moment. That wasn't my agenda. 'Do women ever anger you? Ex-girlfriends, maybe?'

'Sandhurst trains any hothead tendencies out of you pretty quickly. They expect discipline and self-control. I've carried that with me into civilian life.'

'Do you ever lose your temper?'

'Of course. Not often, but I wouldn't be human if I didn't. Do you?'

'Like you, not often. I like to focus my frustration so it doesn't overwhelm me.' I challenged him with my eyes. 'What makes you angry?'

He shrugged. I saw his eyes drift to the ceiling. 'Lying. Cheating. Dishonesty in general.'

He was giving me the answers he thought I wanted to hear but, for once, I didn't push for the truth.

'And you?' he asks.

'Apathy,' I said immediately, not needing to think. 'And resignation.'

My response surprised him. Both eyebrows jumped.

'I never give up,' I told him. 'Once I have my mind set, I'll see it through to the end.'

'Admirable. You'd have done well in the military.' He grinned. It was his turn to try and lighten the atmosphere, for once. I had unsettled him. 'I'd have happily had you in my unit.'

'Were there women in your unit?'

'No, only the local translators in Kosovo, the ones you saw in that photo.'

'How did you get along with them?'

'Very well. They were excellent company, could drink me under the table. They helped me learn the languages.'

'I imagine it was a patriarchal society, the Balkans.'

'Not like the Middle East, but more so than I expected. Most of the other women we encountered were terrified of us. The men were hospitable, but when they invited us into their houses, the women hid themselves away in the kitchen.'

'The kitchen might have been the place they felt safest.'

Richard blew out an impatient breath, as if he couldn't possibly fathom feeling threatened. 'My translator was great. Katya. She had two young kids at home, but she came out every day, stood shoulder-to-shoulder with us even as pot-shots were ringing out all around. In Kandahar, we were surrounded by men, but they weren't half as good as Katya and her colleagues.'

'Did you keep in touch, after the war ended?'

'For a while.' He looked away. 'It was difficult.'

He was becoming edgy, squirming in his seat, crossing and uncrossing his legs. I was slightly perturbed by his nervous energy when he began pinching his philtrum between finger and thumb, tugging on the flesh. I had never noticed him do that before.

'What's the matter?' I asked softly.

'I missed my run this morning. Sorry, am I annoying you? My mother always said I'm an utter irritation when I've not tired myself out with exercise.'

'It's just different, that's all.'

'You normally see me after a morning 10k and a swim. I'm much easier to deal with after that.'

'Why not this morning?'

'Poor timekeeping.'

'We can shorten the session.'

'No.' He shook his head and smiled. 'I don't want to.'

His eyes strayed to my hand as I raised it to brush aside a strand of hair that had escaped my bun.

'May I ask about your scar? I've seen it often. It must have been a bad injury.'

My fingers automatically reached to touch the mark. I considered telling him we were straying into the realm of personal questions again, but the urge was there to answer.

'I was mugged, eight years ago.'

'Christ, where?'

'Oh, close to home.'

'That's an awful thing to go through. Did they get away with much?'

'Too much,' I said shortly, running my finger down the scar. 'He had a knife. I suppose I was lucky it was my palm rather than anything worse, but I still needed two surgeries on it.'

I stared at the white slash mark – a reminder of the darkness in the world, of what that day had cost me. My pulse had begun to thud, as the ghosts of my own cries echoed painfully through my ears. I could smell the grass my face had been pressed into, feel the bruising pressure of fingers on my cheek as much as the searing pain from my bleeding hand.

'Tamsin? Are you alright?'

The flashback was keeping a tenuous grip, but I fought to fix my attention on Richard. 'Sorry. Baby brain.'

'Of all the people in the world, you're the last I'd expect to be susceptible to that.'

'You'd be surprised. Even shrinks can be vulnerable.'

That seemed to capture his attention. His voice dropped to a confidential murmur, inviting me to trust him. 'And what are you vulnerable to?'

I didn't want to go there. I didn't want to open the box, but it was beyond my control, a compulsion I couldn't quash.

'After the mugging, I didn't cope very well. I was afraid to go anywhere alone. I was convinced I was being followed. I became quite paranoid.'

'That's understandable after such a scary experience.'

'It was worse than that.'

I couldn't say it. I didn't know how to say it. But the words were on my lips without conscious thought.

'I was pregnant,' I whispered. 'I lost the baby. The stress of the mugging, I blamed it on.'

'My God, Tamsin, I'm so sorry.'

I barely registered his repeated use of my first name. He leaned forward, gently taking my hand in his. I resisted the urge to snatch it away. I couldn't raise my eyes to his, and focussed on breathing, steadying myself. In and out. In and out. The baby needed me to be calm.

'It's OK if you need to step out,' Richard said.

It would take more than a moment for me to collect myself. The walls were closing in on me. I had to leave the office before I suffocated under its feverish atmosphere.

'I need some air,' I gasped.

Richard was on his feet in a moment, grabbing my coat from the hook and holding it out for me.

'Let's walk,' he suggested, already opening the door. 'Just round the block. We could both do with clearing our heads.'

I should have insisted I go alone. I was breaking every guideline that had ever been established, putting myself at a risk I had always stringently protected myself from.

I stepped past Richard into the hallway, nodding at the security guard as he pulled himself to attention, ready to intervene. I saw his hesitation and made eye contact with him, silently letting him know that I knew what I was doing, but he hovered at the door as we left, shifting from foot to foot, and I could feel him watching our every step.

Drinking in the blissful fresh air, I allowed Richard to fall into step with me. His hand hovered solicitously at my elbow, ready to catch me if my legs couldn't hold me.

We walked in silence, down the steps at the edge of London Bridge, into the jumble of narrow, cobbled streets surrounding the market, until we passed the Golden Hinde and were by the river. Richard stopped at the rail, looking down into the lapping water.

'May I tell you something?'

'Of course.' I was glad to speak. The voices inside my head were close to overwhelming me and conversation was a distraction I needed.

'When I asked you to lunch, it wasn't an impulsive invitation.'

'I never thought it was.'

'I'd been mulling it over for a while, whether to ask you or not.'

'Surely you knew I wouldn't be able to accept.'

'I suppose I wondered if you'd be prepared to break the *guidelines*.'

The emphasis wasn't lost on me, but I remained quiet, giving him no indication of what my response would be.

He turned his head, watching me for a long moment. 'I never imagined I would want to spend more time with someone whose job was to make me uncomfortable.'

'That was never my intention,' I felt required to say. 'Therapy shouldn't be that way.'

'Does anyone enjoy having their deepest thoughts openly dissected?' he retorted.

'Not many people.'

'And yet I've liked coming here. It's not been easy, but I've never come to dread an appointment. All because of you.' He checked my expression, trying to read me. 'I like to think you've found our meetings to be positive encounters?'

'I have.'

'Then would it be so bad, seeing me outside of work?'

I took my time trying and failing to construct an intelligent answer. I couldn't think of anything to say that wouldn't sound ridiculous. He was waiting, tapping his fingers casually against the railing as if my hesitation wasn't an issue.

'You can name the time and place. Wherever you'd feel comfortable. Somewhere no one would know either of us.'

'Richard, what would it achieve?' I managed to say. 'I'm a married woman near to giving birth. More than that, I'm a professional with the influence to affect your appeal.'

'You think that's what this is?' His jaw tightened. 'That I want to smooth-talk you into giving me a positive report, like a badly behaved schoolboy? As if I couldn't have already done that ten times over.'

There it was, that expectation of total command. He concealed it so well and I could imagine many women would never know it was there until he chose to show them.

'Then what is it?' I pressed, my own distress forgotten in the face of this sudden turn.

'It's you, Tamsin. Don't you understand? I can't stop thinking about you. You're never out of my mind.'

It was so clever, how he turned the tables, putting me in control. Handing me the reins, expecting me to defer.

I understood then. With sudden crystal clarity, I knew what I had to do.

'I'll meet you,' I said, my voice perfectly steady despite the churning deep in my gut. The baby stirred, unsettled. 'But not in a restaurant. I can't risk being seen.'

He was quiet for a moment, processing, before a smile tugged at the corners of his mouth. 'Whatever you want.' He stretched out a hand, palm up. 'Though I'd better take your number, to be sure you won't fob me off.'

I had a business card ready. Our fingers touched as I held it out to him, the snap of static making me jump.

I wasn't naïve enough to give him my personal number, but I kept my work phone with me at most times. Unable to switch off, literally and figuratively.

His smile widened, and another brick in the wall crumbled and fell.

I called Lucia as I drove home that evening, my mind far from the road as I navigated Shadwell, heading for the Limehouse Basin without any recollection of my journey so far.

'Would you hate me if I did something stupid?' I asked her, not really sure what I was saying but somehow needing to voice the storm of thoughts reverberating inside my pounding head.

'What's wrong?' she asked immediately. 'Are you OK? Is the baby alright?'

'We're both fine.' I caressed my bump with one hand, even though I was usually strict about keeping both hands on the wheel.

'But you're planning on doing something stupid?'

'It's not actually stupid. It's for a reason, a very good one, but –'

'But it's something that will put you at risk,' Lucia finished for me. 'Tell me what it is.'

'I can't. Not yet.'

'How can I help you if you don't tell me?'

'I just need to know. Would you forgive me?'

'Forgive you for what?' Her voice rose with exasperation. 'Tam, you're scaring me. Are you safe?'

'Yes, I'm safe.'

'You need to tell me what's going on.'

'I will. Soon. I promise. It's important, Lu. You'll understand.'

'I don't understand anything right now.'

'I want you to forgive me, if it goes wrong.'

'I'll forgive you anything, you know that, but this doesn't sound safe, whatever it is.'

'It's a risk,' I admitted, 'but I'm willing to take it.'

'And what will it achieve?'

'So much,' I whispered. 'I'm sorry, Lucia.'

'What are you sorry for? Tam, for God's sake, I'm in Kent but I'll get in the car this second if you keep talking like this.'

'No. Stay in Kent. Have you taken Matty for the weekend?'

'Yes, we needed some space from Ben. We'll be here till Monday. I think we're going to start spending more time here ... and don't change the subject! I know your tricks.'

I huffed a laugh, gripping the steering wheel. 'I'll see you when you're back in London. Love you.'

'Love you lots,' she murmured back. 'Can I trust you not to do this stupid thing while I'm away?'

'You can,' I assured her.

I wouldn't be able to do it this weekend. Not just yet. But I had started something that needed to be finished. And no matter what I chose to do next, the hourglass had been turned. My timing would need to be perfect.

32

Jamie – Now

This time, the meeting takes place at a greasy spoon in Elephant and Castle. When Jamie arrives, his investor is already seated. Even in jeans and a North Face hoodie, Richard looks out of place here amongst the regular clientele. A mug of tea sits before him, untouched, and he tilts his head back, observing his surroundings with hooded eyes.

Jamie goes to the counter to order a bacon roll, just to annoy him, taking his time collecting his own tea before reluctantly sitting down. Richard is already extending his hand for the printouts. He will not accept any electronic paperwork. He scans the figures, pausing only to glare as Jamie's heavily buttered sandwich is delivered.

Jamie sinks his teeth into it, chewing slowly. Richard wrinkles his nose and glares at the food.

'We have some new waitresses waiting for their induction,' he states.

Jamie swallows the bite that has turned to sawdust in his mouth, putting the remains of his breakfast down and pushing the plate away.

'I'll need you to try harder to keep these ones,' Richard says. 'The staff turnover is still far higher than I'd like.'

'You never struggle to find replacements,' Jamie mutters.

'They're easy enough to come by.'

'You make them sound like trophies.'

The other man smirks. 'Something like that.'

Richard folds the printouts and stores them in the inside pocket of his coat, attempting to push back his plastic seat before realising it is attached to the table, which momentarily puzzles him as he examines the structure.

'It's so the chairs can't be thrown,' Jamie explains, permitting himself a brief grin.

A raised eyebrow is the only reaction. 'Are you finished with your food? It's time to go.'

Jamie has no choice but to follow him. The sandwich sits heavily in his stomach, making him feel slightly nauseous, and he is glad to leave the fumes of frying meat behind.

Richard leads him around the corner to a scruffy car park on the site of a demolished tower block. The warden ignores them as they pass the booth, Richard heading straight for an unremarkable silver Volkswagen SUV.

'This is my alternative transport,' he announces, unlocking the doors.

'Registered to an alternative identity, I suppose,' Jamie mutters, as they both get in. It has the neutral smell of a car that is either rarely used or cleaned regularly.

'Careful, Jamie, you're starting to sound like a stroppy teenager. You're welcome to drive.'

'No, thank you.' As if he is stupid enough to put himself behind the wheel of a ghost car.

Richard laughs softly and starts the engine, the tyres crunching on the gravel as they pull out into the traffic.

Jamie despises this process, every time the investor brings in new employees. At best it is shameful to be a part of; at worst, it is dehumanising.

They drive to Shadwell, through the maze of streets behind the hulking estates that flank the DLR tracks, and he knows they will arrive at yet another anonymous house, buried in a neighbourhood used to a highly transient population, where no one will look closely or ask too many questions.

This house, yet another Jamie will only visit once, is just like all the others – a narrow terrace with dirty windows and an overgrown path, which wouldn't warrant a second glance. The faded front door is opened immediately. He doesn't bother to greet the stocky, swarthy man who permits them entry. Jamie has seen him several times now, but the fixer changes so regularly that Jamie no longer asks for any names.

In the kitchen, four women sit at the cheap veneer table, drinking black coffee. They are all in their late teens or early twenties, young enough to be smooth-skinned and bright-eyed, looking forward to their new lives. If they understand the price they will pay, they show no fear of it. Some accept it as part of the deal, to escape unemployment or violent homelives, to provide for families. Others are less compliant, and it is those who don't last long as waitresses.

They look up as Jamie enters the room, interested in his appearance, taking him in. They all smile in recognition of Richard, some greeting him by name, asking how he is. He replies with a wide grin and affable gestures before turning away, taking hold of the fixer's arm to draw him close.

'Where's the fifth?' he asks, his tone abruptly icy.

A shrug. 'Didn't get on the boat.'

A hiss of irritation. 'And you couldn't have told me earlier?' He swings round to Jamie, a muscle flickering in his jaw. 'They're all yours. I'll be in touch.'

Several further questions crowd Jamie's mind, but he knows better than to ask them. He watches Richard stalk out, followed quickly by the fixer. The front door slams a few moments later.

Jamie faces the women, trying to look reassuring, non-threatening. They smile back.

'My name is Jamie,' he tells them, like he always does. 'You will be working at my restaurant.'

He uses slow, simple sentences, not knowing if they all speak English. One nods competently and relays the information to the others in their own language.

Jamie joins them at the table as the fixer returns, his expression dark. The man is carrying the usual messenger bag. From it, he produces a passport and a national insurance card and sets them in front of Jamie. Jamie opens his tablet and notes the details, before the documents are passed to the first woman. The process is repeated three more times. The women are all of the same nationality, but now they are assigned two Latvian passports, one Hungarian and an Estonian. Their real paperwork will already have been taken when they arrived on a lonely English shoreline in the depth of night.

'You are our boss?' the first woman asks.

'At the restaurant, yes.'

'Where do we live?'

'I don't arrange any of that.' Jamie nods to the fixer, who speaks a few rapid sentences. All four nod in unison, eager to please.

The formalities done, the fixer issues another round of instructions, and the women gather their coats, waiting expectantly. Jamie knows the drill. He leaves without any goodbyes, letting the women follow him at a distance, not attracting any attention. They walk quietly, glancing around them at their unfamiliar surroundings, until they reach the DLR station.

It takes all four of them to work the ticket machine, struggling with the money, as Jamie keeps a watchful eye from a distance. They don't raise any suspicion, assumed to be tourists, and they successfully trot onto the next train, sitting at the opposite end of the car to Jamie.

He waits for them at the doors of Porteños, greeting them as if they have never met before when they arrive several minutes behind him. They are smiling in awe of the towering chrome buildings and luxury cars, thrilled at the evidence of wealth and status, chattering amongst themselves in their own language. Jamie comforts himself imagining the hard, grey lives they have left behind.

The maître d' takes them off to dole out uniforms and aprons and give them the brief induction. He is expressionless as always. Maybe he doesn't want to know about the agency who sends them a steady stream of staff. Maybe he just doesn't care.

Jamie tries to deny that he cares, too. But the churning of his gut and the lingering nausea say otherwise.

33

Tamsin – Now

The visitor enters my room so quietly that I don't notice until the door clicks softly closed.

I tense, trying to work out who it is. It is Thursday – I'm not expecting any visitors until tomorrow, when Jamie comes to wish me happy birthday and sign my death warrant. The ghost of cigar smoke finally reaches my nostrils.

Oh God. Richard is here again.

'Hello, Dr Shaw,' he says and my heart jumps at the sound of his voice, bursting out of the silence. 'I'll greet you formally today. You never were comfortable with me calling you Tamsin, were you?'

Maybe not, but it hadn't stopped him doing it whenever he thought my mind was too occupied to notice. I don't like the way he is using it now, as if he is goading me, knowing full well that this time I can't fire back a retort.

He doesn't sit. I listen to him wander the room and imagine him examining any pictures affixed to the walls, looking out at the view.

'This place must cost a pretty penny,' he says. 'Jamie's in a fortunate position to afford the fees. Money wasn't so readily available to him when we first met, was it?'

His words have a dangerous edge. What does he know about Jamie's financial situation? I may have slipped and allowed a brief mention of my husband, but I certainly hadn't stooped so low as to discuss our private circumstances.

'I have to thank you,' he says. 'I wasn't expecting our appointments to present me with a business opportunity.'

What is he talking about? I hold my breath, straining to hear accurately. There is a different rhythm to his voice, and I realise he is teasing, playing with me.

'You were talking to Dan Attwood after one of our early sessions. I happened to have stopped outside your office for a smoke when you opened the window. It was interesting to hear of Jamie's predicament, so I decided to treat myself to lunch at Porteños.' His tone becomes smug. 'And there was Jamie and his idiot of a partner, willing to cooperate. By the time Jamie was worried enough to start asking, it was too late to back out and my operation was in full swing again.'

Comprehension smacks me in the face, so hard I genuinely feel its sting. No wonder Jamie has kept the identity of his miraculous investor so tightly under wraps.

Has he any idea what he's done?

'He had no idea I was a client of yours, of course. In fact, he didn't work it out until he saw the news of my retrial. Not that he could risk drawing attention to his newfound knowledge, once he realised who he was in business with.'

Richard is still moving around the room and his voice is disorienting, coming at me from all angles.

'He's desperate to rid himself of me. His businesses are stable now. He doesn't want to be beholden to me anymore.' I sense his smile. 'Unfortunately, it's not his choice. His profits are useful income, and I can't see any reason for us to part company just yet.'

How can Jamie have been such a fool? In taking Richard's money, he has backed himself into a corner far darker than he can know. What kind of *operation* has Richard trapped him in?

'But, anyway,' Richard continues, as if we are chatting over a glass of wine. 'That's not why I'm here. We have more urgent business to discuss.'

He continues to pace but the genial tone, the relaxed body language, are gone. His strides have shortened, his feet clipping sharply against the floor.

'Did you know Attwood has managed to get an Amnesty International report included in the trial?' As before, he speaks as if he is fully expecting me to reply.

Dan has done well. I had doubted he would succeed in convincing the judge of its relevance. It will not have been an easy report to present to the jury, with its detailed coverage of the abuse suffered by Kosovar women at the hands of foreign soldiers.

'They spent today *analysing* how I might have learned my trade over there. Like they have a clue what it's like in a war zone where any man, woman or child could kill you in a moment.'

His trade. That's a neat way to describe sex trafficking. I wonder how long it took him to reveal his true nature amidst those bombed-out villages.

His agitation becomes palpable. The report has blindsided him, exposed him in a way he couldn't have anticipated. Dan was right. It had all started in the Balkans, exploitation of a population too broken to fight back, and Richard had been part of it.

'It's a feeling no civilian can understand. You have such power, yet you can be made powerless in a moment. That's why you have to take control.'

I understand why he feels compelled to confide in me. The trial has, for the first time, left him wrong-footed. And while it was always my job to listen to his innermost thoughts, I'm in no position to expose them.

'I was a different man when I came back from Kosovo,' he says, as if we are once again in my office, analysing his past. 'Something had changed in me. The things I saw ... they revulsed me at first ... then it started to intrigue me, the depravity men were capable of. I wanted to know what it felt like to have that sort of power. Different from any kind I'd ever had before. It consumed me.'

I have never heard him talk like this. It scares and fascinates me in equal measure. I had been so sure I had got under his skin, extracted his secrets, seen his true self laid bare.

'Maybe you're the first person who's ever really understood me,' he whispers. 'The things we talked about, information I'd never trust another person with. Perhaps I was a fool, Dr Shaw, but I was so certain of our connection when I was under your care. I never thought you'd betray me.'

A sudden sensation sweeps over me as the finality of that statement sinks in. It comes out of nowhere. Electricity courses through me, like lightning is shooting through my veins. The emotions are too much; they are overwhelming me, a suffocating pillow wielded by my own incapacity. My throat is swelling with the scream trapped inside it and my heart is pounding so hard I can hear its frantic beat. My monitors are surely going crazy, but Richard doesn't seem to be showing any alarm. He has gone very still, and I can feel his eyes on me.

A spasm runs down one arm. It is stronger than anything I have ever felt before, a mule's kick.

My fingers twitch.

Then my toes clench.

The breath stalls in my lungs. It can't be. It is a phantom sensation, surely.

I try again with both hands. The fingers all move. I can feel my toes brushing against the soft sheets.

It's really happening.

I hear Richard move, stepping close to me. His fingers come to rest on top of mine and I twitch them again, stretching the joints, pushing them against his smooth skin.

'Do it again,' he urges. 'Move your hand.'

My body is wracked with tension, quivering, as I slowly form a loose fist.

'My God, you really can hear me.' There is wonder in his voice. 'They were wrong. You are waking up.'

He looms over me, so close to my face that I can smell the brandy on his breath.

'I could have killed you long ago if I'd wanted to, Dr Shaw.' His tone lightens again, becomes conversational. 'But your accident took care of that for me. Put you safely out of the way.'

He pauses, watching me, waiting.

'If you're coming back, you're a threat to me again. Aren't you? You know too much.'

The menace of his words chills me to the bone. Because I know exactly what Richard is capable of.

An image flashes in my mind. It is different from all the others. It is clear and sharp with colour.

I see Richard's face. But it is at a distance, contorted with rage, ugly in its fury. For once, the image doesn't flicker away before I can see properly, and I realise it is a reflection in a car's rear-view mirror.

My car, my beloved Mini Cooper. Driving too fast down a winding country lane.

And, as the memory roots itself back into my mind, I see Benicio Aguero in the passenger seat beside me, bracing his hands against the dashboard, his body clenched tight. I see his terror.

'Richard!' The cry is sharp, echoing around the room.

The image vanishes. Richard leaps away from the bed and I hear his breathing quicken; he has been caught off guard.

'Milena?' Disbelief radiates from him, but then he catches himself and I can picture the grin spreading across his face. 'I shouldn't be surprised, my two favourite girls in one place.'

I don't have time to wonder how Milena and Richard could possibly know each other before Milena yells something in the Slavic tongue. To my amazement, Richard raps out a reply in the same language.

Just like that, I understand. Not what they are saying, but the link. I know for sure now that the language is from the Serbo-

Croat family, learned by Richard from his translator during the war.

Milena is not Polish. She is Kosovar.

'Why are you here, Richard?' I have never heard her sound like this. She exudes an animal instinct, fear and defiance meeting head on. 'What do you want with Tamsin?'

'I don't think that's any of your business. I should ask what you're doing here. Your bosses won't be pleased to know your ID is fake.'

'Leave Tamsin alone. She isn't part of this.'

'But she is, Milena. She's one of the biggest parts.'

'You already caused her car crash. Isn't that enough for her to suffer?'

'The crash?' There is mirth in Richard's tone. 'You've decided I'm to blame for that?'

'You wanted her dead. Her case notes were a threat to you.'

His voice hardens. 'I'm losing patience now. Get out of my way.'

I hear sharp movement, the strain of clothing, the squeak of shoes trying to catch purchase on the floor. Milena lets out a cry and panic grips me.

'Sir!' Hannah's voice rings out. 'What are you doing?'

Richard steps smartly backwards, as Hannah's footsteps rush across the room.

'Give it to me, please.' Her command is uncompromising, and I picture her holding out her hand like a teacher confiscating a banned item from her pupil. Hannah is a person I have never associated with true authority but, at this moment, she sounds entirely in charge of the situation.

I don't hear Richard move but there comes the sound of something light, like a cigarette lighter or a pen, being placed on my bedside table before being snatched up almost immediately.

'Why did you have a syringe?' Hannah's voice wobbles just slightly, and I realise she is afraid. Of the answer or of Richard, I can't tell. 'What was in it?'

'It was on the floor,' Richard says, in a tone of pure, breezy innocence. 'Someone must have dropped it. I was only picking it up.'

There is an urgent thump as Hannah hits the emergency buzzer.

'Have you given her anything?' she demands. I hear the creak of her grabbing the monitor's screen, yanking it towards her, examining my vital signs.

'Of course not,' Richard says smoothly. His voice tells me he is now at the door. 'She's fine. In fact, she was wriggling her fingers just now. I'll get out of your way.'

In the rush of footsteps as other staff hurry in, I don't hear Richard leave. My mind is racing so fast I am flooded by dizziness and nausea. There is only one reason Richard would have brought a syringe with him. I know how quickly air embolisms can kill, once even a tiny bubble has been introduced into a vein or port site.

I have a sinking feeling that Hannah has just saved my life.

'Tamsin?' I hear Milena's voice. I hear her fear.

Something strange is happening. I try to flex my extremities again, to prove my accomplishment to them, but nothing moves. I can't feel my fingers or toes. I realise I can't feel anything, just an icy cold seeping through me.

The darkness seems to be getting stronger. My entire body is being crushed by an invisible weight, making it impossible to draw breath. A terrible pain carves through my shoulder blades, exploding through my sternum.

'Get the crash cart!' I hear Hannah yell.

Their voices are fading. The sounds of panicked movements are no longer audible. The darkness has become a black lake, the water shimmering gently as silence flows over me.

This time, I don't fight. It can take me, if it wants.

There is a rhythmic pumping that I can barely feel. Oxygen is forced into my nose and mouth. It continues for a couple of minutes, and I am now certain it is a futile task.

I wait.

Then a punch is delivered to my chest, fast, brutal. It winds me, the breath whooshing from my lungs. It happens again, and this time pain jolts through me, white-hot and sharp.

The darkness lifts. Blurred colour leaks into my vision. At first, I don't understand what I am seeing. I feel a mask over my face, invasive and uncomfortable. I thrash my head from side-to-side, trying to escape it.

Abruptly, I realise what I have been able to do.

My eyelids fly open of their own accord and, just like that, the world is waiting to greet me. I see Milena's pale, beautiful face, stained with tears, for the first time.

And it is like I have known her forever.

34

Tamsin – Before

As I had predicted, Richard didn't wait until we were no longer psychiatrist and client. He didn't even wait until our last appointment.

And so I found myself in Chelsea, in step with Richard once again as we walked along a street lined with multi-million pound properties, in the shadow of the suspension ropes of the Albert Bridge. In one pocket, my phone felt warm with the reassurance of the tracking app tracing my every step. In the other, a slim tube of pepper spray nestled, an insurance policy I prayed I wouldn't need.

And in my breast pocket, a mini voice-recording device, no bigger than a fifty pence piece, ordered just for this occasion.

'Here we are,' Richard announced, turning into a gateway.

It was a handsome period building, four stories of red brick and white facades, bay windows, and gleaming black and gold railings. It was a building that spoke of money and status and gilded lives. The baby kicked once, hard. A warning I had to ignore.

A porter, dressed in a subtle black waistcoat and starched white shirt, opened the door as if cued and greeted Richard respectfully. His presence was enough to stabilise my shaky resolve.

The wide communal hallway was original tiles and ivory walls, leading to the curved oak staircase. Richard led me up the first flight to a polished mahogany door, barred by a series of heavy-duty locks.

That little detail told me more about him than any session so far had.

Inside, the flat was understated, tasteful, the living room large and flooded with light from the bay window at the front and the three tall sashes at the back of the open-plan kitchen. It was scrupulously clean, not a thing out of place. I kept my coat on, mindful of the hidden device recording every word.

'Can I get you anything?' Richard asked.

'Just water, please. Sparkling, if you have it.' I wasn't thirsty, but I needed a moment to compose myself for what was to come.

I moved to the huge window as he busied himself, slicing cucumber and tearing mint leaves to garnish two fizzing tumblers. He cleaned up immediately, washing the knife and chopping board, wiping down the spotless surface.

I took the glass he offered me but didn't drink, watching him gulp his own as he leaned one hip against the chesterfield sofa. I swirled the contents, looking for any telltale distortion; even though I couldn't discern anything untoward, I knew I would not touch a drop.

'I hope I can congratulate you on your pregnancy now. I felt you might think it inappropriate if I said anything during a session.'

I had wondered at his resolute ignorance of my expanding girth. My frame did not suit pregnancy; it made me feel clumsy and cumbersome. I had hidden my bump under loose tunics and flowing shirts for the early months, when I had barely shown, but it had become impossible to disguise. 'How many weeks are you?' Richard asked.

'Thirty-two.'

'You're further along than I thought.'

I caressed the spot I thought was the baby's head. 'She's small but she's doing fine.'

'Your husband must be delighted, especially after your bereavement last time.'

I turned away, looking out at the views of Battersea Park across the bridge. Richard moved to stand beside me.

'It irks you, doesn't it, having to compensate for the pregnancy. You don't like to slow down.'

I knew he was looking at me, but I kept my eyes fixed on the park. 'I find it difficult to switch off. I worry I'm stressing the baby out.'

'And what are you stressed about? Work life or personal?'

He was shoulder-to-shoulder with me now. I could feel the heat of his body as his upper arm rested against mine. He kept both hands in his pockets, but I could read that his easy stance was forced.

I drew in a deep, wobbly breath. 'I suppose you could say both.'

'Nothing I've done, is it?'

I shook my head but avoided giving a direct answer.

His voice deepened. 'The last thing I'd want is to cause you distress.'

He shifted his feet and I was aware of his palm coming to rest on the small of my back. His touch was firm, but he didn't move the rest of his body any closer.

I froze, fighting the urge to push him away. I had to remember I was there for a reason and rejecting him so swiftly would be futile. I forced myself to wait, feeling his fingers gently caress the soft wool of my coat.

'Tamsin,' Richard murmured, barely audible, and it took inordinate courage to make myself turn to face him. I had chosen to wear makeup for the first time in his presence, my hair loose and flowing for once, and I watched him drink in the differences. It was my equivalent of battle armour, my way to announce he couldn't have me like he so arrogantly assumed, that I was beyond his reach.

He swallowed hard, his eyes never leaving mine, as he banished the last gap between us and slid his arms around me. How quickly he crossed the line, as soon as he was in his own domain, away from public eyes.

His biceps were solid, his torso firm and defined, and his breathing was as ragged as my own. Every part of my brain screamed at me to protect myself, but he was perfectly positioned for the microphone to capture his every word, if I played my role right. I had to stay strong, just a little while longer.

He dropped his head to kiss me, and, for a second, I thought I could go through with it. But I couldn't. My fight-or-flight had kicked in and I was helpless to prevent myself cringing away from him.

'Stop, Richard,' I gasped, barely able to draw enough breath to speak.

He went still, his body tightening, and I thought he was going to refuse. I leapt free, skirting to the other side of the sofa, putting a barrier between us.

That seemed to break the spell. He took a casual step back, leaning against the windowsill. My heart was pounding so loud it must surely have been audible to him.

'That's a shame,' he whispered.

I fought to calm myself, slow my breathing, relax my quivering muscles. I had to think of the baby.

I moved towards the door, putting as much distance between us as the room would allow. 'Can we walk over to the park?'

He swallowed hard and I could see an internal battle playing out behind his eyes. I turned the door handle, relief flooding through me when it opened a crack.

It was enough to bring him to his senses.

He was solicitous once again as we retraced our steps, pointing out landmarks when I told him it was my first time taking the Albert Bridge, asking if I needed to sit and rest when I wobbled slightly as we entered Battersea Park.

I made sure we stuck to the paths, but there were so many

winding off through the grassland that it would be easy to become isolated. I took the lead, my hand buried in my coat pocket so I could clutch the pepper spray, and we walked in silence for a time until we reached the boating lake.

We stopped to watch the ducks at the water's edge, the fish blowing air bubbles to the surface, a heron on the opposite shore, scanning for its next meal. I felt Richard's fingers slide into mine again.

He turned my palm up, examining it as if he wanted to memorise every line. He traced my scar with the tip of his little finger, making me shudder. Even after all this time, it was still sensitive.

'You mentioned how scared you were after your mugging, to be out and about alone. Are you still afraid?'

'No. It didn't last long. I became angry instead.' I closed my fist, preventing him from touching the scar again. 'I still am, even eight years later.'

'That's a long time to hold a grudge.'

I folded my arms across my chest, pressing gently against the recording device to assure myself it was still there. I was taking such risks: my safety, my career, even my baby. I could lose everything if this went wrong; I could lose everything even if it went right. But I had to try. I had worked towards this moment from the first day Richard Mandeville set foot in my office.

This would be his confession, whether he realised it or not.

'I told you I was mugged near home. That wasn't true. It was here.'

His eyebrows leapt towards his hairline. 'Here, in the park?'

'I was training for the marathon. I had just found out I was pregnant. Lucia, my best friend, didn't think I should run alone, so she arranged to meet me here.'

Richard had gone very still.

'It wasn't a mugging.' I pressed my fingernails into my scar, using the pain to keep the fear at bay. 'That's what I told the police, and my husband, and everyone else.'

The muscles in his neck tensed, his eyes widening and darkening.

'I wasn't the one you raped,' I told him quietly. 'You wouldn't have forgotten me, would you? I know you never forget.'

'What –?'

'You raped my best friend as she waited to meet me.'

I didn't give him chance to react, forging on.

'Then you came across me as you made your escape, and you couldn't resist, could you? Except I fought back.' I thrust my palm into his face like a stop signal, the evidence of his knife's blow as he'd tried to overpower me. 'I was wrapped up for the run. You wouldn't have seen much of my face, only the blonde hair that you liked so much. I was the icing on the cake, until I got away.'

He didn't speak. I wasn't sure he was able to.

'Lucia was the opposite of your type. You didn't stalk her, did you? Not like Inga or Bryony. I think you'd already made an attempt on someone else. Did the woman you actually targeted escape, before you stumbled across Lucia?' I kept using her name, determined for him to know who she was, for him to realise exactly why we were here. 'You didn't beat her up like the others. You didn't have time. But you still hurt her, Richard. You broke her.'

Richard was barely breathing, his eyes locked on mine.

'Two women were brave enough to come forward. Lucia couldn't do it.' I took a step closer to him. 'I helped her scrub away any trace of you, burned her running kit in our fire pit. I threw away any chance of identifying you. And I promised her no one would ever know what happened to her, what you *did* to her, because she was so ashamed she hadn't been able to stop you like I did.'

His entire body jerked at the abrupt change in my voice, to a tone he had never heard me use before. A tone of hot fury, the internal rage that had driven me ever since that early morning in this very park.

'My pregnancy was found to be ectopic at ten weeks. I needed emergency surgery.' I gritted my teeth. 'I still believe the attack caused it; the trauma, the guilt, it all led to a hormonal imbalance. I was late that day. I was *never* late. If I'd been on time, I'd have been able to save Lucia. You wouldn't have attacked us in a pair. You're too much of a *fucking* coward for that.'

'Tamsin …'

'Admit it, Richard,' I snarled. He took an instinctive step back, trying to get away from me, but I moved closer still, needing to be sure the microphone would pick up his words. Fury blinkered my vision. All I could see was him, those grey eyes that now looked as cold and hard as paving slabs. The same eyes that had bored into me behind that ski hood as he had pinned me to the ground.

'Listen to me,' he started.

'Say it!' I yelled. 'Are you not brave enough without your mask and your knife?!'

He turned on his heel, attempting to walk away from me. I followed, struggling to keep up with his long strides.

'I don't understand.' He stopped in mid-step, swinging round to face me. 'You're my psychiatrist. I chose you! Out of them all, you were the only one who stood out.'

'I stood out that day as well, didn't I? Me, not that broken, helpless woman you left discarded behind a bush like she was rubbish.'

Rage made his handsome face irreversibly ugly. I saw then, for certain, how he released that anger he kept locked away inside him. He took it out on women who couldn't defend themselves.

'Shut the fuck up, Dr Shaw,' he snarled. 'You think you're so clever, sitting there in your little office, trying to trick me into giving you evidence against me.'

'You revealed your true self years ago, Richard.'

A sneer contorted his features further and he took a step back towards me, reaching out. 'Letting you go was my mistake. I should have finished what I started. I should have put you in your place, like I did your friend. Lucia, was it?'

He seized my upper arm. I pulled away but he wrenched me closer, his knuckles brushing against my breast pocket, and my breath stalled.

He noticed.

His long digits reached into my pocket and he withdrew the recording device, pinching it between his thumb and index finger as he examined it. As if in slow motion, his head came up, his eyes fixing on mine, devoid of human emotion.

'You recorded me?' he snarled.

I reacted purely on instinct and, before I knew what I was doing, I had snatched the device off him. His soldier's reflexes, for once, deserted him.

As I span round to flee, he lunged.

I screamed.

'Tamsin!' A male voice rang out.

Dan was running towards us, his long legs eating up the ground. He grabbed hold of my fisted hand, hauling me into his embrace, shielding me from Richard with his body.

'What the hell are you doing?' he thundered, and I couldn't tell if he was addressing me or Richard.

Richard made to walk away again, his face now a picture of bemusement, as if he could not for the life of him understand what had caused my reaction.

'Stay there!' Dan barked the order with such ferocity that even Richard paused. Dan took my shoulders in his hands, turning me to face him. I could feel him shaking but he was careful not to handle me too roughly. 'Why are you here? What were you thinking?'

I shook my head as if lost for words, clutching his coat sleeve with one hand. The other was occupied burying the recording device safely in my inner pocket.

Richard took the opportunity, striding away from us without a backward glance. Dan took a step, as if prepared to chase after him, but I kept my grip.

'No,' I croaked. 'Let him go.'

I had what I came for. There was no need for Dan to pursue his quarry.

'Are you seeing him?' Dan's voice was incredulous as he looked from Richard's retreating back to my face. 'Is that why you've been so odd about him?'

'I'm freezing.' I let my teeth chatter, not entirely an exaggeration. 'Can we just go? I need to get warm.'

I could see Dan wanted to push me for answers, but he tamped down his impatience, wrapping his arm around me as if he didn't expect me to be able to walk unaided. He steered me back to the road, held open the BMW's passenger door and guided me into the low seat before hurrying round to the other side.

Turning the heat up full blast, he urged, 'Tam, talk to me.'

I couldn't tell him. Dan had been such an integral part of this plan, without ever knowing it. I couldn't admit that on the night we spent together in March, I had gone back to his hotel room knowing he would have brought his secure laptop with him, ever the workaholic. That, when he had passed out, I had used his compliant fingerprint to access the probation service network. How I had made sure my brief was included in the file of psychiatrists that would be presented to Richard Mandeville. Unsurprisingly, Dan had left me out of the running. So I took the chance to insert myself, and carefully reword my profile to spark Richard's interest.

Dan had snored away, naked, his memories of the night blurred by whisky. I had never dared imagine such an opportunity would present itself to me in those first sleepless nights after the attack, when I had dreamed of revenge. But now I had taken it, and I wasn't going to waste it.

I had assumed Dan wouldn't remember us returning to his room, the kisses I had allowed him on our stumbling walk through the hotel corridors. I hadn't expected him to assume we had slept together but, really, what other conclusion could he have reached?

What I hadn't banked on was pregnancy. That really had thrown a spanner in the works. Even though I was certain it wasn't Dan's, to tell him that would have led to questions I couldn't answer.

He was still waiting, drumming his fingers against the steering wheel, his body coiled tight as a spring. I buried my chin in my coat.

'Have you been following me?' I asked.

'No! I've been following Mandeville.'

'Are you mad?'

'He'll attack again, Tam, we both know that.'

'You're a bloody director; you can't go around stalking clients!'

'What else was I supposed to do? Let another woman go through something like that? Risk you being his next victim?'

I shuddered at the chill that ran through me. At least I now had the evidence that would prevent that from happening. To me, or any woman.

'Talk to me.' Dan demanded. 'You're scaring me.'

I kept my eyes straight ahead, fighting to control my soaring heart rate.

'You were right about Richard Mandeville.'

35

Jamie – Now

Jamie is putting Elise to bed, or trying to. She resists this process most nights with a stubborn streak as wide as her mother's.

'Where's Matty?' she asks.

'In his room, I guess.'

'I want Matty to tuck me in.'

It isn't the first time she has demanded this recently. She wants to spend all her time with Mateo, even more so since she has learned of Tamsin's imminent demise.

'What does Matty do that makes you feel better with him?' Jamie can't help but ask.

A shrug. 'He knows.'

'Knows what?'

'How I feel.' Elise touches her head. 'In here. We draw it.'

Jamie frowns. 'Can I see the drawings, sweetheart?'

Seizing the opportunity to evade sleep, Elise scrambles out from under the duvet. She grabs her latest artworks from her little desk and proudly spreads them out on the floor to show her father.

It is the first time Jamie has really studied any of her efforts. He looks from city landscapes to country scenes surrounded by fields; from a blue car to a blonde figure lying in a bed.

They are too accomplished to be the child's work. She has done the colouring but there's no way she is able to sketch with such detail.

'Did Matty help you with these?' Jamie asks, a sense of dread creeping over him. She nods. 'Did you tell him what you wanted to draw?'

'We were talking.'

'About what?'

Elise shakes her head, pressing a finger to her lips. 'Secret.'

Jamie has no idea how to persuade her to tell him.

'Can you tell me, Els?' Lucia asks softly from the doorway. She has joined them without Jamie realising. 'Is it just Daddy who can't know the secret?'

Elise nods, clearly relieved. She reaches up to wrap her arms around Lucia's neck and whispers in her ear. Jamie's fingers itch with the urge to take his daughter and make her reveal the truth to him.

Finally, Lucia hugs the little girl close and plants a gentle kiss on her forehead. 'You did well, sweetie. I'm proud of you.'

'Trouble?' Elise asks as Lucia lifts her back onto her bed. She snuggles under the duvet, wary eyes peeping out at Jamie.

'No trouble. I promise. You go to sleep while I talk to Daddy.'

For once, Elise doesn't protest. Sleep must be a better prospect than letting her father know her secrets.

'What was that about?' Jamie mouths as they tiptoe out of the room.

Lucia closes Elise's door and beckons him further down the hallway. Jamie has no choice but to follow her to Mateo's room.

She enters without knocking, reaching back to grab Jamie's sleeve and pull him inside. Mateo leaps from his oversized beanbag, ready to object to the invasion of his privacy, but Lucia beats him to it.

'Matty,' she says, in a low voice so the younger child won't overhear. 'What have you been telling Els about the crash?'

Mateo's lips move, but no sound comes out. He rakes his fingers through his hair, stepping backwards, putting distance between himself and his mother.

'What's she been saying?' he asks hoarsely.

'That you've described how the crash happened. You told Els you hear your dad crying and shouting.'

Mateo starts to shake his head, but the movement dies before it begins. He clenches his fists, moving even further backwards, until his back thumps against the wall.

'Why have you told her you hear those awful things?'

'Because I do.' Mateo's eyes flash in Jamie's direction. 'I hear it every night since Dad died. Every time I go to sleep. I hear him in Tam's car, yelling at her to slow down.'

'And now Els believes she hears her mother crying for her,' Lucia says, her voice catching.

'She told me she was already having nightmares. I just explained them.'

'How could you upset her like that?'

'I didn't mean it. I wanted to fuck with Jamie, not Els. I didn't know she'd take it like she did.'

'Fuck with Jamie?' she echoes. 'Why are you so determined to ruin this?'

'Because he's not Dad!' Angry tears spill down Mateo's cheeks.

'No one's trying to replace your dad, Matty.' Lucia sighs. 'But we've talked about this. Even if Dad was still here, he and I wouldn't be together now. He really hurt me. Do you understand that?'

Mateo lets out a bitter laugh. 'I understand better than you can imagine. He hurt me too. Didn't stop *me* loving him, though.'

Mateo's tone has darkened. Jamie seeks Lucia's eyes, but she's staring at her son, pale faced.

'He hurt you too?' she repeats, her voice trembling.

Mateo grips the front of his T-shirt, tugging at it as if the neck is throttling him. 'One time, before he died. He wanted me to shut up and I wouldn't. He tried to strangle me. I couldn't breathe.'

Jamie hears Lucia's razor-sharp intake of air. 'He did what?'

'He was high, Mum. I was trying to tell him he didn't need drugs – he had us – but he lost his temper.'

Lucia takes him in her arms, holding him tight as he buries his face in her shoulder. For a long moment, he cries, no longer a teenager, but a frightened child, attacked by the person he had put on a pedestal.

'Taking it out on Jamie won't make it better, Matty,' she murmurs. 'He isn't the one who harmed you.'

Mateo's chest heaves. 'That grief therapist said I needed to find a way to let the anger out.'

'I don't think she meant you should accuse Jamie of trying to kill your godmother.'

'I didn't actually believe it.'

'Then why say it?'

A shrug. 'I wanted someone else to hurt too.'

'You could have talked to us, instead of trying to battle through it by yourself.'

'There's never been any truth in this house, not from anyone.'

Thank God he doesn't know how accurate that statement was.

'I think we need to organise another therapist for you.' Lucia speaks over Mateo's head, looking at Jamie. He nods his agreement. 'This isn't healthy, sweetheart.'

'I don't want to.'

'You need to find a coping mechanism that isn't trying to break up Jamie and me.' Lucia's voice takes on a wry tone and she throws Jamie a smile. 'And I think an apology is in order.'

She eases her son upright, turning him so Jamie can see his salt-stained face. The kid looks exhausted – haggard, even. Jamie wouldn't wish this kind of twisted grief on anyone, let alone his godson.

'No apology needed,' he says softly. He watches the tension drain from Mateo's stance. Could this be the start of a truce? His phone rings. He glances at it out of reflex. The screen says it's Milena.

'Leave it,' Lucia pleads.

Jamie looks again at the number. 'I can't.' He steps out into the hallway and taps the answer icon.

'Jamie.' The voice on the other end is trembling. 'He came back again. Richard was here.'

Jamie's brain stalls. For a never-ending minute, he has no idea how to respond.

'Jamie, are you there?' Milena gasps.

'I'm here. Tell me what's happened.'

Milena's words run into each other in her haste to get them out. Her breathing is so loud he can barely hear her. 'I think he came to hurt Tamsin. I disturbed him and he left.'

'Are you both alright?'

'Tamsin's heart went crazy. We had to shock her. I'm not supposed to tell you over the phone, it's against the rules, but fuck the rules after this.' She is forced to stop to gulp air. 'She's OK. She's better than OK.'

Milena's voice cracks. 'She opened her eyes, Jamie. Tamsin is awake.'

36

Tamsin – Now

My unexpected return to the waking world causes quite a commotion. Doctors rush from London, a pilgrimage to see the miracle. They ask me questions I can't yet answer, give me instructions I am too fatigued to follow. Blood tests have found nothing to suggest Richard managed to inject anything into my system and there is no giveaway pinprick anywhere on my skin.

It is not how I pictured my fortieth birthday, but it is a triumph to be here.

Milena stays by my side. It is a joy to see the features of strangers I have known for over a year. I am pleased that my deductions and assumptions have so far proved to be mostly accurate. Milena is as small and slight as I had imagined, and her hair is the exact shade of magenta she had described to me. Her pretty, symmetrical face is familiar to me even though I have never seen it with my own eyes.

She brings me pen and paper when we both realise I have no voice, but I can't coordinate my fingers enough to pick up the pen, let alone find the strength to grip and move it. For the moment, my communication is limited to nods and head shakes, weak smiles and mouthing basic words.

The sentences are there, crowding my brain, bursting to spill out, but even moving my mouth is a struggle, the muscles unwilling to respond to my commands.

It isn't as I had envisaged, the triumphant moment I had carefully created in my mind and rehearsed over and over again. Instead, it is almost as frustrating as before. The one bright spot is being able to see, and my eyes are moving almost constantly, greedily drinking in my surroundings.

A consultant from the Royal London tests my pathetic grip strength and reflexes, tells me to track his finger with my eyes, checks my pupils with a penlight that blinds me momentarily. He gives me more commands I fail to respond to.

'We're going to take you for a scan, Tamsin,' he tells me. 'It'll let us see what's really going on. Is that OK?'

It is the first time my permission has been sought for years, and the temptation to refuse, just to see what they do if I say no, is tempting. But I get a grip of myself. I also want to know what's going on and, for once, I won't have to rely on eavesdropping to find out.

I am bundled up in blankets and wheeled carefully out to a waiting ambulance like a precious china doll. The autumn sun feels so intense that my eyes water, but I strain to look around me, to see Rushmore as it really exists. The colours and furnishings I pass by are different, but the architecture and layout are exactly as I had worked out, and I flush with pride.

I expand my lungs, greedily drink in the fresh air, as I admire the red and gold leaves and watch birds flitting about the sky. Life surrounds me and I want to absorb it all.

The Royal is discombobulating, a hive of activity and piercing sounds. I hadn't thought I'd be afraid of MRI equipment but, once I am inside the tight cylinder, surrounded by mechanical knocking, I am terrified. The consultant asks me to perform a variety of tasks I know will stimulate blood flow in different areas of my brain – language, memory, motor control – but I barely respond when I am directed to state my date of birth, open and close my eyes, tap my index fingers left and right.

The whole exercise exhausts me, and I sleep the entire journey back, another missed opportunity. At Rushmore, I only wake when Milena comes to check that I haven't slipped back into a comatose state. Another woman is with her, wearing a severe suit and bright-red lipstick.

'Hello, Tamsin,' the woman says. 'I'm the director of Rushmore. I came to see how you are. We're glad your recovery is gathering pace. And happy birthday! I didn't expect to be congratulating you like this.'

I wonder if she drafted her little speech beforehand, to make sure she got it just right. Her words sound robotic, like they've been memorised.

'The consultants have advised that you need to rest, so you don't risk any setbacks. We've been keeping your family updated but we've told them it's better to wait until you've regained a little strength before they visit.'

I don't know how she expected me to respond, but she seems disappointed when I can only manage a weak nod. Milena tries to reassure me with a smile, but I am already drifting again.

When I finally wake, a new stranger is by my bedside, a woman who introduces herself as a neurologist.

'I've been asked to come and conduct another test here.'

'She's already had too many tests,' Milena protests.

'I know it's a lot, but it's important that we do these examinations quickly before any evidence is lost.' Like I am a petri dish in a laboratory. 'The fMRI scan didn't show as much activity as we would have liked. We're going to try with an EEG instead; it's possible Tamsin found the scanner too much to cope with.'

I decide I like this doctor from that statement alone. She is perceptive.

Milena holds my hand, but I'm not afraid this time; I'm focussed, determined to prove my brain activity is not to be dismissed.

It takes a long time to position the multiple sensors all over my head, but the doctor talks to me throughout, seeming to sense my intended replies.

'Has your husband visited yet?' she asks. 'You've got a daughter, haven't you?'

I shake my head, then nod.

'The director thought it was better to get all the tests done before allowing visitors,' Milena says, her face reflecting her disapproval. 'They will come later tomorrow.'

I can finally show Milena I appreciate her protectiveness.

'You must be looking forward to seeing them,' the consultant said.

I can scarcely wait to look at my daughter for the first time, but the delay is useful for me, as much as I want to rage against it. Elise's visit must be a success. She must see me as a real person, finally. I need to be able to speak to her, stroke her hair, squeeze her hand.

I can't say I've afforded Jamie much thought. He isn't mine anymore.

'Do you have any questions before we start?'

I slowly raise my hand to tap my lips.

'Speech? You're asking about when you'll be able to talk?'

I nod vigorously. My thoughts are operating at full capacity, but I can't direct them to my lips.

'Your vocal cords are the same as your muscles. They've wasted from inactivity, so they need to be strengthened. It'll take time but you'll get there. Your occupational therapist will do exercises with you. You could use a tablet to communicate for now? Get someone to hold it close to your hand so you can type more easily?'

I nod again, mouthing *today*.

'Don't rush and push yourself too hard. This isn't going to be an easy process of recovery.'

I take a deep breath, tamping down the frustration.

'I'm going to start the tests now, Tamsin,' the consultant says. 'Are you ready?'

Another nod, careful not to upset any of the sensors. Milena has not seen EEG equipment before, and her apprehension is palpable. I sense she is holding my hand as much for her own reassurance as mine.

The doctor positions herself in front of the screen, her eyes roving constantly over the readings. She begins to ask me questions, instructing me to think of the answers rather than trying to voice them. My full name, simple addition sums, my favourite colour, my favourite food. The concepts become more abstract – do I believe in God, am I a leader or follower, how do I define happiness? I am directed to follow a flashing light with my eyes and think of how to describe it.

I apply all the strength I can muster to proving that, not only am I mentally present, but I remember enough to make some people very, very uncomfortable.

Finally, I am allowed time to collect myself. My ears are ringing, and I am dizzy, disorientated from all the activity. Exhaustion is threatening to drape its heavy cloak over me, but I resist it for a little longer.

Milena is still here, sitting quietly, aware that I am trying to ground myself.

'I have something for you,' she tells me, a grin spreading across her face as she shows me a small parcel wrapped in shiny paper.

My fingers don't have the dexterity to open the present and Milena has to do it for me. She shyly shows me the silver earrings nestled in the jewellery box, pretty studs in the shape of butterflies.

'Elise loves butterflies,' she explains. 'She shows me her drawings. She'll want you to see them too.'

Tears spring to my eyes. 'They're gorgeous,' I mouth. 'Thank you.'

Milena gingerly threads them into my ears. The piercings have closed up over time but she is gentle as ever until they are in place.

'Happy birthday, Tamsin.'

She gives me a hug and I cling to her momentarily, breathing in the comfort of her familiar scent.

'Are you OK?' she finally asks. 'It's crazy, isn't it?'

I nod to both questions. *Tired*, I mouth.

'The police will be coming, Tamsin. They will have questions about what Richard came here to do. But I think they can't prove anything.' She lets out a shaky breath. 'I can help, but I'm scared. If it goes wrong, I'll never be safe from him. What should I do?'

She looks at me with such trust that I feel an intense weight of responsibility. I still haven't been able to connect the dots of her story and, without all the information, I cannot offer her advice.

I indicate the iPad on my bedside table. She smiles at my insistence and moves it so the screen is directly beneath the pads of my fingers.

You know Richard Mandeville.

She meets my gaze, and I see her answer in the depths of her eyes.

Tell me everything.

She doesn't speak immediately, staring at a spot on the far wall as she steadies herself. Several deep breaths and she nods again, ready. Her fists clench.

'I told you I was Polish. That's not true. I had a Polish passport, but it's not mine. Neither is my national insurance number. I couldn't tell the truth to anyone here.'

I hold her fragile eye contact and will her to continue.

'I came to the UK from Tirana, but I was born in Kosovo. I was a carer back home, that bit is true, but I wanted more.' She pushes her hair sharply out of her eyes so she can look directly at me. 'I came to work for Richard Mandeville. We all knew him, during the war. Did he tell you about the war, when he was your patient?'

I nod hard.

'He saved my baby brother and me. We were taking cover in a basement when a mortar hit it. Richard came through the flames and carried us out. He was my hero then.'

I remember him telling me about being decorated for that courageous act, but it gives me goosebumps to know Milena was one of those children he rescued.

'We had so little. My father was away fighting – he never came back. Richard was like an uncle to us. He'd visit our house to see our mother, always brought us sweets and Coca-Cola. We loved him. Even after the UN left, he would send money. It kept us going.'

She sighs softly. 'I saw him a few times, after I moved to Tirana for work. He promised he would bring me to the UK. My mother warned me not to trust him, not to go. I didn't listen. I wanted out of the Balkans. I wanted a new life. I was stupid. He always treated me well when I was a child, and I thought I was safe with him.'

She leans forward, taking my hand.

'I wasn't safe. I found that out soon enough. Richard Mandeville is a monster. He takes whatever he wants from women who cannot fight back. He took so much from me.'

Her eyes swim with tears but she refuses to allow them to fall.

'Richard supplied waiting staff to Porteños. I met Jamie there. He was always nice to me. He knew what was happening, but he was helpless too, and it hurt him, so he tried to look out for me. Then your crash happened, and he didn't have time for me anymore.'

I squeeze her hand, a pressure that must be barely detectable, but it is enough to rally her.

'Richard got worse. Fuck, it was bad.' She shakes her head as if trying to clear it. 'I was dying inside. I had to get out before he killed me. Jamie was the only person I told – I trusted him. He was looking for a place for you and, when he found Rushmore, they were advertising for staff. I thought it was far enough from London for me to be safe here. Jamie wrote a CV for me, brought me for the interview. He even got my fake passport for ID checks and put it back without Richard knowing.'

Slowly, the dots are all joining, but I am still struggling to fully comprehend the intricate web that had been spun around me.

Milena is speaking again and, although my brain is slowing, I strive to tune back in.

'I've been thinking, if I tell the police my story, will it be enough to stop him?'

I am desperate to reassure her, tell her it absolutely will be enough, but I can't give her false hope, not after everything she's done for me. I don't know what sway her words will have, an illegal migrant with forged documents, who is the strongest, bravest woman I have had the fortune to know, but who, in the eyes of the law, may be considered an unreliable witness.

I maintain eye contact, trying with all my might to convey every ounce of gratitude I have for her, before tapping insistently at the iPad.

We need more.

Milena swipes at her eyes as she reads. I type again, underlining the two words.

Dan Attwood.

She swallows audibly. 'He will help me, if I talk to him?'

I nod as forcefully as I can. Dan has lived this for so long, driven by his determination to prove Richard's guilt. He will know what to do.

Milena is on her feet.

'I have to go now, Tamsin. I'll come back, I promise.'

I hope that she will but, at the same time, I will understand if I never see her again.

37

Tamsin – Before

Dan had dropped me off at home, insisting on walking me up to the apartment, making chamomile tea, gently pressing me for more information I wasn't prepared to give him yet. When he finally gave up and left, I stood under the shower, the temperature as high as it would go, scrubbing myself with soap until I had cleaned away the insidious dirt I could feel clinging to my skin.

I had to go to Lucia. I had to tell her what I'd done and play her the recording. She needed to hear what Richard had admitted to. Now I had the evidence of his guilt, Lucia may find the courage to report her attack. The retrial would be prevented, and Richard Mandeville would be back behind bars.

I would finally have my revenge, for all Lucia had suffered, for the baby I had lost, for everything Richard had taken from us.

Back in the kitchen, I slipped the little implement into the pocket of fresh jeans as I fired off a text.

Where are you?

She didn't reply. She always replied within moments. I pressed the call button. It went straight to voicemail.

I set the phone down harder than was necessary and poured a glass of water, gulping it, spilling some down my chin in my haste.

A text chirped and I lunged for it.

I'll get to your friend before you do.

My numb fingers nearly dropped the handset. I stared at Richard's message, forcing myself to read it several times to make sure I wasn't hallucinating.

I know where she is. Give me that recording, or she's mine again.

I wasn't aware of moving to the hallway, of shoving my feet into trainers without bothering to undo the laces and making my way to the lift.

I moved as speedily as I could to the next street, along to Lucia's house. My legs shook as I glanced continually around me, checking for threats. The baby seemed especially active today, drumming her feet against my ribs in protest at my stress.

At first, there was no response to me hammering on the knocker or ringing the bell but, eventually, the door was flung open.

Ben stood there, shirtless. He looked a decade older than his years. His face seemed grey and strangely baggy, as if the skin around his eyes had slipped. He sniffed uncontrollably, his eyes bloodshot.

'Tammy? What you want?'

'Is Lucia home? Her phone's off.'

'No, she go to Kent. The Wi-Fi no working so she getting it fixed.'

He had no reason to lie to me, and it would explain her apparent lack of phone signal, but I needed to be sure. I barged past him, brushing off his cry of pique, and hurried upstairs, checking each room before returning to the ground floor, once again pushing Ben out of my way when he tried to bar me.

'Are you crazy? The hell you doing?'

'I need to see her. I have to talk to her.'

'What about?'

This was getting me nowhere. 'You don't need to know!'

I wasn't sure if it was my emotion or my erratic behaviour, but something flipped a switch in Ben. His face tightened as his eyes grew darker, and his fists clenched. 'Tell me!'

'I'm going to Kent,' I said, striding past him for the door.

'Tammy, wait!'

I turned back, about to tell him in no uncertain terms that I wasn't interested in providing him with answers, but he was already on my shoulder. It occurred to me that any male presence, even Ben's, might make us all safer.

'Lucia's in danger. I need to get to her, stop her coming back to London.'

He took too long to process that garbled information and I wanted to scream in frustration. 'Danger from who?'

'There's no time, Ben! We have to go now. I'll explain, I promise. Just come with me.'

We strode back to Apollo Point's car park, Ben panting in my wake. The street was deserted. The recording device lay heavy in my pocket, although it weighed practically nothing.

The entirety of the hour-long journey, I fed Ben half-truths about a dangerous client who was out for revenge and prepared to use those closest to me to reap it. It didn't occur to him to question me. He muttered to himself in Castilian and was such an irritant that all I wanted to do was tell him to shut up. Somehow, I prevented myself.

I retreated inside my own head to speak calming words to my baby girl. The A-roads gave way to B-roads, then to winding country lanes. I glanced in my rear-view mirror, certain the silver SUV had been behind us on the motorway too. But my paranoia was unsettling enough without inventing conspiracy theories, and I resolved not to look again.

I could see the house a few minutes before we were scheduled to arrive, standing out amid the landscape. It was a beautiful building, dark weatherboarding, the centuries-old wood still standing strong, and orange-red roof tiles. I had sought sanctuary there on many weekends, and now it would have to shield Lucia too. London would not be safe for either of us until I could ensure Richard Mandeville was back behind bars.

I became aware of strange movements in the passenger seat. Ben was leaning forward, his shoulders rounded to try and conceal his actions. I nearly missed a bend as I finally comprehended what he was doing.

'For fuck's sake!' I struck out with one hand, knocking the little baggie from his hand.

'I need it!'

'You *need* to protect your wife! How can you do that when you're high?'

I checked the rear-view mirror again, trying to keep my fragile control. It was still there. The silver SUV.

It was following us.

I slammed on the brakes, bringing us to a juddering, screeching halt in the middle of the road. Before I knew it, I was out of the car, clinging to the door to keep me upright as I wavered on the rough tarmac. I thrust my other hand into my jeans pocket, squeezing the recording device like a talisman.

The SUV approached. The sun visor had obscured the driver's face at first, but now it flipped up and I could see for sure who was behind the wheel. My stomach dropped. I had chosen to toy with the Devil, and now he had come for his final dance.

Richard Mandeville accelerated and, with a sudden roar of his engine, swung out onto the other side of the road, barely missing the back wing of my car. Then he was gone, powering away out of sight around the wide, curving bend.

He hadn't known where Lucia was. But I had led him right to her.

I leapt back into the Mini, not even remembering my seat belt. I howled into the windscreen, and something shattered within me.

'Tammy, what's happening?' Ben cried, throwing off his own seat belt as if preparing to dive out. His eyes were pinpricks.

I barely acknowledged him. I was shaking too much to maintain a grip on the steering wheel and I was certain I was about to vomit. I had messed this up so badly, when all I had wanted was justice – for Lucia, for myself, and for the baby I had lost.

Beyond the bend, a long straight road stretched out for well over a mile, giving me a clear view.

The silver SUV was charging back down the road, right at us.

38

Tamsin – Now

A bang startles me, my eyelids leaping back to attention at the same moment my heart jumps.

The door has flown open, and Elise hurtles into the room. I am so shocked by her arrival that I can't move. This isn't how I wanted her to find me, unprepared and thrown into a panic. As much as I have been desperate to see my family, it has also been a relief to be alone as I sought a grasp on my surroundings, my capabilities, my limitations.

'Els, wait a sec!' Lucia's voice calls from the corridor. 'This visit is different; we need to talk to Hannah first.'

'No!' Elise is already halfway across the floor towards me. 'Mummy sees me!'

She leaps onto the bed, ending up almost nose-to-nose with me. Her hands take my cheeks, so she is looking at me squarely. I smile and she jerks back with a gasp.

'Mummy?'

I nod manically through the tears that blur my vision. I can see my child for the first time in her life.

She is exactly as I had pictured. She has my features, but with golden hair and a deeper complexion that comes from Jamie, and she has his cheeky grin. But her sapphire eyes are purely mine.

We stare at each other for what could have been forever.

'Elise,' I mouth, and I let out a croak I worry will scare her, but she only leans closer.

'Mummy's here,' she whispers.

Her finger runs across my cheekbone, down the length of my nose, traces the outline of my jaw and caresses the shape of my lips. For that moment, it is only us, mother and daughter united at last, and no one else matters.

'I love you,' I mouth, the same hoarse noise emerging again.

'Love you,' Elise mouths back, dropping her own voice to match mine.

Jamie finally approaches the bed and leans down to kiss my forehead. Lucia is close behind, pressing her lips to my cheek as her hands grasp both of mine. Her hair is shorter now, warm strands of chestnut weaving through her dark waves. She has that glow that comes only from happiness. Lucia has found her place in the world, but it is with my husband and my daughter, and the taste in my mouth is bitter as she steps back and beams at me.

'Welcome back,' she whispers, her eyes filled with tears.

I keep my eyes on Jamie, drinking him in. He has aged; there are crow's feet around his eyes and lines creasing the sides of his mouth. His stubble is untidy, and his frame no longer boasts the honed muscle it used to, but I still feel the magnetism of him, a pull I have never been able to resist.

'How are you?' he asks, his words stilted.

'I'm not sure,' I mouth, battling to produce even the smallest voice.

He is distracted by Hannah's arrival. I was smugly vindicated, when I first opened my eyes, to find she was exactly as I pictured her, right down to her swollen ankles and pinched expression. Nearly two full days have passed but she has yet to address more than a few words to me.

'Where's Milena?' Jamie asks her.

'That's what I'd like to know,' Hannah bristles. 'She was due in this morning but didn't show. She isn't answering her phone. The police wanted to speak to her.'

'Police?'

'We had to report what happened with Mr Mandeville. They came to take statements while Tamsin was asleep.'

That enrages me. They hadn't even bothered to speak to me. I still counted for nothing, even with my eyes open.

'What did they say?' Lucia asks.

'There's no evidence of a crime being committed.' Hannah draws herself up to her full height. 'It was one of our syringes he was holding, he hadn't brought it with him. Besides, why would Mr Mandeville have come to hurt Tamsin?'

A grim look is exchanged between Jamie and Lucia, and I flinch at the ease of their wordless communication. A couple's secret code.

'Thank you, Hannah.' Jamie dismisses her with a brisk nod. I see her disappointment that her part in my recovery goes unacknowledged. I suppose she did save my life, but I can't bring myself to like the woman.

'How do you feel, Tam?' Lucia asks.

I ignore her. I want to focus on my daughter first.

'Mummy OK,' Els murmurs, snuggling into the crook of my neck.

'Do you remember anything?' Jamie leans over the bed but doesn't sit down. 'What's the last thing you recall?'

I shrug, avoiding his gaze as stubbornly as I avoid the question. Jamie startles visibly as the door opens again, clenching his jaw in irritation. I look to see who is interrupting my reunion with Elise this time.

To my surprise, it is Dan.

He crosses the room in a few long strides, peering at me as if to check this is real. I raise my eyes to his, my lips curving of their own accord.

'Tam? Hi.' His face splits into the broadest of grins and he gently slides his arms around me, lifting me off the pillows, drawing me into his warm, safe body. He doesn't so much as glance at Jamie and Lucia, entirely focussed on me. 'God, it's good to see you.'

His sleeve is close enough for me to grip and I take it between my fingers even after he carefully lays me down again.

'You do remember me, don't you?'

I smile and nod, watching relief flooding his eyes.

'How are you?' he asks, dragging the chair as close as he can, as if Jamie and Lucia aren't even in the room. He gives Elise a wave, but she only has eyes for me. 'Does anything hurt?'

I shake my head, laboriously raising my hand to tap my lips. It is a relief to interact with him, to block out the others.

'Yeah, Hannah said you can't talk yet. Guess there'll be a lot of stuff you'll have to learn again. But it'll be OK. You're here, that's all that matters.'

His relief, his joy, is palpable and, for now, it's nice to simply bask in this brief moment of happy reunion, before it all starts to fall apart as the inevitable questions are asked.

'What are you doing here?' Jamie interrupts. 'It's not good for Tam to have too many visitors at once.'

'I won't stay long.' Dan dismisses him. He lets go of my hands and reaches to grab the TV remote. 'I had to come. We just got out of court – we're in recess. You need to see this.'

At his command, we all look obediently to the screen as he selects a news channel. In the studio, the presenter is speaking directly into a camera, delivering a monologue, as a still of the Royal Courts of Justice frames her. A headline runs across the screen beneath her.

Battersea Park predator's re-trial halted amid new evidence

'The Right Honourable Richard Mandeville, fifth Earl of Southvale, had been on course to have his convictions overturned until police today reported the presentation of two new alleged victims of his reign of terror. The women, a mother and daughter from the Balkans region, had both been subjected to his predilection. The daughter was brought to the UK by Mandeville years later as part of a people-smuggling operation he established during his time peacekeeping under the United Nations.' She pauses for a dramatic silence, to let her words sink in.

'Mandeville has been free on licence for the duration of the trial, but the judge ordered he be immediately returned to prison, having broken the terms of his parole. He will be held in Wandsworth until the trial concludes.'

A sharp noise erupts from Lucia and her body jerks instinctively to try and conceal any further sounds.

'Oh my God,' she breathes. I watch her reach for Jamie's hand as they both stare at the screen, pale-faced, mouths slightly open in shock. Jamie is too wrapped up in the report to notice Lucia's reaction, but I don't miss it.

She has finally made the connection that I had been racing to explain to her three long years ago.

'Do you know who the daughter is?' Dan asks me.

I can't bear to tear my eyes away from Lucia, but I make myself look at him as I nod, to show him my competence, to prove myself for the first time in years.

'Milena came to you,' I mouth.

'I knew you'd be one step ahead of me. As bloody usual. I've brought her with me. Let me go and rescue her from Hannah. Hang on.'

He hurries out of the room, leaving me to watch Jamie and Lucia exchanging glances. I can sense their maelstrom of emotions, see it being played out across their faces. Fear and hope are an unstable combination.

Lucia makes eye contact with me, and I see her terror. Some cruel part of me wants to hurt her but, no. All of this, everything I've gone through, was for us, for the pain and terror we shared, for what we were both robbed of. She needs to know, needs to understand what I tried to do for her.

I flick my eyes to Jamie. Through her haze, she recognises what I'm trying to say, and I watch her internal battle to decide whether she wants Jamie to be part of this. I nod hard, needing her to understand that he has to know. However inadvertently, he has become a part of this twisted web, and he needs to recognise just what his decisions could cost him.

'Jamie, take Elise to Milena for a few minutes.' Lucia speaks hesitantly, as if she is awakening from a deep sleep. 'Tell Dan to give us some time alone.'

Jamie frowns. I can see he has picked up on Lucia's distress, but he is clueless as to what has caused it. For once, he does as he's asked, luring Elise with the promise of chocolate and a swing they must have set in the gardens for any young visitors.

I flap my hand at the iPad.

'What is this?' Lucia stretches out an arm like a sleepwalker but fails to move the tablet. 'I don't understand.'

I flap harder and finally she places it in the right spot. The small muscles in my wrist burn as I strain to type quickly: *I need to explain, but so does Jamie.*

Confusion darts through her frantic eyes. She really was in the dark about Jamie's investor. She has no idea that her attacker is the one who kept them from bankruptcy and has controlled her lover ever since.

Jamie returns, reluctance clear in his slow movements and tense body. He sits beside Lucia but doesn't take her hand. His own guilt is writ across his rigid face.

I turn my palm over, tapping my scar. Jamie frowns, uncomprehending. Lucia pales even further and her head twitches, trying to silence me.

'I'm sorry,' I mouth at her. Our secrets will do us no good remaining hidden.

I tap slowly at the iPad, gritting my teeth against the ache in my fingers. It takes a long time to type out our shared story, angling the iPad so Jamie can follow along as the text appears. The blood drains from his face with each sentence and he swallows repeatedly, trying to stem his nausea.

'Why didn't you tell me?'

I'm not sure if he is asking me or Lucia. Lucia can only shake her head, wordless.

You were never meant to know, I type my admittance. *I couldn't risk it.*

His voice is incredulous. 'You planned all that, right from making sure he became your client?'

I don't have the strength to type what I want to tell him, to explain what Lucia and I had suffered because of Richard, how I needed to ensure it wouldn't happen a second time. I have to settle for short, stilted replies.

He got away with it once. Not again.

'You took a huge risk, Tam.'

So did you, I fire back on the iPad, watching his cheeks colour.

'Were you going to tell me about confronting him?' Lucia whispers.

I nod emphatically. *Wanted you to know*, I type. *Hoped you'd report him after you saw evidence.*

As I watch her read and baulk at my words, something nudges at me. My brain is trying to get my attention, a hazy reminder beginning to form. I close my eyes for a moment, frowning as I try to focus.

'You kept a record of evidence?' Lucia asks.

My entire body jerks, but I don't notice even though my visitors startle at the physical reaction. *Record*! I *recorded* Richard!

That's why I was driving to see Lucia. To play her the tape.

'Tam, are you OK?' Jamie taps my arm, trying to break my reverie.

I ignore him, frantically searching the recesses of my mind. What happened to the recording? I saw myself putting it into my jeans pocket. I remembered touching it throughout the drive to Kent, checking it hadn't vanished.

Richard's text message echoes through my memory. His threat to retrieve the device that signified his downfall.

Where is it now? Would it have survived the crash? Dan has

never mentioned it. How will I find out, when I was the only other person who knew of its existence?

I become aware of Jamie and Lucia staring at me, and I realise I have been mumbling to myself. I shake my head, trying to clear it.

'Did Dan know you deliberately went after Richard?' Jamie asks.

I shake my head rapidly. *No idea*, I type. I can't let Dan take any blame for this. *Just me*.

And, in a way, it had been. I was the one who drove it all, from the moment I saw Mandeville's name appear on the parole list.

Jamie blows out a long breath, glancing across at Lucia, who can't bring herself to look at him.

Your turn, I type, not about to save him from his own explanation. I need to get this conversation over with, so I can apply my concentration to solving the device's whereabouts.

Lucia's body jolts like she has taken another blow. She wraps her arms around herself as Jamie hesitantly begins to speak. He tries his best to give an explanation that sounds rational, reasonable, but there is only so much he can do when the reality is so damning.

I understand his fear. He doesn't want to end up in the cell next to Richard, and he's right. Elise needs him.

'How could you do business with someone like that?' Lucia demands when he finally runs out of words.

'I didn't know,' he whispers. 'I had no idea he was Tam's client, or an offender. He was just another customer when I met him.'

'He destroys women's lives. You saw that for yourself.'

'It was too late by then. His dirty money was already in my business accounts and, unless I cleaned it for him, it would only have been traceable back to me. His real name never appeared on anything.'

Lucia wants to trust him. Her body is angled towards him, but she is wringing her hands together to prevent herself from reaching for him.

Jamie lays his palm gently on her arm.

'If I'd have known what he did. If I'd even had an inkling what he put you and Tam through …'

'I never wanted anyone to know,' she says hoarsely. 'I felt so dirty. Not like a real woman anymore. Until you and I started seeing each other, I didn't think I'd ever be complete again.'

It hurts to lie here and listen to this, but I can't rally against it. Lucia wouldn't have been attacked if *I* hadn't wanted to run, if *I* wasn't late to meet her. Richard's primary motive for targeting Jamie's business was because he wanted another way to control me.

Richard is the culprit in all this: the offender, the aggressor, the sadist. But I am the reason we have all ended up in this room, in this facility, all of us broken.

39

Tamsin – Now

I don't get the chance to figure out what could have happened to my hard-fought-for evidence of Richard's guilt.

Jamie has barely finished speaking before Milena slinks into the room, as if expecting retribution. She looks exhausted and so very young, her wan face free of makeup, hair carelessly dragged into a messy ponytail, wearing leggings and an old hoodie. Elise is in her arms, and Milena sets her gently on Jamie's knee.

She comes straight to me, sliding her arms gently round my neck. 'Thank you,' she chokes out. 'I wouldn't have been brave enough without you.'

I want to tell her that it is her courage that has inspired me, not the other way round.

'Milena's been a star,' Dan says with real feeling, following behind her. 'She let me take her to the police after she told me her story.'

'He hurt your mother too?' I mouth to her.

Milena worries at her thumbnail with her teeth. 'She was the one always calling me when I answered my phone in your room, if you heard me.' I nod my confirmation. 'I rang her on my way to meet Dan. I needed her advice whether I should go through with it or not. She had some stories to tell me. Things she has never talked about. I never realised Richard had hurt her too. It made me sure I was doing the right thing.'

'The police are arranging to go to Kosovo, to fully interview Milena's mother, Katya,' Dan adds. 'They've both agreed to take the stand, if necessary.'

Katya. I know that name.

Milena's mother was Richard's translator. He had abused his own colleague, whose purpose had been to help him communicate with the locals, risking her life to aid him.

'It wasn't only her,' Milena says. 'Other women too, in our village and others.'

Jamie doesn't know where to look. His eyes flit continually between all three women, his jaw working as if he is frantically chewing gum.

'Why now?' he asks hoarsely. 'Why not before, when it was at its worst?'

'Because I thought it was just me, and I could handle that. Now that I know it wasn't, it's changed my thinking.'

'You're brave to stand up to him,' Jamie says.

Milena gives a sharp laugh. 'I was stupid to trust him in the first place.'

'Desperate people do desperate things,' Jamie mumbles.

'No.' Milena's voice finds strength. 'Bad people do bad things.'

She pauses to take my hand.

'You kept me safe, Tamsin. You gave me a reason to be here, and I hope I took care of you well enough. I tried my best for you.'

I can't apply much pressure in return, and tears are blurring my vision, but I mouth my thanks as clearly as I can. She has kept me safe too. Without her, Richard's syringe would surely have found its target.

'I think I will go and talk to my colleagues. Dan, thank you for being with me. You made me feel strong enough to tell the truth.' She turns to my husband. 'And Jamie, you saved my life bringing me to Rushmore. I would never have survived Richard if you'd left me with him. I've told the police you had no idea what was going on. Richard just supplied waiting staff to you.'

Jamie's shoulders slump and Lucia closes her eyes in relief. She leans across and takes Jamie's hand.

Jamie releases a long breath. 'Thank you,' he manages to say. He reaches for Elise, drawing her close against him, resting his chin gently on top of her golden head.

Dan clears his throat, his shoulders angling away from the display of affection. 'Tam, do you remember the day of the accident? You'd gone to meet Mandeville in Battersea Park.'

The question throws me. I had expected it to be asked, but not by Dan. 'A little,' I finally mouth.

'After I took you home, you said I was right about him. You wouldn't tell me what you meant. Can you tell me now, if you remember?'

I should explain, but I know I can't. This has to end, all of it. I have a second chance and I don't want the darkness to rule me again. I need to live in the light again, something I have failed to do ever since Richard Mandeville sent my mind to a place so black I feared I would never have the power to see beyond it.

I shake my head, managing to shrug, hoping Dan will realise exactly how vulnerable I am like this. It is no effort to bring tears springing to my eyes.

To his credit, he doesn't push me. He reassures me with a squeeze of my hand and tenderly wipes my eyes with the pad of his thumb.

'Can I have a minute with Tamsin?' He is pleading, and I see Jamie recognise it. 'Please. Then I'll go. I'll leave you all in peace.'

Jamie is shaking his head as he opens his mouth to argue, but Lucia puts a hand on his arm and, again, I see the true depth of their relationship as he looks to her and allows her to guide him. It stings.

'Take all the time you need, Dan,' Lucia says softly. 'We'll go and speak to the director.'

Elise attempts to refuse this time, but Jamie swings her into his arms, whispering reassurances that we will not be separated for long. Dan's gaze follows them from the room, focussed only on my daughter.

'The DNA results came back,' he says, as I knew he would. 'I faffed about for ages deciding whether to send the damn thing or not, but I thought we were going to lose you, and then I'd never get near Elise.'

He rakes his hair back, his jaw tight.

'She's not mine, Tam.'

I force myself not to look away, swallowing hard, wishing I could use words to deflect or soothe, but there are none, even if I could speak.

'You already knew that, didn't you?'

I nod. I can't lie to him about anything else.

He smiles like he has calmly accepted the truth, but his eyes tell a different story. 'I don't know what I imagined would happen if the test was positive. I couldn't bring myself to take her from the only life she's ever known. She's happy, I can see that.'

Are you? I try to ask him.

'I'm doing OK.' He reads me perfectly, forces a grin. 'Better now I know you're going to be alright.'

I close my eyes momentarily, unable to bear the rush of emotions fighting for supremacy within me. It isn't fair on Dan. He's done nothing except try to protect me, blinded by a love that, for him, had never been extinguished.

I've caused so much harm by trying to do what I thought was right.

40

Tamsin – Now

Several days pass in a blur of tests and professionals. Milena's continued absence bothers me, and I picture her in a police interview suite, answering the sort of questions that will open up chasms of pain. Milena would be here if she could, which can't be said for everyone.

Lucia has not visited again since Saturday, and I am glad. What could we say to each other, after all this? I can't even bring myself to confront Jamie about his willingness to pull the plug on me. That is a conversation for another time, when we have all regained enough strength to withstand it.

This morning, Jamie arrives with Elise who has brought a little backpack stuffed full of her favourite possessions. She kneels on the bed, proudly showing me each item one by one. Alongside her Squishmallows and My Little Ponies are her artistic creations, drawings of butterflies and unicorns that I will never tire of looking at.

When she has finally exhausted herself, Jamie sets her in the easy chair and plugs her into her tablet. The excitement has been too much for her and I watch her drift off to sleep almost immediately to the faint sound of *PAW Patrol*.

'I need to tell you something,' Jamie says awkwardly.

God, what now? What else can he possibly throw at me?

He grasps my hand. 'Richard Mandeville is dead.'

I inhale so sharply I choke. The coughing fit alarms Jamie and he reaches for the call button, but I wave my arms to dissuade him. He grabs water from the bedside table, not realising he has to hold it to my lips. In my agitation, I take a clumsy grip on the plastic glass, spilling more than I drink as I try to raise it to my mouth. Jamie finally understands, taking a straw and positioning it for me. The coughs gradually subside.

'Dead?' I gasp.

'He hanged himself in his cell.'

I stare blankly at him, unable to take it in. I swallow hard, corralling all my strength to form my next words. 'Are you sure?'

'Dan messaged me. It happened last night.'

'News?' I am reduced to mouthing single words again. My throat muscles are already burning from the effort of speaking.

Jamie grabs his phone, types rapidly and scans the results before turning the screen for me to see. A few of the daily papers have picked up the story, but it is apparently not enough to be front-page material, and the write-ups are scant.

Suicide in custody.

Death at troubled London prison.

Earl of Southvale takes his own life behind bars.

It's true. A shudder runs through me, deep into my bones. He really is dead. We are all safe, but he will never face justice now, and that leaves a sour taste in my mouth.

'The full story won't have got out yet,' Jamie says. 'Dan was only told the bare minimum.'

I flap my hand at my tablet, miming typing. He understands, positioning it so I can tap my index finger slowly against the screen.

Did you know? Richard hurting the women?

284

'I wouldn't have agreed to any of his terms if I had known,' Jamie says tightly.

I am determined to get answers, as if I am interviewing a recently paroled offender instead of my husband. Jamie hesitates – so much of him wants to refuse to answer – but everything he has done over the last three years has led to this moment. I know he doesn't believe in fate any more than I do, but if he did, he would easily believe it has finally caught up with him. His guilt is palpable. He has kept so many secrets – his affair, his investments, his deal with the Devil, his intention to let me die. And they have broken him. Jamie is no longer the man I married.

When he finally speaks, the story leaves him so readily it feels like it was bursting to escape.

'It was OK at first. He was demanding, but I could deal with that. I knew the women were illegal, but I thought they were just coming over for work. I had no idea what he did to some of them.'

I am hitting the screen hard enough to feel reverberations running into my wrist.

But you found out.

'I couldn't walk away by then,' he says quietly. 'It was never meant to be like this. I needed his money, but I had no idea what it would involve. Then he had me over a barrel.'

I type one more word, making it bold and underlined.

Milena.

Jamie flushes as he reads, much to his annoyance. 'He was obsessed with her, like she represented something.'

She did. She represented his prize. He had known her since she was a small child, and he had waited for her. When he was finally ready to claim her, he would have seen her as the ultimate trophy.

'I couldn't do anything to Richard directly to harm him,' Jamie continues, 'but I could keep what he wanted the most out of his grasp.'

I let out an incredulous laugh. 'You helped Milena to piss him off?' I croak.

Jamie shrugs, shamefaced. 'She told me she'd been a carer back home. When I found Rushmore for you, and it had a staff vacancy, it seemed the right thing to do.'

The next words I type cost me more than I am prepared to show. 'Are you and Lucia OK?'

He sighs softly. 'I think we will be. We cleared the air last night, as much as we could.'

He looks to our sleeping daughter. 'What are we going to do, Tam?' he asks.

I have no answer to that, but I no longer feel tormented by the uncertainty. I have one piece of knowledge that will soothe me through the rest of this terrible mess: the knowledge that Richard is gone for good.

The darkest moments are behind me now. They died with Richard. Lucia won't have to be recognised as a victim, Jamie won't be an accomplice, and Elise won't lose her father. We have the chance to repair whatever is left of our lives, whether together or alone. And when I am ready to be completely honest with myself, I will accept that alone is for the best.

The door opens, granting Jamie a brief reprieve, but his relief is short-lived when he acknowledges the two strangers who troop in. They wear office attire, but their stances tell me they are police officers even before they show their ID.

'Hello, Dr Shaw, we're from the Serious Collision Unit,' the first man explains slowly, as if speaking to a child. He's the younger of the two, and built like a rugby forward. 'We investigated your crash three years ago.'

'We'd like to talk to you about what happened that day,' the older officer says, shorter and slighter than his colleague. 'The nurses have said you can't speak much yet, but we'd be grateful for any help you can give us to fully close the investigation.'

My fingers tremble as I grasp the bed control, weakly pushing the button to raise me more upright. Jamie pulls Elise onto his lap but doesn't move away. She stirs and settles more comfortably to sleep against his chest. To outside eyes, we look like a complete family unit.

'There was no CCTV around the area of the crash,' the younger one continues. 'As you didn't have dashcam and there were no witnesses, we've pieced together what we think happened from the evidence recovered from the scene, but you're the only one who really knows.'

'We found a small amount of cocaine in the car,' the other says. 'That has been attributed to Mr Aguero. Your phone records show you weren't using it at the time of the crash. The only other thing we found was a little recording implement. It was on the road, smashed to pieces. Too damaged to retrieve anything. Was that yours, Tamsin?'

I try to hide my sharp intake of breath by coughing, indicating for water to buy me time. I hope they think my shaking hand, as I grasp the straw, is the result of my physical condition.

'I used to record my work notes for transcription later,' I rasp. 'I must have left it in the car.'

'My wife had a traumatic brain injury,' Jamie interjects. 'Her memories will be affected.'

'We understand. We're not expecting miracles. Anything you can remember, Tamsin, even the smallest thing can help us conclude your case.'

I try to make eye contact, to prove that I am a reliable witness, but it is impossible. I can't focus on them when a carousel of images is tearing across my mind. I close my eyes.

I can smell the stench of petrol. I can hear slow, deliberate footsteps treading across broken glass. I see Richard looming over my prone figure, feel his hands roughly frisking me.

'Where is it?' he pants in my ear.

His fingers wrench the pocket of my jeans, and I glimpse the tiny recorder in his grasp. For just a second, he looks at me. He smiles.

As he stands upright, I hear the crunch of the delicate device beneath his boot's sole.

'Tamsin?'

I don't hear the detective. My ears are filled with the growl of Richard's engine as he speeds away, leaving me to my fate, no witnesses to see him flee.

The images don't stop. More and more pile in, brief snatches of awareness, from before the moment of impact. A reverse chronology unfurls before me. I see a road stretched out before me, a wicked, curving bend. I see my foot hovering above the accelerator. I see Ben's head lolling in the passenger seat, his own seat belt forgotten just like mine.

I am crying before I realise it. The tears spill from my closed lids, cold against my cheeks. Surely they should be hot with the emotions that are overwhelming me but they are icy, like my heart was that day.

I look up at the police officers.

'I'm sorry,' I whisper. 'I don't remember.'

41

Tamsin – Before

The plan was there, like it had been fully formed all along, waiting for this very moment. I knew exactly what to do as I watched Richard's car draw nearer.

My own voice shrieked inside my head, trying to wrest back autonomy. But I was already lost, my sensible, structured, responsible mind no longer in charge. I was another person, one who craved revenge by whatever means. It had been happening so slowly, over the months, that I had barely realised the dangerous grip it had taken.

It had become a cold, constant, invisible rage. My mind had been poisoned by that morning in Battersea Park when my life changed forever.

That's the thing with obsession: it becomes insidious. Before you even notice, you're a shadow of your former self, a mere host for the parasite that consumes you.

And when you finally recognise that the things which used to mean the most to you now feel inconsequential, it's too late. The mania has already won the battle, and now you are powerless to stop the destruction it wreaks on your life.

My skin grew slick with sweat as the realisation struck me. *You can't! You're a doctor, for fuck's sake!*

You're supposed to improve lives, not take them!

But it was too late to prevent me.

I had already hit the accelerator, aiming straight for Richard's car. Not to collide with him, but enough to force him to take evasive action, enough to make him lose control at the speed he was travelling. I wasn't going to risk my life, or my baby's – the madness was not that far beyond my control. But I was going to take Richard's. Of that, I was certain.

I heard Ben scream out in his own language. A plea? A prayer?

The wheel yanked itself from my hands as the tyres lost their grip on the slick road. I grabbed at it, fought to correct my mistake.

I tried to hit the brake, but my foot blindly found the accelerator instead.

My ears filled with the awful, tearing crunch of metal on metal, friction screaming from the tarmac as the car rolled over and over, a blinding kaleidoscope.

Then the jolt of stillness, the creaks of the car coming to rest upside down, and the agonising silence that followed.

I didn't see Richard's car speeding away from the scene. I didn't see Ben's life slip away from him. I didn't see the terrible reality of my choices.

All that was left was darkness, and the voices that would become my closest friends until I could find my own again.

Acknowledgements

The Voices came from a dream about a woman trapped in her own body. I could hear her strong, intelligent voice and sense the terror of her predicament, and I knew I had to learn more about her. Tamsin's story wrote itself, but it needed a village of people to make it what it is today. My heartfelt thanks go to:

My agent Liza DeBlock, who promised me a book deal as a wedding present and secured it as she went into labour. If that's not dedication, I don't know what is! To have this strong, smart woman in my corner is something I will never take for granted.

Daisy Watt, my incredibly talented editor, who has believed in me and *The Voices* from the moment we met. To publish my first hardback with her feels incredibly special. Daisy has shown such a depth of understanding and compassion for Tamsin and *The Voices* has grown immeasurably under her clever, meticulous guidance.

The HarperNorth team, a group of people whose company I immediately enjoyed, and who are always happy to share a cake. Thank you to publicity and marketing extraordinaires Alice Murphy-Pyle for the straight-talking Northernness and Hilary Stein, who has been an absolute hero these past months. To Genevieve Pegg, Sarah Emsley and Kate Elton for their unwavering support and belief in this book. To Taslima Khatun and

Megan Jones for always making me feel welcome and answering every stupid question I have. I'm so grateful to you all for this incredible experience.

Henry Steadman for a chilling, foreboding cover I adore. CJ Harter and Joseph Barnes for their attention to detail and eagle eyes.

Chris McDonald and Serenity Booksellers – Chris and Kelly Willocks – for introducing me to the amazing northern book scene and all its opportunities. And to the high street and indie bookshops who have been so enthusiastic as I've excitedly waved proofs under their noses.

As always, my wonderful parents who share every step of each book's journey and never stop believing. I'm very lucky, and always thankful, to have them by my side.

My favourite geek Lee, now my husband, who quoted Taskmaster at our wedding, cannot be trusted with charcoal cheese, and whose unwavering support makes my writing dream possible. Love you 3000, Mr C.

Kim, my sister from another mister. Don't know where I'd be without you. Definitely lost on a road trip. Here's to Porto and forty!

Sara Link for being a legend of a beta reader and someone who never fails to make me LOL. Reading your missives is one of my favourite activities.

Liam Jackson for having the patience of a saint trying to get a decent headshot of me. This creative force has a very bright future ahead of him.

The canine crew – Indy, Nanci, Nala and newest baby Rollo, for all the snuggs, the smiles and the questionable help figuring out plot points on walks. And the fur babies now over the rainbow bridge who gave so much love to everyone who knew them – Zep and Betsy, Molly and Poppy, Charlie-dog.

And to everyone who dug into their pockets to purchase a hardback – THANK YOU. I know in these times, books often can't be a priority, but I value each and every sale for helping to keep the dream alive. I hope you love Tamsin as much as I do.

Harper
North

Book Credits

HarperNorth would like to thank the following staff
and contributors for their involvement in making
this book a reality:

Sarah Allen-Sutter
Jospeh Barnes
Fionnuala Barrett
Peter Borcsok
Laura Braggs
Sarah Burke
Alan Cracknell
Jonathan de Peyer
Anna Derkacz
Tom Dunstan
Kate Elton
Sarah Emsley
Simon Gerratt
Lydia Grainge
Monica Green
Natassa Hadjinicolaou
CJ Harter
Emma Hatlen

Megan Jones
Jean-Marie Kelly
Taslima Khatun
Holly Kyte
Rachel McCarron
Alice Murphy-Pyle
Adam Murray
Genevieve Pegg
Amanda Percival
Florence Shepherd
Colleen Simpson
Eleanor Slater
Henry Steadman
Hilary Stein
Emma Sullivan
Katrina Troy
Daisy Watt
Ben Wright

For more unmissable reads,
sign up to the HarperNorth newsletter at
www.harpernorth.co.uk

or find us on X at
@HarperNorthUK

Harper
North